Welcome to the Carnival

Welcome TO THE CARNIVAL

F R WITHERS

Copyright

Cover design created by Erik Mclean
Self-published
authorfrwithers@gmail.com

Authors Note

The world created in this story is purely fictional, as are the characters and the experiences they live through.

However, please take the TW's seriously.

Trigger Warnings include: drug abuse, graphic descriptions of self-harm, suicidal tendencies, discussions of mental health, murder, prostitution, non/dub con, explicit scenes, language some may find offensive, death, sexual assault, exhibitionism, minor stalking, and trauma.

If you have any concerns before reading this book, please reach out.

Your Mental Health Matters

What you should know.

Welcome to the Carnival is book one in a duet and ends of a cliffhanger.

It involves a morally grey man tangled up in illicit and illegal activities.

It's duel POV and covers subjects some readers may find triggering.

If you've made it this far, ***Welcome to The Carnival.***

For anyone fighting an invisible battle, for those who want to escape to another world, and for those that have more strength than they give themselves credit for.

This is for you.

Chapter One

Harriet

My relationship with Felix could have ended for a variety of reasons.

His unhealthy desire to justify his worth through the commitment he had to his job, his relentless inability to separate work from our home life, and the weekends he spent away leaving me isolated and alone in our tiny apartment.

Or perhaps it was his lack of self-control that prevented him from restraining himself around other women, and his forgetfulness that led to him ignoring the fact he was already engaged.

To me.

Standing in the doorway I stared at his pale, and very naked body, watching his encounter with yet another woman that wasn't me. When a shrill cry filled the apartment, I knew this was it.

I knew it was the moment I walked out and never came back.

I met Felix when I was eighteen, just after I'd moved in with my dad. He was an intern at my father's company, and we immediately hit it off. Looking back now, maybe I was just desperate for someone to take care of me, make me feel loved. He was charming with his words and chivalrous with his actions, not to mention he was incredibly career driven.

The number one trait in a future husband, my father would say.

But as I stared at him, still skulking over the blonde woman spread out on our dining room table, I knew my father was wrong.

Desirability had nothing to do with someone's capability to have an aspiration. It had everything to do with morals, and staying loyal to the person they'd promised to dedicate their life to.

Even more so when you're engaged to the daughter of the city's most prolific businessmen.

Not that I ever made a point of sharing who my father was. Apart from a few photos online and a couple of articles, I didn't exist in his world.

I liked it that way.

My father, Richard Wolston, was a renowned mogul in North Callie, but not for the right reasons. Whilst most financial companies aimed to support and aid families being hurt by the financial crisis, my father's company aimed to cripple them, take every last penny they could, and then force them to take out credit they'd spend the rest of their lives repaying.

There was no other way to describe it apart from filthy daylight robbery.

By association, I should have known that anyone who would want to work for Richard would be a power-hungry lowlife.

Even if they did come with pretty blue eyes and a dazzling smile that would break even the stoniest of hearts.

Skin slapping skin pierced my ears. I needed to leave. My breaths were starting to turn shallow, and the wheeziness that often battled in my lungs was beginning to come out from hiding.

I refused to give Felix the satisfaction of knowing he was breaking me, and I knew if I didn't leave now when he begged for forgiveness I would crumble.

I always crumbled.

I needed to remember this wasn't out of character for him. We'd been here so many times, enough that I'd lost count.

I wasn't afraid to admit that I needed comfort and familiarity, maybe that was why I always forgave him, always allowed myself to believe his seedy lies and excuses.

Slowly, I tiptoed backwards until I was over the threshold of my brightly painted yellow front door, and back into the apartment building's hallway. My hand stayed glued on the handle as I pulled the door closed and pushed the side of my face up against the smooth laminate surface.

The sounds didn't stop. They hadn't heard me.

When I reached the elevator at the end of the corridor the woman's fake winy moans still bounced around, and the images that were burned into my eyes made my face scrunch. Apparently they had been too engrossed by each other's genitals to notice my interruption.

I wasn't naïve enough to think it would be easy to move on from Felix. After five years together and an impending wedding, he had taken over most of my young adult life and left an imprint that would be difficult to escape.

I couldn't ignore that he had helped me through my mother's death and been the rock I desperately needed.

Apparently he was being a *rock* for other women too.

The sad thing? I wasn't even surprised. When it happened before I'd ignored it, pretended it was my imagination playing unfair tricks on me. I didn't want to believe that the man I had sacrificed so much for was capable of such a cruel act. I wanted stability and comfort, I wanted to feel like my life was something I actually enjoyed, not just tolerated.

Felix helped to distract me from the numb chaos in my head, even if only temporarily.

Shoving through the large double doors that kept the building secure, the cool rain hammered against my skin and plastered my chocolatey brown hair against my face.

I needed to come up with a plan, find some way of getting as far away as I could before he noticed I'd gone.

Preferably a plan that didn't involve me sleeping in my car for the night.

Think stupid.

Fishing my keys from my bag, I directed them towards my electric blue Mustang's door, and it flashed twice as it unlocked.

Sliding into the driver's seat, I firmly wrapped my grip around the steering wheel and leaned my head back, attempting to calm the rapid breaths fleeing my mouth.

Silently I counted.

One, two, three, four, five.

My shrink told me to practise taking deep breaths, she told me it would help.

It didn't help.

I argued that it was genetic. Completely inevitable that I'd become a victim of mental illness, just like my mom.

My beautiful chaotic mom.

A few days before my eighteenth birthday I had come home from school, excited to tell her that my writing had been nominated for an award in one of the literary programmes it hosted.

But the house had been uncomfortably silent.

By the time I got home it was barely seven, and I'd expected the lights to be on at least, but when I opened the front door I had been met with a chilling quiet and unnerving darkness.

It didn't take long for me to find her. I followed the trail of beer cans and broken glass to the living room, the shapes illuminated by the streetlamps pouring light through the window.

Despite the lavish world my father lived in, when he and my mom divorced, she'd walked away with nothing apart from a broken heart and fractured memories. His toxic need for power had left us scraping by on the money I earned from a weekend job delivering papers, and the minimal child support he offered.

I was only three when they divorced, and any memories that I'd had of him were tightly locked away in my subconscious, never daring to come out from hiding.

Our home was off a side street in an area most people referred to as the slums. Broken wiry fencing lined the small shack, and uneven concrete steps guided visitors towards the front door.

Not that we had many visitors, we were destitute. No one wanted to know the addict and her weird child.

My mom loved bright colours. She'd painted the front door in an assortment of rainbows and clouds, said the brightness reminded her of the world she had created in her head.

She always made it sound like such a happy place, the one in her head. As a child I told her I wanted to move there.

She told me one day I could.

My father blamed the psychosis for her chaotic and unusual behaviour. He also blamed it for the breakdown of their marriage, and refused to take any responsibility for the role he'd played in driving them apart.

Secrets. Lies. Affairs. That's what *really* drove them apart.

My mom was just innovative though, her mind controlled her imagination, and she harnessed it with every inch of her being.

Even when she was strung out, barely able to hold her body, she was still dancing in the moonlight of her vivid mind.

No one understood her like me, no one let her dream like I did. I had the same wild creativity burning under my skin.

Angie's substance abuse was a secret from everyone apart from me and my dad, how would anyone know?

No one checked on her, no one checked on me. We became isolated in this overcrowded life.

Nobody wanted to be associated with the freaks that painted their home in bright colours, and had picnics in the pouring rain.

I had always hated that my mom resorted to drugs when she needed a break from life, I hated that having me wasn't enough, that I couldn't *be* enough to soothe her mind through the voices. But now I kept the same company in my own head, I understood it better.

No one spoke to me like they did, no one *knew* me like they did.

Her arm hung off the sofa and underneath, two empty needles and a plastic bag camouflaged into the murky carpet, along with the remnants of crushed white powder.

I'd wanted to cry for her, wanted to be angry that she had chosen to leave me alone in this unpredictable world. But a part of me understood, and after that, the voices in my mind shrieked louder, their shrills offering me new comfort.

Seeing my mom dead flicked a switch in me.

I became reckless, unbothered by the consequences of life. The once quiet murmurs in my head were now dictating every part of my being.

I became a puppet controlled by invisible strings.

My dad forced me to move in with him, told me he was *worried* for my wellbeing. My dad didn't care about me. the only thing that Richard cared about was his image and reputation, both of which would have been tarnished if people found out about his junkie ex-wife and the unhinged child he'd abandoned.

After staying with him for a few months, and content that I wasn't still exciting my reckless habits, Richard offered me a job within his company, nothing particularly difficult. I was hired to help with general office admin; photocopying, arranging timetables.

Despite my reluctance to be connected with his shady work, I needed the money, and at eighteen I wasn't going to turn down the opportunity to make an income, one that would probably be the easiest to obtain in my life.

One that would help me escape this life.

As much as my dad had been obsolete for most of my childhood, he did help me through the challenges after Angie's death.

A few months after living with him, he put me up in an apartment he owned with minimal rent and helped pay for me to see the shrink. It didn't make up for the years he'd taken no interest, the years he'd failed to acknowledge that I even existed, but I knew somewhere in his hollow blackened heart he cared, and he was trying.

He even paid for me to undertake courses in computer science and tech, something that I had a genuine interest in and kept me occupied.

Felix helped too, but I knew he struggled with my outbursts and the anxiety that would render me paralysed, unable to leave our home.

I had unhealthy ways of dealing with the memories that had branded themselves behind my eyelids, coping mechanisms that only my shrink knew about. I was careful to hide the scars and burns that painted my thighs, and no matter how much I tried to stop, I didn't want to.

They always tell you in order to help someone they have to want to help themselves. That was the problem.

I didn't *want* to help myself.

I enjoyed the corrupt feelings that the pain gave me. I didn't want to feel numb anymore, and every time I had to plaster a smile on my face, I just became more and more exhausted.

On the outside, I was a bright young woman investing in and creating her future. On the inside, I was dying. Or at least I wished I was.

I'd managed to avoid anything intimate with Felix for over a year, something he frequently reminded me of. He scolded me daily, told me that relationships didn't survive without sex.

Our relationship wasn't surviving though, it was barely existing.

I stretched over the passenger side of my car towards the glove compartment, and as it fell open a pack of cigarettes, a lighter, and a stack of crumpled-up leaflets tumbled out.

I reached for the pack of cancer sticks first.

I wasn't a religious smoker, but I kept a pack in case of emergencies. My argument was that they helped to guide the deep breaths and calmness exercises my shrink wanted me to practise.

She couldn't tell me off for exploiting the loopholes.

The lighter came into my grip next, its metal casing cooling my fingers. With a quick flick, the flame sparked to life, and I was soon inhaling the dark smoke, begging it to poison my body.

I closed my eyes, and the voices rioting in my head began to sedate, clearly pacified by the toxic habit sitting between my fingers. I let my head roll to the side, keeping my eyes closed, and listened to the sound of rain spilling onto my window, its gentle rhythm helping to ease the turbulent thoughts.

My eyes flicked open, and I stared at the papers and leaflets littering the passenger seat. Most of them had been given to me by the people standing outside supermarkets, the ones that harassed you until they forced you to stop and listen to whatever propaganda they were churning.

My shrink suggested that I worked on saying no, she said that the reason I got myself into uncomfortable situations was because I was constantly on a loop of trying to keep everyone in my life happy.

I knew I was a people pleaser, it was a personality trait I'd gone through life despising, but one I couldn't seem to escape from.

Growing up I was forced to find comfort and solitude in companions that I didn't really have, and I quickly learnt that saying yes got you more friends. Even if most of them did abandon you when things got tough.

Everyone wanted friends though. I was no different.

But right now, staring at the pile of messy pamphlets, I was grateful for my reluctance to say no.

Lying on the top of the stack, a rental ads leaflet sat crisp, and bright colours shone from the glossy covering. Snatching it up, I took another drag from the cigarette in my hand, savouring the harsh scrape as it burnt down the back of my throat. I turned the flyer over in my hand and one of the ads caught my attention; a single female occupant looking for a roommate in the town of Bromlin.

Bromlin was only a few hours from here, but far enough away that I could escape seeing Felix.

Though I'd never been there before, I'd read news articles and stories online about the town. It was quaint but on the more poverty-stricken side. Its wealth didn't bother me, I'd only been privy to the lavish lifestyle for the last few years, so readjusting back to my roots wouldn't be a problem.

The clock on the dashboard blinked, its orange lines flicking rhythmically. It was already ten, and if I didn't want to spend the rest of the night in my car, I'd have to hope that whoever the owner of the ad was they didn't mind having a late-night enquirer.

Digging for my phone in the back pocket of my jeans, I took one final drag of the cigarette balancing between my fingers, and flung it out the car door. After tapping the number into the keypad I held it up and it rang into my ear.

"Hello?" A cheerful voice answered, the owner of it sounding young. I relaxed in the seat as tension unfolded from my body. It didn't sound like I'd woken her up, and knowing I was one step closer to escaping this hellish nightmare sent floods of relief hurtling under my skin.

"Hi. I'm calling about the ad for a room." I stared back towards my apartment building's door, just as a tall leggy blonde sauntered out into the showers of rain.

Probably the same blonde that had just been railed by my fiancé over *my* dining table.

I hope she gets swept up by a tornado.

The numb stroked the anger in my head, keeping it hidden from the surface.

"It's ten, what kind of maniac calls about a room at this time of night?" There was a slight laugh that followed the voice, but it didn't sound annoyed, more amused. I returned a breathy sigh into the speaker.

"The kind that's sitting in their car trying to find somewhere to stay— My name's Harriet."

"Delilah. I need a month's rent upfront; can you do that?"

Fortunately, I could. My father had been generous with his finances, if not a little hasty when he took me in, I guess he felt guilty for all of the years he hadn't been around.

All the years I had been alone with my unstable, drug-addicted mother.

The words he used to describe her rattled around in my ears. I wouldn't let him tarnish her memory, wouldn't allow him to make her into an uncaring monster.

"Sure, in fact, I can give you six." There was a whistle from the other end of the line and another brittle laugh.

"It's all yours. You coming tonight?" I smiled and looked back at the clock blinking on the dash.

"I'll be there in about three hours."

"Cool. You drink your coffee black?" I liked this woman already.

"Black. And I hope you've got something stronger to go with it."

Chapter Two

Harriet

The drive to Bromlin didn't take the three hours it should have done.

In my desperation to get away from Felix, I ran several red lights and easily broke the speed limit for most of the journey.

When I reached the town's perimeter a small, boarded sign engraved with the words 'Welcome to Bromlin' stood proud. It was a mixture of bright red and green paint, as though someone had recently given it a new coat.

Regardless of the town's status, it was apparent the residents cared about first impressions. That was promising.

I slowed down and watched as clusters of people staggered along the overcrowded sidewalks. Bromlin was obviously privy to late night parties as much as any other town.

I looked down at my phone sitting on the passenger's seat when I slowed to a stop at a red light, its screen acting as a map. One that was guiding me to a beacon of freedom, or so I hoped.

As soon as I cast my eyes down, a message pinged through at the top of the screen.

When will you be home baby? It's getting late.

I scoffed and stared wide-eyed at the lit-up screen. I didn't believe that Felix actually cared where I was, *or* what time I'd be back. It was much more likely he was trying to decide whether to risk inviting another woman into our home.

I rolled my eyes at the message and swiped upwards, my fingers frantically tapping a reply. Suddenly the driver behind sounded their horn and the blaring noise startled me. In my panic, the phone slipped from my hands and tumbled to the ground.

"Great," I mumbled as I dug around beneath the seat. The horn sounded again, and a sigh dragged from my mouth.

It was a shame arseholes like the one behind me gave towns a bad name. *Patience is a virtue,* someone should tell them.

With the map to my destination now firmly back in place, I started to pull away, but the horn from the motorbike blared again and I slammed my foot on the brake. Whoever they were, they were really beginning to test my patience.

I rolled the window down and flung my arm out, giving the driver behind me the middle finger. A smug smile sat on my lips. I was never very good at confrontation, but I'd be lying if I said I didn't get some satisfaction from my passive aggressive tendencies.

However, the driver didn't seem to appreciate the gesture, and they quickly manoeuvred their bike to the side of my car, and the now open window.

I was too tired to be diplomatic.

Coming face to face with a black visor, I stuck my tongue out and yelled. “It costs nothing to be patient arsehole!”

The driver barely moved apart from a slight tilt of their head. Something was unsettling about the way they just sat there staring, and tightness curled inside me.

Did they recognise me?

Had Felix known I’d left and sent someone to bring me home? His text earlier could have been a trick to make me think he had no idea where I was, when in reality he always knew. *Was there a tracker on my phone?*

Maybe a little over dramatic, but the voices loved theatrics. Besides it wouldn’t have surprised me if he actually *had* sent someone to retrieve me, take me back like a misbehaving child.

Before I could hurtle more of my sleep-fuelled words at the driver they sped off, the tires of the motorbike screeching as it left me behind.

Normally I wouldn’t allow something as stupid as a minor road altercation to rile me up, but I was feeling emotional and tired. I just wanted to get into bed and sleep for eternity.

Even if that bed ended up being a sleeping bag on the floor.

After a few minutes of slowly shunting my car down back roads and unnamed streets, I pulled up at an apartment complex. The lamppost outside flicked, and each time the light beamed it lit up the building.

The brickwork creating the structure was a dark mossy shade. Colourful graffiti marks and tags covered most of it, and bags of rubbish rolled around against the path in the heavy winds.

It must have been six floors high. My tired aching legs cried, and I prayed that I wasn't going to be walking up hundreds of flights of stairs. I was pretty sure I wouldn't even make it up three.

The street had a nostalgic familiarity about it. It wasn't too dissimilar to the street I'd grown up on; I was used to litter and graffiti.

What I wasn't used to was the smell wafting through the air. For someone who had been exposed to drugs for a long time, I'd forgotten what the smell of marijuana was like.

It surrounded me and invaded my senses, but I couldn't see where it was coming from. Apart from me, the street was empty.

When I looked up at the apartments, I spotted a gentle fog of smoke floating from one of the top floor windows.

Please don't be Delilah's. I'd had enough of drugs for one lifetime.

Grabbing my bag, my only possession from my car, I slammed the door and anxiously tiptoed up the steps towards the enormous metal double doors.

Get a grip Harriet. It's just an apartment.

The numbers one to ten were handwritten on small scraps of paper lodged into plastic slots under buttons, and I looked at the ad in my hands again. Pushing down the one for number four, I silently thanked that I wasn't going to have to walk up too many stairs, or closer to the putrid smell.

A cheerful voice answered after a couple of rings, "yeah?" Her tone was questioning.

Had Delilah already forgotten that she had a new roommate arriving?

You're intruding.

"I'm here for the room." I tried to keep my voice elevated like hers, but the fatigue was making it difficult, and my throat was scratchy from the hundreds of cigarettes I'd smoked on the drive over here.

A buzz, and the sound of a latch unlocking, had me pushing against the door quickly, eager to get inside and escape the winds of the outside world.

"We're on the second floor. Door should be open now." I barely heard the instructions as I threw my body down the first corridor and to the bottom of a stairwell.

The stale smell followed me, and I paused for a moment, looking up at the dingy staircase. Vivid graffiti lined the walls in patches, some still hanging on, other parts peeling from the plaster stripping away.

It was poorly lit, with only two lights working, and even they flicked as I started to walk. I was pretty sure this was how most horror movies started.

It was a good thing I was still numb, otherwise I might have let my fears drag me back home.

Inside I could still hear the street, the traffic outside jumping through the walls encasing me.

Bromlin wasn't quiet. The articles online had led me to believe that because it was recluse it would also be peaceful.

I couldn't have been more wrong.

Voices shouted outside, and cans clattered as they were kicked against the sidewalk. If I closed my eyes I would have thought I was outside, the blares clear enough to be next to me.

Still, I continued up the stairwell, my feet bouncing off each metal step as I climbed further. I counted each one as I moved, an attempt at keeping my mind from wandering to my old home, and the man I was leaving behind.

No matter how much of a cheating scum bag Felix had been, he made me feel safe. *All I wanted was to feel safe.*

I swung around the last step, and my body hung over the railing of the second floor. Thankfully the smell wasn't as strong down here and was replaced by a more familiar one, cigarettes. Whilst I wasn't particularly keen on the scent of burning tobacco, I could tolerate it a lot more.

I was a hypocrite, but I could live with that.

At the end of the corridor a door stood out amongst the rest. Promiscuous red paint coated most of the surface, sections of it stripping off and revealing a rusty metal underneath.

Tiny holes were scattered around the unpainted surface, the red had obviously been used to camouflage the bullet holes. I tried not to let it bother me, but with each one my confidence was slowly chiselling away, and I held my bag tighter over my shoulder.

The voices in my head were having a field day, they provoked my imagination into creating scenarios that explained the door's chaotic exterior. Every possible explanation forced my body to shrink smaller and smaller, and encouraged the voices to scream louder and louder.

I crept forward. I didn't want to wake any of the other residents with my heavy footsteps, and as I got closer I used my phone's torch to highlight the apartment number that was etched into the paintwork.

It was as though someone had used their nail to carve the lines.

Four.

Taking a deep breath, and trying to pacify the itch that was starting to gnaw at my chest, I knocked gently on the door. After a few seconds a latch on the other side was swiped across and it swung open.

I had to blink a couple of times; Delilah wasn't what I had imagined. She was petite, and couldn't have been much taller than five feet. Ribbons of black hair were bundled on top of her head in a messy heap, and her skin was gently tanned giving her a badass Latina vibe.

I instantly wanted to be friends with her. She looked like one of the cool kids at school, the ones who would torment me about my vivid thoughts.

Still, she radiated kindness and that was exactly what I craved.

I shifted and held my hand out, mustering the biggest smile I could, though I'm sure it just made me look twitchy and weird.

"Harriet. Nice to meet you." Delilah stood there looking from my hand to my face for a minute, before suddenly grabbing and wrapping me in a hug.

My body stiffened. I wasn't against physical contact, but it felt unwarranted to be offering affection to a stranger.

Delilah smelt like strawberries and lime, the scent flowing from her wild hair tickling my nose. It was a nice smell, like walking on a beach.

Stepping back she beamed at me, and I instantly relaxed at her welcoming gesture.

"Hi Harriet, come in. I wasn't expecting you quite yet, so I haven't boiled the kettle, but I have a bottle with our names on it."

I followed her into the apartment hallway, and she closed the door behind me, bolting the latch again.

I wasn't sure whether to feel grateful that security was a priority for her, or that she felt it necessary to *have* a latch in the first place.

I silently scolded my paranoia as I trailed behind her further into the room.

The rent Delilah was asking for felt undercharged.

The apartment was large and airy. Lightly painted walls surrounded the open plan living room and kitchen, and posters of bands and half naked women were taped up everywhere.

I kicked off my trainers and began to lap the room.

Dark brown floorboards groaned under my steps as I explored, and my feet softly touched a circular rug that sat in the centre. I wriggled my toes under the softness, not realising how much they ached until the threads eased them.

Delilah distracted me in the corner of the room when she dropped a couple of plastic cups onto a small two-seater dining table, and poured a generous amount of vodka into them both, topping them off with cola.

I should have told her not to bother with the cola.

Above the table, two large floor to ceiling windows sat giving a panoramic view of the town surrounding us, though most of it was blocked by similar brick apartment complexes.

Taking a sip from one of the plastic cups she hummed as the liquid ran down her throat.

"So what happened?" Delilah pulled out one of the chairs, rounded the table and pulled out the other before taking a seat and lounging back, her eyes never looking away from me.

I walked to the other wooden chair, took the cup in my hand, and in a couple of swift gulps allowed the liquid to coat my mouth and sit in a warm pit in my stomach.

The butterflies convulsed in the heat.

"What makes you think something happened?" I rose my eyebrow but kept my stare glued to the cup in between my hands.

I didn't want to see how she was looking at me. It would either be in pity, or with wariness, both of which I was too tired not to take personally.

"No one calls about a room at this time of night. You turn up with one bag looking like you've been dragged through a hedge backwards and don't expect me to jump to my own conclusions?" Wow, Delilah didn't hold back.

She was right though. I hadn't thought to check I was presentable, and after having been out in the rain I probably *did* look like I'd crawled from a park bench.

I shrugged and looked over at her.

"Just needed a new place to stay, that's all. I didn't have a chance to grab any belongings." She leant forward and topped my cup up, and again, I knocked it back in a couple of swallows.

Delilah smiled. "You're going to be great fun at parties."

I didn't answer her, not that she was really asking me a question. I refused to delve into the truth of my anxiety and crowds just yet, I needed to fit in with her if I was going to survive here. I looked around the room again, counting the posters hanging on the wall.

"You have a thing for the female anatomy?" The remnants of the vodka were still delighting my tongue, and I welcomed the sensation with each word I spoke.

"I enjoy female company, if that's what you're asking?"

I bet that broke many men's hearts. Delilah was beautiful, if I was attracted to women there was no doubt I would be tempted to crawl into her bed.

"I found my girlfriend in bed with another woman, hence the room. I can't afford the rent here by myself." I froze but quickly masked my surprise with a nod, and feeling a little confidence flow into me from our similar situations, I raised the corner of my mouth.

"Me too. Well, my fiancé, and it was over my dining table. He doesn't know I saw him."

When I polished off my third drink, I became very aware that Delilah was still sitting with her first and made a mental note to slow down, I couldn't afford to be kicked out of here just yet.

Delilah whistled and folded her arms as she smirked. "Man, I'd burn the table." I copied her smile, even if it was half the size.

"Did you burn the bed?" She laughed and it was cheery, just like when she spoke. I was already enjoying her company, she made me feel relaxed. As though I didn't need to try around her.

She reminded me of how I used to feel around my mom.

"Yes, and her belongings. She was pretty angry about the designer shoes I turned to ash." She paused as if reliving the moment all over again. "She's lucky I didn't lock them both in the apartment and burn the whole bloody place down."

I didn't know if Delilah was serious, but even if she was, I could understand where her need to cause hurt was coming from.

I wished my need burned as strongly as hers.

Deciding to change the subject, I pulled the bag from my shoulder and dug around for the envelope I knew was sitting in its depths.

"I have six months' rent in cash; I hope that's alright. After that I'll pay in transfer." I pulled the sealed envelope from my bag and slid it across the table to her, she didn't even check the contents before flinging the packet into a drawer behind her.

"Sure, whatever works for you. Did you want me to show you your room, you must be tired?"

As if on cue, a yawn crept from my mouth and I nodded. Delilah rose from her chair and moved further through the living room. Like an eager child, I scurried after her and took in the space in more detail.

Sitting between two doors was a large leather brown sofa adorned in patchwork squares, and in front of it, an enormous box back TV perched on top of a unit covered by a thick layer of dust.

"We never watched much TV. It's there if you want it, but it's old, don't expect much from it." Delilah motioned her arm towards the door on the right, "this is you. I'll be next door if you need anything."

Delilah left me standing in the open doorway of my new home, and I tilted my head as I walked in.

The walls were the same here as they were in the living room, minus the posters. But in here, the white paint was peeling from the walls in strips, and damp marks sat in each corner of the room. The floorboards were the same as outside, and as I reached the centre of the room several of them groaned under my weight, my footsteps shifting them slightly.

At least I knew no one would be able to creep in here without me hearing.

Who would be trying to get to you in here Harriet? I shook my head, ignoring the irritating voice.

The paranoia was getting worse.

In the corner of the room, a mattress was pushed up flush against the wall. A crumpled duvet and two pillows were bundled into the middle, and above it fingerprints were imprinted onto the wall.

At least this explained the reason for the cheap rent.

Unease curdled around inside of me again, the swirling pit in my stomach pleading to come out and play. I begged it to subside, to give me a night off.

Around the side of the bed, the wall homed a window that protruded slightly from the wall, and the windowsill was littered with an ashtray filled with cigarette butts, a semi melted black candle, and a spider plant.

The plant was limp, its leaves turning a dead shade of brown. I wondered if that was what would eventually happen to me, maybe I'd just wither up and die covered in dust and cobwebs.

Maybe no one would even realise.

Dirt coated the wooden edge, and I ran my finger across the surface. The window was blurred with droplets from the rain outside, the gentle sound helping to soothe the knot forming in my throat.

My phone buzzed from inside my bag, distracting me from my turbulent thoughts. There was only one person who would be calling me at nearly one in the morning.

As I took it out I blinked. Felix's name stared at me in bold letters, with an image of us standing arm in arm on a beach lighting up the screen.

We looked happy. Another life.

I considered answering it for a moment, but I pulled together the remaining fragile strength I had and sent the call to voicemail. Throwing the phone down beside the mattress, I began to undress, not caring about being naked in a place I didn't know.

I would only ever admit it to myself, but I enjoyed being naked, having the air kiss my skin. It felt empowering, and I could use all of the strength I was being offered right now.

But if other people could see me naked, I was certain they'd turn their noses up at my body riddled with trauma and chaos.

I crawled onto the bed; it was surprisingly comfortable despite its appearance. Sitting back and leaning against the wall, I searched for the bottled water and meds that were loitering at the bottom of my bag, and quickly took two.

I needed to get some sleep before the side effects would start to wage a war with my head.

Tucking myself in I allowed my eyes to flitter closed, but when I did, images of Felix and the woman flashed behind them. Rogue tears escaped the corners of my eyes and I desperately swiped them away from my cheeks.

I just needed to get through tonight.

I could get through tonight.

Chapter Three

Harriet

My eyes were heavy, and they struggled to open against the weight keeping them tightly shut.

Secretly I begged them to stay closed.

I'd had a restless night's sleep, most of it spent tossing and turning, and it had taken me so long to finally drift off that I hadn't been able to avoid the side effects of my meds.

Sickness swam like waves in my stomach, and I'd contemplated running through the apartment naked twice to get to the bathroom, just in case.

Despite my unsettled night, it wasn't the nausea that had forced me awake this morning. It was shouting coming from the living room, and Delilah yelling incoherent words.

I wasn't going to complain to her about the early wakeup call after my first night here, but if it was a regular occurrence I was going to have to mention it.

I rubbed the palms of my hands against my eyes and pulled my knees tightly to my chest. Leaning my head against my folded arms, I peered around the room as I gradually became more awake.

The room looked different in the natural daylight. The walls were still light, but it was easier to see the stains that covered various patches, and there were more damp spots than I had thought.

I'd buy paint today. Try and make the room feel a little homier.

I was finally ready to face the world and, feeling brave, I peered down at my phone. Part of me didn't want to look, but I knew I couldn't ignore it forever. I needed to let Felix know I was safe at least, stop him from sending someone to find me.

As much as he had pissed me off, I wasn't cruel. I wasn't going to let him unnecessarily worry.

That's assuming he was actually worried in the first place.

I tapped the screen and it came to life. Scrolling through endless notifications, my eyes narrowed when a couple from my dad appeared.

Great, Felix must have called him.

Taking a deep breath, I picked the phone up from the floor and entered my password. My finger hovered over the call button under Felix's name before I quickly pushed it and held it to my ear. I couldn't back out now.

Two rings later he answered, his voice sounding tired and panicked. It pulled on my heart.

Stupid. Stop it. He caused this.

"Baby. *Harriet.* Where have you been? Are you alright?" A tightness wove its way around my chest, and the sickness from last night returned. Felix sounded genuinely worried about me, maybe I had been too quick to leave.

"I'm fine, I just needed to get away for the night."

My voice was raspy, the sleep still lodged in my dry throat. I ran a hand through my feral hair, and on the other end of the phone a door closed in the background.

It was too early for Felix to be at work so who was he keeping our conversation private from?

"Harriet, you know you shouldn't be anywhere by yourself. Something might happen. You should come home, let me take care of you." His sincere tone quickly turned patronising.

He thought I couldn't take care of myself.

I sat upright and pulled my shoulders back. "I can take care of myself," I bit my cheek to stop myself from blurting out the words, but it was too late. "Clearly I can't take care of *you*."

The line stayed silent for a moment, and then he laughed. The sound rose the hairs on my arms. "What are you talking about Harriet? This is ridiculous you're behaving like a child. Come home."

My voice didn't carry the edge I wanted it to, but I didn't let that stop me from throwing my hate filled emotions into the phone.

"No. Call the blonde, you sounded like you were having a great time with *her* last night." Refusing to give him the chance to respond, I ended the call and threw my phone towards the other end of the bed.

Grabbing one of the pillows from behind me, I squashed my face into the plush material screaming as loudly as I could. It muted the sound, just as I'd hoped it would.

When I finally ignored the temptation to suffocate in it, dampness began falling from my eyes. I didn't want to cry, I didn't want to feel hurt. This had happened so many times before, I was used to feeling second best.

This time though, it felt different. Final.

I looked at my clothes bundled on the floor and gently rose from the bed, when a small pile of folded material caught my attention by the door.

I walked towards it puzzled, and picked up two t shirts, a pair of leggings and a jumper. Delilah must have snuck them in this morning.

I was harshly reminded that I didn't have any of my own belongings with me. At least it gave me a chance to start over without any baggage.

Physical baggage anyway.

I hurriedly stepped into the leggings and yanked one of the T-shirts over my head. I was grateful she had opted for something that covered me up, there was no way of explaining the stories behind my scars to her that didn't make me sound like a complete psychopath. I didn't want to scare her off in less than twenty-four hours.

I know how people used to treat my mom, they thought she was crazy.

She wasn't crazy. *I'm* not crazy.

After pulling the hoodie over my arms, I zipped the front up, hiding my body under the comfort of the material. Everything fit perfectly. Considering Delilah was so much smaller than me, I was surprised that we wore the same size.

The shouting coming from the other room towed me from my daydream, and I swiftly opened the door.

On the other side of the room, Delilah hung out of the window as she shouted. "Yeah! Well, why don't you come up here and say that!"

I nervously trod my feet into the floorboards as she pulled herself back from the window and turned in my direction.

"Shit. Did I wake you?"

I smiled and shook my head, "no you're fine, I didn't sleep particularly well." Delilah moved across to the kitchen's island and poured a mug of coffee, before sliding it to the other side and in my direction. I thanked her and greedily took the mug in my hands.

"What's going on out there?" I nodded towards the window she'd been hanging from, but she just waved her hand dismissively and chuckled.

"Just kids, nothing to worry about." We both stayed in comfortable silence as we drank our caffeine boost. At first the hot liquid scolded my throat, but I soon settled into the warmth.

"What happened?"

I raised my eyebrow at her question, not knowing what she was referring to. Sensing my confusion, she continued.

"Why did you come here? I know you mentioned walking in on your fiancé, but is there more to it than that? Call it instinct, or experience, whatever you'd prefer." Delilah took a sip from her mug and looked down when she spoke.

"Does it have something to do with the marks on your legs too?"

My eyes widened; how did she know about those? Looking down, I checked my legs were covered. Racking my head, I tried to figure out how to explain as the familiar lace of panic began stroking my skin.

"When I brought the clothes in this morning, it was kind of hard to ignore them. I didn't mean to look, but you were… on show." So Delilah hadn't just seen the marks, she'd seen my entire body. A scorching heat crawled up my neck, and I drank more of the coffee, buying myself some time to think.

"Felix is my fiancé. Was. I'm not sure if he still is." I picked at the corner of my nails.

"He's mostly a good guy, but he battles to stay loyal I guess. The girl last night wasn't a surprise, it's happened before. I have a lot of things I'm trying to figure out, and he finds it difficult to help me."

Delilah's expression remained flat. "Don't defend him Harriet." When she looked at me, her eyes were stern. "He knows his girl is struggling, and his first reaction is to find another one to ride his dick. You need to sack him off."

I laughed at her bluntness, but it sounded sad, and as tears formed in the corners of my eyes my voice broke.

Delilah came to stand next to me, her hand running down my back in an attempt to offer some comfort.

"Why did you start self-harming?" I wasn't going to get into this now, I barely knew her. As much as I was hoping we would naturally grow close because of our new housing arrangement, I didn't trust or know her enough to spill the secrets of my past.

"This and that, it's a long story." Delilah nodded and moved across to the window, perching on the edge as she lit a cigarette.

I rabidly guzzled the remainder of my coffee, and moved next to her, taking one of the cancer sticks from the packet and lighting it. The smoke wound through me, and my eyes closed absorbing the silky feeling.

My senses bowed to the calmness it granted and when the anxiety began to subside, the voices in my head retreated into the background.

"What's your plan for today?" I dazed out of the window as I considered her question. I didn't really have any plans besides making it through the day.

With the way I was feeling, that would be a miracle.

Despite giving Delilah six months' rent upfront, and even though I had enough money to get me through, I wasn't sure how long my father's generosity would fund my rebellious trip and I wanted to be able to support myself when he inevitably cut me off.

"I think I'll find a job." Delilah nodded.

"What kind of work are you looking for?" Apart from the admin work for my dad and the paper round, my experience was limited. I'd recently finished my computer course though, so maybe something in tech or with computers would be a good place to start.

"Any tech shops round here?" Delilah's eyes glanced around for a moment in thought.

"You could try Smithy's. It's a few blocks away. They sell computers, phones, and a bunch of other gadgets. They were looking for help a few weeks ago. I'm sure a pretty face like yours would be a welcome change of scenery for the place."

I lifted my mouth in thanks and threw my cigarette out of the window.

As I strode off Delilah called after me. "The Carnival opens backup tonight, there's no show but they have all the rides and games. We should go, it might help to take your mind off everything."

How could I politely tell her that going to a Carnival was the last thing I wanted to do when she had done nothing but try to make me feel at home?

Maybe it was time I started at least attempting to create some positive changes to my miserable life. Delilah was making an effort with me even though I was a stranger in her world. The least I could do was try and look excited to do something with her.

I turned and smiled as I entered my bedroom, "sure, sounds fun." She smiled back as I closed the door.

Throwing myself onto the bed, I dragged my bag closer and fished my purse out. Unzipping it, I pulled out a small Polaroid photo that was hidden in a compartment in the back.

Staring at me was a beautiful brunette woman, whose smile lit up the room she was standing in. Her hair hung in tight ringlets around her face, creating a lion's mane around her features.

Bringing the photo to my mouth, I gave it a kiss and hid it back away in my purse. "I miss you, mom." I wonder if she felt like this before she decided to inject another needle into her arm? Before she decided to give up.

I was feeling hopeless, but I knew I wasn't her; I knew I wouldn't give up yet. I just needed to find my reason.

After changing for the hundredth time, I ended up opting for a pair of Delilah's black ripped jeans and a chequered shirt.

I'd argued with her that I should wear a blazer, but she just laughed at me, and said if I wore anything smart Smithy would think I was *'the man'*. Whatever that was meant to mean.

From the stories Delilah was reeling off, it sounded like the people of Bromlin held a strong aversion to authoritative figures, something I could appreciate. I'd never had many good encounters with those in positions of power, my dad included.

Teachers, police. Doctors in white coats.

It seemed that was the first thing I had in common with this little recluse town.

As I left the apartment and travelled down the stairwell, I thought about the sense of unease it had provoked in me last night. The walls were still covered in graffiti and scribbles, but the sunlight stopped them appearing as intimidating.

It was surprising what a bit of sunshine could do.

Despite the brightness, when I left the building's main door a cold wind knocked me back, and I wrapped the shirt tighter around my body.

Delilah said the shop was a few blocks away, and even though I'd only drunk a little alcohol last night, I didn't want to risk being behind the wheel in an unfamiliar town. Besides, the fresh air would do me some good, it always had a way of clearing my mind and quietening the voices.

Rounding the corner, the cool breeze aided my strides, and the remainder of my unstable thoughts soon washed away from my body as I fell into a rhythmic stride.

I spotted the tech shop at the end of the street. It looked a bit like a dive bar, one of the windows was boarded up and above the main door, paper had been taped together making up the word *SMITHY'S.*

Peering through the door, I hesitated for a moment before forcing the heavy weight open. A bell above jingled, alerting the man behind the counter to my arrival.

His hand was rummaging around in a bag of crisps, and crumbs had fallen onto his white stained top that was two sizes too small, the material riding up showing off his belly button.

His hair was slicked back into a low ponytail. At first, it looked like he'd overdone it on the wax, but up close it was more obvious it was swimming in grease.

When he finally dragged his attention away from the magazine he was engrossed in, he appeared as though he was looking straight through me, until he seemingly focused and his eyes widened.

He looked surprised for a moment, and then his eyes trailed over my body before returning to my face. I ignored the defensive bark that was ready to scream from my lips and decided to settle on a smile instead as I pulled my shoulders back and neared the counter.

Stretching my hand out, I assembled the cheeriest voice I could muster. "Hi, I'm Harriet, it's nice to meet you."

The man met my hand, and as soon as he did I had to stop myself from immediately pulling away from his grip. Thick salt and an oily residue coated my palm, the sensation almost forcing my face to scrunch.

"Smithy."

Of course this was the owner. Bit of a cliché to name your shop after yourself, but who was I to judge?

"I heard you're looking for help?" I gave Smithy my biggest smile, but he just sniggered and returned his attention to the magazine lying on the counter.

Now I was closer, I could see the pages clearly. The two currently open showed two topless women straddling a motorbike. I rolled my eyes.

"What do *you* know about computers?" He didn't bother to look at me when he spoke. Great. Another sexist man who thought a woman couldn't possibly understand tech. I'd met enough of them on my course.

The store bell rattled again, signalling the arrival of another customer, but I ignored it and leant forward, smiling sweetly and commanding Smithy's attention.

"That depends. Are we talking mainframe computers or hybrids?"

That caught his attention.

He leaned back in his seat and crossed his arms, a smirk toying with the corner of his mouth.

"What do *you* know about mainframes?" He was challenging me, but I was happy to rise to it.

"I know they're expensive, and high capacity. I wouldn't have thought any of the organisations around here would use one. They're too small. Unless of course, they're focusing on bulk data processing." The man raised his eyebrow and nodded as his eyes lit up with a spark.

Good. He *should* be impressed.

"Hybrids?"

I stood upright and mimicked his posture. "A combination of an analogue and digital computer, even rarer than a mainframe. Is there anything else you need me to teach you, or are you going to admit you were wrong?"

Normally I wouldn't dare speak to a potential recruiter so directly, but when it came to people questioning my skill I tended to get carried away. This situation was no different.

Besides, I was pretty sure in Smithy's case it would warrant some kind of respect.

There was a silence between us for a moment, before the man laughed and stretched his hand across the space between us. I looked at it, mentally preparing myself for the coating of salt and grease that was about to scratch my hand.

"You've got spunk Harriet; I'll give you that. Jobs all yours if you want it, come by next week and we can sort out the paperwork."

A large grin crossed my face, and I shook his hand firmly.

"I'll be here, thank you." He nodded his head and I turned to leave, but as I did I came face first with a leather jacket, a helmet, and a smoky scent that made my legs go weak.

The figure barely even budged as I shoved into them, and I had words of apology on the tip of my tongue, but before they could spill out of me I narrowed my eyes.

The helmet looked similar to the one on the rider from last night, so similar it might well have been the same. But my need for sleep had stopped me from noticing any details, and I hadn't been paying close enough attention to know for sure.

My eyes trailed the closed visor and the figure stepped around me as if I wasn't even there.

That wasn't unusual, I was insignificant in most people's eyes.

I watched Smithy interact with the mysterious figure for a moment, but when it was clear I wasn't going to get a second glance I shrugged my shoulders and left the shop, beginning my pursuit in the direction back to the apartment.

I had chosen to do a loop of the area, get to know my new home a little better, and as I rounded the street to the back entrance of the apartment, I heard voices chattering from across the other side of the road.

About five or six people were busying themselves behind a small gate in what looked like a park.

As soon as I crossed the road, I caught the attention of an older woman who was standing in the centre and holding bunches of weeds in her gloved hands.

"Can I help you dear?" She smiled gently and leant over the metal railing.

"I was just being nosy, I'm new to town. What are you doing here?" I observed the people gathered. All of them were either moving, pulling or planting various shrubs and flowers.

The woman's grin widened, "my name is Josie, we're the town's community garden group. We're focusing on this one at the moment, trying to raise some money to bring it back to life."

I beamed, my mom had always loved being outdoors and gardening. We had this tiny plot at the back of our home that we would spend hours tending. We'd plant the brightest colours we could find and have little gnome ornaments scattered in amongst the dirt.

When I was a child I would talk to the gnomes and pretend they could talk back, as though they held the key to life's greatest secrets.

I loved that garden.

When my mom's addiction became debilitating I tried to keep it alive, but between caring for her and school I didn't have much time and it eventually withered away.

Before I could re-think it, I offered my help.

"When do you meet? I would love to help. My name's Harriet, I've moved in just across the road." I held out my hand, and Josie removed her glove and shook it gently, her face glowing.

"Lovely to meet you Harriet, I do hope Bromlin is welcoming you. We meet here every Monday, depending on the weather we sometimes pop down on other days, but we'll take anything you're able to offer."

My eyes were bright as I began backing away. "See you next Monday then."

I waved as I crossed back over the road, and began climbing the steps to the apartment complex. Plastered to the door was a colourful poster. A clown sat proudly in the centre and the word *Carnival* arched around its red frizzy hair. This must have been what Delilah was talking about.

I leant in closer to look at the small print, it promised a night of fun and freedom with rides, games, and interactions with the Carnival's performers.

Only if you dare was scribbled in bold letters across the clown's face, and despite the thrilling fear it was obviously designed to evoke, the chaotic words just made me laugh.

Today had been a good day, and as I entered the code to access the building, I reconsidered attending the Carnival.

Maybe a night of fun was just what I needed to unwind.

Chapter Four

Seb

"Tony. *You're the fucking tech guy.* What do you mean you need more wires? Don't you keep spares in the draw with your porn mags?"

My patience was skating pretty thin. The Carnival was due to reopen today, and even though there wasn't a show, I needed to make sure everything ran smoothly.

But fuck me if it wasn't getting more and more difficult as the day went on.

After one of the performers twisted their ankle, and another was too hungover to stand up straight, I was starting to twitch at the thought of crowds being unleashed on this place tonight.

We had a reputation to uphold, one that would be quickly destroyed if we didn't have the basic necessities.

Lights and effects were all essential components that added to the atmosphere we were renowned for creating. The mysterious, albeit terrifying, waves of chaos that would reap the streets were part of our trademark, and being told a few hours before we opened that the wires we needed were missing was agitating my already tested mood. As usual, it would be down to me to fix the problem.

Sebastian fucking Everett. The Carnival's knight in shining armour.

"Sorry Seb, I thought I had everything, I don't know where they've gone. I called Smithy though; he's put one aside at the shop."

The oaf probably lost them when he was having a wank, too busy to notice them being stolen from under his nose. He should have learnt by now that some of the performers have slippery fingers.

I was already pulling my jacket on before he finished his pathetic attempt at an excuse, I had too much other shit to deal with without worrying about his fuck up too.

"Want me to come with you?" Cherry's seductive voice travelled into my ears as she passed me my helmet.

"No. I need you to stay here and make sure everything's sorted for tonight. We could do without any more cock ups." I looked at Tony as I said the last bit, and his curly red hair hid his face as he looked down sheepishly.

His body even trembled slightly. Good, he should be scared.

I held the helmet under my arm and began walking from the tent and towards my bike. Smithy's tech shop wasn't far away, I should be able to get there and back within the hour.

Hopefully that was a short enough amount of time to stop anything else from going wrong.

The walk from the tent to the performer's parking lot didn't take long, and I looked at all of the shacks covered with tarp that would soon be brought to life with colours, music and willing customers ready to part with their hard-earned cash.

Yanking the helmet onto my head, I threw one leg over the seat and began pulling against the handlebars.

My motorbike howled to life, and I let the noise engulf me. I loved being on the bike, the freedom that came whenever I was on a ride.

If I could, I'd spend every day riding around, travelling to different places. But my loyalty had to remain to The Carnival.

It had to remain to Saffron.

As I closed in on the shop, I spotted a familiar brunette with her hands squashed against the glass looking inside. It was the same woman who had given me the middle finger at the lights yesterday.

The same woman had crept into the crevice of my nightmares and stopped me from getting an ounce of sleep last night.

I turned the handlebar on the bike, and the engine quietened. Leaning back I folded my arms over my chest and watched her with fascination.

Her body was slender, and I enjoyed the way her jeans hugged tightly to her arse.

There was something about her that intrigued me. I knew most of the residents of this town having spent the last ten years here, but I'd never seen her before.

I would know if I had.

When I'd seen her yesterday, her hair had been plastered around her head in a mane of frizz, but now it hung delicately down her back and swayed against the breeze in the air.

I continued gazing at her until she pushed against the grimy door and disappeared inside. The smart thing would be to wait until she left to start my business with Smithy, but my curiosity got the better of me.

What was she doing inside there?

It was rare to see the women of Bromlin in a computer store, she probably just needed help setting up a phone or something.

Abandoning my bike on the side of the road I stalked in after her, keeping myself concealed with the helmet.

The tech store was quiet, nothing unusual about that.

What was unusual was the vanilla scent that camouflaged the musky stale smell that normally clouded the store.

Only the brunette and Smithy were inside, caught in what looked like an intense debate. He was questioning her about different computer types, shit that would go over most people's heads.

But as I busied myself tapping keyboards and clicking the mouse buttons around the shop, I heard her answer all of his questions with ease.

The fact she was fucking smart was a bigger turn-on than that arse she flaunted around.

Even though her voice was low, I still caught parts of her words. She spoke softly but with a challenging bite that drove right into my senses.

When I looked back over at her again she was leant over the counter, the position causing the shirt covering her back to ride up slightly. Slowly I moved as though a magnetic force was pulling me forward.

When she yelled at me yesterday, I couldn't hear her properly over the noises on the street, but here each word rippled through the air clearly.

Every intellectual sound sent waves of need straight to my cock, and I wanted to push her further over that counter, teach her to use that challenging mouth in other ways, but I was quickly torn from my imagination when she crashed straight into me.

Her mouth opened in a fluster but tightly closed as a wave of hesitation filtered over her face and she raised her brow.

The expression reminded me of the one she had given me yesterday— A daring look written all over her features.

For a moment I considered removing my helmet and revealing the glare that was hidden by my visor, but I didn't have time, I had too much to do to be distracted by her.

Shoving around her body, I barely gave her a second glance before she was walking out the door, the jingle of the bell alerting me to her disappearance.

The room felt empty without her teasing scent to fill it.

I wanted to follow her, but I had business to attend to. Fucking Tony was to blame for me not getting what I wanted.

I would make sure he knew what his carelessness had cost me.

Smithy's chin raised as I approached the counter. "Seb, good to see you. I assume you're here for the wires that Tony called about." I nodded. I didn't have time for conversation, I wanted to be in and out as quickly as possible.

Smithy dug underneath the counter and threw a bundle of wires across to me. Grabbing them, I shoved them into the inside pocket of my leather jacket.

"Tony said Cherry will be around tonight." A smirk appeared at the corner of his mouth, the sleaze always did have a thing for redheads.

I pulled a twenty bill from my pocket and threw it on the counter, but he raised his eyebrow and slid it back towards me.

"Not necessary Seb. The girls always suffice." His tone was miry, and I ground my teeth together.

Without saying anything, and without picking the twenty back up, I stalked from the store and headed back in the direction of my motorbike.

The Carnival took me in when I was just fifteen years old, and I've run with it ever since. The lights, the performers, everything about it dazzled me, and as a kid I was in awe of the masterpiece that had captured the small town.

As soon as I turned twenty-one, I was introduced to the private side of the business. A woman named Saffron ran the Carnival, and many others littered throughout the country.

The shows, the spotlights, it was all a canvas, a charade to hide the underbelly of what the Carnival was really about.

During the day, performers were sent on errands, ones that involved acquiring goods and services with no money. Those who were no good at stealing were sent as drug mules.

At night it was a completely different world. The women served the most elusive part of The Carnival, the part I despised the most but had wound up closest to.

As I twisted the handle of my bike the engine came to life once again and I began to move away from the path. From the peripheral of my visor, I spotted the ends of brunette hair winding the corner.

I'd caught her name in the shop.

Harriet.

Her name caressed the demon in my head, and without thinking, I followed in the direction she had walked, making sure to keep a suitable distance and remain hidden.

I wouldn't stay hidden forever, but for now until I figured her out, it would be safer for everyone if I remained in the shadows.

I was a willing player in the game of obsession, and I'd just found my new target.

Harriet paused at the community garden on the other side of the road, and I watched as she interacted with one of the volunteers, her face lighting up as smiles passed between the pair.

The way her eyes shone at the woman was fucking devastating. She was breathtaking, her porcelain skin glowing in the sun's rays.

I wanted to run my fingers over her naked body, find out if she was all bark or whether she would surrender to my touch. It would be interesting to hear what objections would spill from her mouth when I forced her to her knees. If any.

The thought stirred my cock, and I narrowed my eyes as she laughed along with the female on the other side of the gate.

My phone started to vibrate in my pocket, distracting me from the siren on the other side of the road. I swiftly pulled it out and Cherry's name lit up on the screen.

I flicked open the visor on my helmet to speak clearly into the speaker. "Yeah?"

"We thought you'd be back by now; did you get the wires?"

"Yeah. I'm headed back now. Smithy will be around tonight, he asked for you personally."

I could see the roll of her eyes in my head.

"Great. The guy is a lump, and he makes the weirdest noises." I chuckled to myself, "Saffron is coming by soon to assign us all. Make sure you're back by then Seb."

"Yes ma'am."

I pushed the end call button on my phone just in time to see Harriet crossing back to the other side of the road, and up the stairs to an apartment complex.

This must be where she's staying.

I wonder if she's met Lilah yet, that would be one way to get closer.

I contemplated walking after her for a moment, watching to see which door she went into, but I needed to get back and find out what costume I would be wearing tonight.

Whether we agreed with it or not, we all knew we had our roles to play at the Carnival, and as it was opening night we were sure to make a good taking. We all needed to be prepared for carnage.

Reving the handlebar, I flew back in the direction of my home and tried to extinguish Harriet's perky arse and husky voice from my head.

I threw the wires at Tony, who was sprawled out asleep on the sofa. The cables hit his chest and tumbled to the ground as he spluttered awake.

"Wires. Don't fucking lose them again." He nodded his head as I crossed the room and headed in the direction of the kitchen at the back. Cherry was leaning against the island, her head lying on the cold countertop as she whispered incoherent words.

"Seriously? Smithy?" She wined against the marble.

I grabbed a bottled water from the fridge and loosened the cap, gulping back half in one go.

"Yep."

She groaned and leaned her elbows on the counter, her head being held up by her hands. Before she had a chance to respond, tapping heals echoed on the floor and a woman appeared in the entryway to the performer's tent.

My body immediately tensed.

Her eyes scoped the room and her dirty blond ponytail whipped around as she looked from person to person.

Satisfied that everyone was present, she placed her hands firmly against her hips.

"Everything ready for tonight?" Saffron oozed power, each of her words carrying through the air with authority. Every person in the room responded to her presence. Most of the newer recruits feared her.

They should.

She held the power to destroy us all and put us through hell, something I had experienced only once, and I swore I would never disobey her again.

"Tony, tech as always. Sandie, I need you on routes tonight, I'm sure there will be a lot of influential people in attendance." She scoped the room, her eyes landing on me.

"Seb, I need you on merchandise, I have some important friends arriving tonight that I need you to make sure are taken care of. Cherry, you'll be in the back room—"

"I have one client booked already." Cherry's voice was quiet.

None of us interrupted Saffron, we knew the punishment.

"The tech store guy did us a favour, it's payment." Saffron's head nodded, and she walked towards us in the kitchen stopping inches away from Cherry's face.

The room was silent, every person there holding their breath.

Suddenly, a loud slap bounced against the wall, and Cherry's head swung to the side on the impact of the slap. A slight whimper escaped her as she cradled her cheek, before Saffron roughly gripped her hair, yanking her head upwards.

"Don't *ever* interrupt me again." She spat, "let's hope that mouth of yours gets you a good payout tonight."

Saffron released her grip on Cherry's hair, and walked from the room, leaving us all standing there in silence. I moved attempting to comfort her, but she stomped away towards the bathroom.

"That man's dick isn't going anywhere near me without a condom." She shouted as she slammed the door behind her.

Tony was standing up in front of the sofa when I walked over. My body towered over his, forcing him to take a step away. When he fell backwards, my arms gripped the back of the sofa, caging him under my glare.

"Lose the wires again, and next time *you* can be his payment. I heard the guy has a thing for tight arses." His throat bobbed when he swallowed, and his body shook with his frantic nod.

We all knew what we needed to do to survive the Carnival, some of us were just better at wearing our masks than others.

Chapter Five

Harriet

"You have to be kidding, you can't wear that! I give you full reign of my wardrobe, and *that's* what you pick?"

Delilah frowned as she folded her arms and took in my outfit. An oversized red jumper covered my neck down to my thighs, and skintight black jeans hugged my legs.

"What's wrong with it?"

I hadn't had a chance to go out and pick up some clothes yet, and Delilah's wardrobe was mostly low-cut crop tops and miniskirts, neither of which appealed much to me.

"Hang on, I'll find you something."

I remained silent as she walked past me standing in the middle of the living room, and headed through her bedroom door. No doubt whatever she offered as an alternative would make me feel naked.

I wanted to be invisible. Skimpy clothes in the middle of the Carnival sounded like the *opposite* of invisible.

Patiently waiting for her to return, I wandered towards the window beside the kitchen and leant over the sill. Outside the streetlamps illuminated the path, and a couple of people walked past, their arms around each other as they turned the corner.

My chest ached when a man took a woman's hand and pulled it towards his lips, planting a kiss on her knuckles.

I didn't miss Felix. I didn't miss Felix.

Opposite, the similar apartment building was shaded in darkness, as if no one lived there. Maybe they didn't, maybe it was deserted.

From the sofa, my bag began whistling the familiar chime of my ringtone, demanding my attention.

I rushed over and dug around until the silver phone was lying in the palm of my hand, and the word *DAD* was lighting up the screen. Taking a deep breath I peered into Delilah's room, she was still rummaging through her wardrobe. I had a few minutes of privacy to take the call.

Digging my finger into the green answer button I held the phone up to my ear.

"Hey Dad." I tried to stop the shake that was jittering from my voice, but it was no use. Answering the phone to Felix was one thing, but answering it to the man who had the power to cut me off and leave me out to dry, was another.

"Where are you?" I let out a thin laugh and shook my head. Of course, straight to the point. My dad had no time for niceties.

"I'm safe, I'm staying with a friend for a little while." The line went silent, and I had to check the screen to make sure we hadn't been disconnected. "Hello? Dad?"

"No daughter of mine would run away in the middle of the night. What were you thinking? Felix is beside himself."

I gripped the phone tightly in my hand. "Can we do this another time dad, I'm in the middle of something."

"What kind of woman leaves her fiancé in the middle of the night, with not so much as an explanation? You're twenty-three Harriet, It's a bit old to be playing hooky." Anger bubbled inside me, Felix was being treated like the victim as always.

My father had always prioritised Felix's wellbeing over mine, coming to his rescue. Of course he would defend him without knowing both sides of the story.

He had no idea what he had done to me, *done to our relationship*, but he still ran to his defence.

"You're behaving like your mother. Do you have any consideration for how your behaviour affects others?"

Something inside of me snapped at the mention of my mom, and I took a moment to focus on the words he had spoken, my eyes dancing with a concord of flittering shapes.

The sharp corners of my phone dug into my palm, and a burning heat clawed against my chest with my breaths that had become wispy.

"You know nothing about my mom!" I shouted down the phone. Quickly hitting the end call button before I could hear what he had to say, I lunged the phone across the room.

It smacked against the wall, leaving a dent in the plaster, before clambering to the ground with a thud.

I desperately tried to calm the rapid air that was leaving my mouth, but my vision was turning hazy and my mind became disorientated.

Hanging my body forward, my legs held my weight as my fingers gripped around my knees.

"One, two, three, four, five." I counted and then counted again. Each number gave my mind something to focus on apart from the lack of oxygen I was getting into my lungs.

A gentle hand rubbing my back startled me, and I lurched upwards. Spinning around, Delilah stood there staring at me, her eyebrows creased and concern swirling in her eyes.

"It's okay." Her soft voice did little to soothe the chaos that was holding me hostage, and my breaths were short and sharp, each inhale audible in the room.

I needed space, needed a distraction.

Throwing myself down on the bench at the window, I pulled the pack of cigarettes from my pocket and wasted no time lighting one and taking a long shallow drag. Delilah watched me from across the room, her face worried as I took another drag.

"I'm okay," I said, trying to convince myself more than her. She crossed the room and sat down next to me.

We stayed there in silence, and I took frantic puffs on the cancer stick until the red glow travelled towards the end and closer to my fingers.

"Was that the ex?"

I shook my head and flung the cigarette out the window, watching as it fell through the metal steps. The flamed end still shone as it hit the pathway and narrowly dodged the unaware pedestrians.

"No, my dad." I ran my hand through my hair and looked over at Delilah. "He wants me to go home. He's worried about what my late-night escape is doing to Felix."

Delilah scoffed and pottered towards the kitchen counter. From one of the cupboards above, she pulled out the same bottle of vodka we had drank from last night.

She obviously had a thing for the spirit.

Delilah wasted no time pouring it into two shot glasses, and when she brought them back over to the bench, she held one out to me.

"Fuck em'"

I couldn't stop the laugh that rolled off my tongue, and we quickly clinked the glasses together before throwing the contents down in one go. The liquid burned, and tiny knives ran down my throat.

I'd missed that burn.

"I found you something else to wear," she nodded towards the sofa, where a pile of black fabrics were hanging over the arm. One thing I was learning about Delilah was that she had an unquestionable ability to read a room, that was the second time she had changed the subject with no arguments.

I was grateful for her talents.

"I guess I'll get changed then." I rose from the bench, and my trainers gently tapped the floorboards as I scooped the clothes up and bundled them into my arms, heading for my bedroom.

"Harriet trust me. You'll love them." A confident smile beamed from her face, and I smiled back, closing the door.

Once inside, I removed my jumper and jeans and leant my head at her selection. Black fishnet tights hung from my hands, along with a pair of black denim shorts and a tattered T-shirt that had the word MISFIT printed across the front.

Delilah was right, I *did* love them.

After I'd finished dressing I stared at my reflection in the mirror.

The tears in the shirt were scattered chaotically. Most of them did little to hide my lacy red bralette and showed off a generous amount of cleavage. The shorts barely covered my arse, but at least the fishnets helped to camouflage the scars on my legs.

The mark I'd carved into my left thigh four days ago was raised and red, its angry colour pressing against the black lace.

I ran my finger across it. It was still tender.

Four days ago, I'd been shopping at the local supermarket, when a man had reversed into the back of my Mustang. When I'd gotten out of the car he towered over my tiny frame, and hurtled words of abuse at me. Clearly an intimidation tactic, and It had worked.

The oxygen soon began playing games in my airways, and I'd felt my head beginning to cloud. I hated feeling out of control, and when the counting didn't work against the riots, I'd resorted to more extreme methods to bring myself back to reality.

It always worked. The pain helped to unblur the lines in my imagination and force my mind to surrender its control.

Refocusing my eyes on the mirror, I gave a little twirl. Despite how much of my body was on display, I was also modestly covered.

It had been a long time since I'd liked how I looked.

A knock on the door hurtled me back to the present, and I turned from the mirror to find Delilah's eyes raking over me.

"Shit. I wish you weren't straight."

The corners of my mouth curled as I walked back out of the bedroom and threw her a quick wink. "Who says I am?"

Delilah fanned her face and pretended to fall against the door, forcing more laughs to spiral from my body. "Don't tease a girl. It's rude." She hooked her arm through mine as we moved towards the apartment's front door.

She pulled me back slightly before we left, and grabbed something from the counter.

"It's a good thing you're working for Smithy now. You're going to need a new screen on this."

Delilah held my phone out, the remaining glass on the screen shining with cracks and scratches. I took it from her and shoved it into the back pocket of my shorts, along with my purse.

"I guess it's a good thing I'm not expecting any calls."

We took a cab to the Carnival, the ride over had been quick, perhaps only about twenty minutes. An unfamiliar excitement made my fingertips twitch as the lights ahead beamed into the sky.

Turning the corner to our destination, swarms of people littered the pathways and roads, making it impossible to get close to the entrance gates.

Delilah called to the driver, asking him to drop us where we were, and flung a twenty into the front seat.

Stepping out of the cab, my eyes widened at the busy scene playing around us.

The crowds were rowdy, and I was beginning to reconsider whether this had been the best idea. The excitement quickly morphed into nerves, and they were begging to be given another chance to come out and play.

Begging to expose me.

Delilah rounded the cab and was standing beside me in seconds. Slipping her arm through mine again, she gently led us towards the gates framing the entrance.

Enormous towering pillars created the opening to the Carnival, and an orange lit-up sign made of tiny bulbs shone from above. It was clear it should have read CARNEVIL, but blown and flashing bulbs had blacked out most of the outlines, and the word EVIL was left in its place.

A shiver danced over my skin.

I stared through the metal fencing that outlined our destination. It was dark, the only light source coming from the stalls that were inside, along with a Ferris wheel in the distance.

Weaving through the crowds and entering the fairground, we were engulfed by a shadowy thick smoke wafting through the air, a mix of cigarettes and marijuana skating through my senses.

I began to feel disorientated, but it wasn't from the usual panic.

The lights and crowd were all starting to shove around in my head, and I had to blink to keep my vision focused. Looking down at my clothes, I suddenly felt naked and exposed.

Should have covered up. Should have worn more clothes.

Slut.

It wasn't as though any of the people here were wearing much more than me, but the hungry eyes of the men that we passed stung against my skin, and I wanted to wrap my arms around my body.

What if someone spotted me? What if Felix found me here and took me back to my miserable pathetic life as his housewife?

"Let's go to the high top."

Delilah's voice shouted over the noises battling in my ears, and I smiled at her, grateful that she was taking us in a direction away from the crowds.

Bodies intertwined with ours as we sauntered across the muddy field. Characters on stilts towered into the night sky, and actors dressed as clowns jumped out behind shacks and trees.

As we got closer, a group of people in matching black and white mime costumes started waving at us as they performed exaggerated movements on the spot, their limbs bending in chaotic directions.

The high-top tent didn't look like much from the outside, its red and white stripes appearing like any other circus-styled tent. But when we slipped through the opening in the fabric, my eyes widened.

At the far back was a small kitchenette that had everything you could possibly need. A large double doored fridge, marble covered counters, and even a top of the range coffee machine was sitting at one end.

Over at the right side of the tent was a lounge area, three large black leather sofas were positioned in a horseshoe shape, and above them, posters of various artwork were scattered around the wall. In the middle of the sofas, a pool table caught my eyes, with two ques laid over the green fabric on the top.

The left side of the room was covered by doors, five of them, and I wondered where they led, but before I could think about it, a woman with bright red hair emerged from the furthest one. She was wearing even fewer clothes than me, and her hair was hanging in wild strands around her face.

"Cherry!" Delilah squealed from next to me, and ran towards the woman, wrapping her in her arms.

"Delilah! I missed you." The two were obviously good friends by the way they shrieked with each other. I shifted nervously on my feet, feeling like a third wheel.

When Cherry stepped back from Delilah, she looked me up and down, narrowing her eyes.

"Who's your friend?" Delilah waved me over, and I moved slowly towards the pair.

"This is Harriet, she's new in town." I smiled, but it was forced. Cherry's stare felt like judgemental knives piercing into me.

Could she see straight through my mask?

Suddenly her arms wrapped around me, and I stumbled into her tight hold, the unexpected contact causing the wind to get lodged in my chest.

"It's about time Lilah found a new woman. I'm jealous."

I stuttered. "Oh we're not—"

"What the fuck is going on in here?" A deep voice yelled from behind me, and as I spun to find the person responsible, the remaining air evaporated from my lungs.

Good gods, the man looked like he'd been carved in stone by the deities.

A scowl was set on his face, and tight arms folded over his chest as he stared at the three of us.

Jet black hair and glaring coal-coloured eyes were aimed at me, looking anything but happy. I allowed my vision to wander down his body, and butterflies ignited in the pit of my stomach.

A dark grey T-shirt clung against his body, his muscular arms struggling against the sleeves, and black artwork decorated every inch of skin on both of them.

On one of his hands, I spotted a skull inked over his knuckles, and on the other, a snake wrapped around his wrist and slithered across his hand, its fangs sharp, protruding from his thumb and finger.

When my eyes finally finished their hungry violation, they returned to his face, and my chest tightly wound when I realised he wasn't looking back at me.

Instead, his glare was fixed on the redhead.

Why did I even think he might have been looking at me? This man was devastatingly handsome, there was no way he would be offering me any of his attention.

"Seb, you know Delilah. This is her new *friend*, Harriet."

My cheeks burned.

I didn't like the way her voice trailed around the word friend, but I couldn't correct her. Tightness clung to my throat, and I coughed a couple of times, pleading with my words to work.

"Harriet." That was all I managed as I stuck my arm out.

Seb looked at my hand, his face emotionless, before he ignored me and continued his glare at Cherry.

"You have an appointment."

She pouted and turned towards Delilah, wrapping her in another tight hug.

"Wait for me, I won't be long." With that she disappeared through the door she had originally emerged from.

I bit the inside of my mouth as I folded my arms, and balanced my weight between each of my feet. My eyes wandered around the tent again, looking for a distraction to absorb me from the room.

"You need to leave."

It took a moment to realise the harsh words were aimed at me, but as I whipped my head back up to face Seb, his body was suddenly inches away from mine, and I had to step back to stop my neck from craning to see him.

"Leave it Seb. Harriet's with me." Delilah moved closer, her body acting like a wedge keeping us apart.

As much as I was grateful she was there, I also wanted her to move from between us. I could feel the heat that was pouring from his body, and my own wanted to surrender to it.

"I don't give a shit who she's with. She needs to go."

One thing that got on my nerves more than anything was when people spoke about me as if I wasn't there, and the sudden nerves that were assaulting my body froze.

"What's your problem?" The corner of Seb's mouth lifted in a lethal smirk, and he moved around Delilah, forcing me to take another step back. But he didn't stop. He kept stalking me until I was leant flush against the pool table.

Until we were out of earshot of Delilah.

"Princess, you don't belong here." His words were low, and with each one, The throb intensified between my legs. An unwelcome distraction if there ever was one.

My bottom lip began to shake and I bit down on it to stop the tremble.

I thought it was my imagination playing tricks on me when I heard a growl simmering from his body, but when I finally dared to meet his eyes he was radiating a look that fanned the roaring flame in my stomach.

"Harriet…" My name was sugar on his tongue.

Seb's hand rose and I flinched for a moment, not expecting the gesture as the back of his hand ran down my face.

His eyes darkened as though that was even physically possible, and when he removed his hand, he took the flame with him.

Slowly he stepped backwards.

I wanted to beg him to come back, but I'd made the mistake of speaking once already.

"I said you need to leave. This area is for performers only." The bite in his words seemed to have disappeared, but an authoritative tone still rang around each syllable.

"Cherry said to wait for her. You heard—" My roommate shouted.

"I don't give a fuck what Cherry said. Your friend needs to leave Lilah before I personally drag you both from here."

An airtight memory began to stroke my mind. I hated when people shouted, I hated it even more when I knew it was because of me.

"It's fine, I'm going." My voice was shaky and quiet, and I quickly clamped my mouth shut, not trusting the words that were dancing around on the tip of my tongue.

Seb didn't move to let me past. Instead, I cowardly dipped around him, and when my bare arm brushed against his, every inch of my skin scorched into a furnace.

Not sparing another glance in his or Delilah's direction I scurried through the opening in the tent, desperate to escape the oven I had been locked in.

I welcomed the cool air as it invaded my lungs and trampled over my raging skin. Seb reeked of danger, and I had enough of that in my life to even begin entertaining the fantasies that had sprung to life behind my eyelids.

I knew it would be a mistake coming here tonight.

Maybe it had been a mistake coming here at all.

Seb was right, I didn't belong here, and if that was so easy for him to see, how long would it be until others saw through the costume I was wearing.

Chapter Six

Seb

"What the fuck Delilah? You know the rules." Delilah huffed in front of me, it was almost comical. Her tiny frame made her look like a child when she was mad. If it wasn't for the fact that Harriet had been here, so close to the underbelly of the Carnival, I might have laughed.

Anybody could have been back here; anyone could have mistaken her for a performer and forced her into one of the other rooms, thinking her cries of protest were some form of roleplay for their fantasies.

The thought sent whiplash up the back of my neck, and flaming anger to the tips of my fingers. It was a good thing I had been around before that happened.

"Harriet's my new roommate Seb, I just wanted her to feel welcome. Besides, we're allowed back here. Cherry said—" Why the fuck was it always someone else's fault?

"I don't care what *Cherry* said. Your friend stays the fuck away from this tent Lilah. Is that clear?" I didn't give her a chance to respond, I needed to get some fresh air before I said something that would get me in trouble.

The breeze hit me as soon as I was outside, and I welcomed it.

Opening night at the Carnival had the opportunity to go one of two ways. It either went well, the girls played their part, the mules fed the addicted and we all got a generous payout from Saffron.

But there was also the possibility it could turn sour, and having someone like Harriet in the performer's only area created that possibility.

I didn't want her anywhere near this toxic cesspool, let alone in the tent that entertained the most corruption.

The moment I'd stepped through the entrance, I was distracted by the perky arse standing in front of me, and I immediately knew who it belonged to.

I'd wanted to grab her, and drag her kicking and screaming into my own private room, but I couldn't risk her being there. I refused to complicate her in this, she was too innocent to be scared by the dive world I lived in.

And when she bit back at me, seeing that fierceness in her eyes, *that challenge.* Fuck. It had my cock stirring.

Everything she did had my fucking cock stirring.

Normally it took more than the innocent lips of an attractive woman to catch my attention, but the way her tits begged me to grab them when she folded her arms, and the way she'd bitten her lip. All of it had me fighting the intrusive thoughts that rampaged around in my head.

I needed a drink.

Heading in the direction of the customer bar, I looked into each of the stalls as I passed. Crowds of partygoers were swarming around each one, and roars of victory were erupting from them all.

Everyone loved opening night.

The visitors didn't know, but it was the one night we made the games easier to win. We laced the odds to make them work in their favour, it ensured they would return and encouraged more of their guiltless spending.

I paused in front of one of the stands and watched as a group cheered their success at the ring toss when a man's voice spoke behind me.

"Sebastian?"

I peered over my shoulder at the man, his body dressed in a smart charcoal suit and his dark greying hair neatly combed back.

He looked like the kind of man I'd spent my entire life avoiding. Conceited businessmen who thought they could buy you with their money.

"I'm John. Saffron said you were expecting me."

I turned to give him my full attention and held my hand out between us. His shake was tight as he gripped, a way of asserting his dominance.

"It's Seb. She mentioned something."

John smiled at me, but it wasn't kind. Fortunately I had a lot of experience dealing with unkind men.

"It's good to finally meet you. Am I right in thinking your stock resides in that tent?"

Fucking stock.

I'd heard the girls being referred to as numerous things, but stock? That was a new one.

I ground my teeth together, not attempting to hide the agitation he was fuelling. "Yeah. Go wait in there, I'll find someone to help you."

John nodded and disappeared into the crowd.

Stock? Arsehole.

Rounding the corner, I noticed Tony emerging from the crowds, his body freezing when he spotted me making a beeline for him.

"I need you to find some stuff out for me." Not only was Tony our resident tech guy, and had been for the past five years, but he was also an excellent hacker. He could find information on anyone with a few clicks of a mouse. I didn't like pulling the rest of the performers and staff into my personal business, but I needed to know everything about Harriet.

I wanted to know who she was, where she grew up, and most importantly why she was here. Hell, I wanted to know what she'd eaten for breakfast this morning.

The first few interactions we'd had had been from afar, she didn't even know I was there. But now, having seen her up close, letting the vanilla scent of her skin infiltrate my senses, she had me hooked.

I was a starving man, desperate to taste her.

Harriet was like a deer in headlights when she'd seen me earlier, and her beautiful brown opal eyes carved their way into my nightmares. I didn't want to feel too smug, but noticing the bob in her throat hitch when our bodies nearly touched, and the way her chest rose and fell with each of her breaths fuelled the obsession.

I needed to make sure Delilah chose more suitable clothes for her for next time though, I couldn't have anyone else seeing the parts of her body that would belong to me.

But fuck me if she didn't look fucking delicious.

"Lilah's new roommate, Harriet. Find out whatever you can. I need it by morning." Tony nodded and walked past me, back in the direction of the circus tent.

I liked that he didn't ask questions. It would be easier to keep my new game a secret the fewer questions that were asked.

Images of Harriet's body leant over the counter in Smithy's began overrunning my head. The way that peachy arse had stretched around the back of her jeans, the way her husky voice purred in my ears. It was like she was fucking made for me.

My fingers twitched.

It wouldn't take much to get her on her knees, I saw how she responded to me, I knew the effect I had on her. And that fucking mouth, how good her lips would feel when they were wrapped around my—

Nails on my arm dragged me from the frenzy that was starting to untangle in my head as Cherry stepped into my view.

"That was quick." I hung an arm around her shoulders as we manoeuvred through the hoards and attempted to give her my full attention.

"Smithy never did know how to pace himself." A quiet laugh shook her body, but her words were camouflaged in sadness.

Each of us had been forced to partake in the extracurricular activities of the Carnival since we joined, and though most of us were privy to some kind of law-breaking, it didn't mean we enjoyed it.

Cherry was one of seven girls who had been brought in purely to satisfy the loyalist customers at the Carnival. Saffron had a long list of high paying clientele that donated a lot of money for a few hours with one of our top performers.

Many of them had needs, *fantasies*, ones that weren't fulfilled by the wives and girlfriends they kept at home, but ones that Saffron was happy to provide for them.

Other performers were tasked with taking advantage of the clumsier visitors, those who were naive to the wandering hands of thieves. Over the years, we'd managed to get our hands on cars, house keys, even legal documents that had been used for blackmail.

Most of the time though it was money, that was always the easiest thing to steal undetected.

Alongside the girls, the most profitable venture of the Carnival was the drugs. That was where I came in. I negotiated with the suppliers and then distributed the wares to the mules. As well as that, I was the only male performer that doubled as the *help* to Saffron, the kind of help I despised above everything else. The kind that had my skin crawling.

"I hope he didn't give you too much trouble." Cherry shrugged under my weight and wrapped her arm around my waist.

"Smithy's one of the nicer guys." I knew what she meant.

I'd met Cherry when I first joined the Carnival, she was the same age as me, and we instantly hit it off. We kept each other sane in the chaos.

When she turned twenty-one, she moved from being a greeter, an entertainer for the clients, and became one of *the girls.*

She'd been exposed to every kind of fantasy the men would have, carrying each one to her doorstep and often on her body, leaving her more and more numb. The more extreme, the more money Cherry made, it was just a shame that money didn't end up in her hand.

We rounded the corner of the parking lot, and I wrapped her against my chest. We'd all made our beds with the Carnival, it just bothered me that some of us ended up in them more often than others.

"I have some stuff to take care of, you should head back before anyone notices you're away from the tent. I just sent a guy over. I think he's after a chat with Saffron. You should keep him company."

The roles we had to play may have made us immune to our feelings, but the consequences of defying the rules of the Carnival were what caused many to topple the edge.

Or to just disappear.

I had only done it once, and once was enough for me to learn never to do it again. I still wore the scars from five years ago, a sign I refused to be broken.

Cherry smiled up at me, and I gave her a kiss on the forehead before stalking in the direction of my motorbike.

"Seb," she called after me. "Why did you make that girl leave? You've never had an issue with Delilah coming into the tent?"

That's because Delilah wasn't a goddess like Harriet. Sure, she was good-looking, but everyone knew who she was. There was no mistaking the cannonball for a performer. But Harriet…

"She doesn't belong here." I didn't turn when I answered, Harriet's face coming to life behind my eyes and the reminder of her presence skirting underneath my skin.

When I got to the bike I unhooked the ratchet strap securing the helmet, and it fell to the ground with a thump.

Quickly dragging it up and pulling it over my head, I swiped the visor down and turned the handlebar. The engine came to life under my body, and I quickly moved from the lot, skidding in the direction of the apartment complexes in town.

In the direction of my new obsession.

Chapter Seven

Harriet

I'd been lying on the floor staring at the ceiling for over an hour. Seb's phantom touches danced over my skin, and every time I closed my eyes his striking dark glare paraded through my mind like a marching band demanding my attention.

My imagination ran away with images of his body, or at least how I pictured it, and the tattoos that snaked over his arms caressed my skin.

I clenched my thighs in an attempt to sedate the throbbing, but each movement caused more friction, and I let out an exasperated huff.

It had been a long time since I'd experienced any raw, hungry need. This was so intense that with every motion I could feel the frustration growing, and my willpower to ignore it draining.

I sat up and looked at the clock flashing on the oven, it was midnight, Delilah would probably be home when the Carnival closed, which was about an hour away. That gave me a short window of opportunity for some privacy.

Lifting my heavy body from the floor, I turned the latch on the front door and began walking towards the bathroom we shared.

The room wasn't large, but it also wasn't small. At the far end, a bathtub underneath a showerhead lounged, and I narrowed my eyes, a wanton bliss hovering beneath my skin.

I was itching to get out of my clothes, the fabric latching onto Seb's smoky smell from where he'd been pressed up against me.

It had been hard to ignore the way his cock twitched against my body during our contact, and I craved to feel it again.

Craved to feel *him* again. The voices in my head were causing a riot, one that could only be soothed by the hand of a devilish man.

What is wrong with you. He barely even looked at you.

I pulled my T-shirt over my head, followed quickly by my lacy red bralette and the jean shorts that were stuck to my clammy skin. Finally, I shimmied from the fishnet tights and stared at myself in the full-length mirror pinned to the tiled wall.

My eyes immediately narrowed on the scars and burn marks that painted my legs, my fingers tracing each one as unwelcome memories resurfaced in my mind.

Every ugly welt and raised etching provoked the numbness to consume me, begged the chaos to come out and play. Shaking myself from the thoughts, I stepped over the edge of the bathtub and turned the tap, bringing the shower to life.

The immediate blast of cold water jolted me, and I stepped back to shield myself from the harsh icy coldness. After a few minutes, the water warmed and my fingers waved under the stream, trickles pouring between each one.

Content that the water was now a comfortable temperature, I stepped forward and allowed it to waterfall over my skin.

My eyes closed, and Seb immediately appeared behind them. The way he walked, the gruff sound of his voice as his breath fanned my raw skin.

Every inch of his powerful demeanour demanded my attention, and I was happy to bow to him.

Ghost touches of his hand over my naked skin, and the feel of his lips on my body flittered in my imagination, my fantasies edging closer to the surface.

Fantasies I didn't even know existed.

Allowing myself to give in to my needs, my left hand began trailing down my body, whilst my right held my weight up against the shower wall. My fingers danced across my chest first, delicately swiping over my perk nipple, before they closed tightly and squeezed.

I'd always enjoyed rough hands and heavy touches, a desire that Felix had struggled to sedate. He scolded me for the lucid yearnings that I had, often making me feel ashamed for wanting to try different things.

I never allowed his words to stop me from using my own hands to throw me into pleasure he could never create.

The throb between my legs was growing frantic and needy with every pinch of my chest, and I allowed my hand to explore further down.

As my fingers brushed the skin across my stomach and then further, small breathy moans fell from my lips, and my head leaned forward. Water ran down my face, but I welcomed it, the stream provoking goosebumps to explode across my skin.

Seb spoke into my ear.

"That's it princess, show me how you touch yourself."

I had to give my imagination credit, she was working overtime. The fact the bathroom had filled with thick steam only helped to guide my mind. Nothing could distract me.

Using the words as encouragement, I let my fingers fall further down, and when they hit the throb of my nerve-riddled clit, my whole body ignited.

"Faster."

The desperate, gruff voice echoed through my ears again, and I bit my lip to stifle the moans that threatened to scream from my lips as my fingers quickened their assault.

"I want to hear you. Let me hear that sweet voice."

The coil in my stomach was growing tighter with each swipe of my fingers, and my throat sang with moans, desperate to please the imaginary man in my head. My voice grew louder as I threatened to topple from the edge.

"Good girl. I want you to come for me. Let me see you fall apart."

"Seb—"

That was all I needed to throw myself over the edge, and as waves of pleasure barricaded through my body, my legs became limp, and I pushed my palms harder against the wall to stop myself from falling.

"You did so well Harriet. You look fucking delicious when you're falling apart for me."

I stood there, panting, and trying to calm my beating heart for what felt like an eternity when a sudden crash from outside startled me, and I was ripped from my ecstasy-filled trance.

Quickly turning the tap on the shower, I raised my still trembling legs over the bath and wrapped a towel tightly around my body. Creeping the door open, I peered through the crack. It was empty, quiet.

My bare feet snuck over the floorboards, leaving a trail of water dripping from my hair behind me, but as I entered further into the room there was still no sign of what had caused the noise. I must have imagined it, my senses once again playing tricks on me.

I looked over at my bedroom, the door was closed.

I'm sure I'd left that open.

Maybe Delilah had closed it before we left, and I hadn't noticed.

Not wanting to take any chances, I quietly tiptoed to the kitchen and pulled a knife from the utensil drawer.

I had no idea what I would do if someone was in my room, but feeling slightly more prepared I snuck towards my little sanctuary.

My hand shook as I pushed down the handle, and the door opened with a screech, the noise heightening my nerves.

It was empty.

I let out an anxiety fuelled laugh and threw the knife onto the TV cabinet before walking over the threshold into my room.

Satisfied that I was still alone, I went straight for the pile of clothes that Delilah had left on my bed, pulled out an oversized black T-shirt from the pile and dragged it over my head, before pulling my hair and braiding it into two sections. Sitting down on the mattress, I gave my chest a chance to stop its rabid thumps when my consciousness poked out.

What was I doing? I had a fiancé, and here I was fantasising about another man.

A fiancé that cheats on you. What you did doesn't even come close.

I needed to call Felix, I needed to end things. Try and pacify the guilt.

A lump formed in my throat, and my eyes stung with tears threatening to spill. I had only been here for three days, and I was already getting caught up in a game I didn't want to participate in.

In search of the one thing I knew would bring me comfort, I headed back towards the jean shorts I'd abandoned in the bathroom, and the photo of my mother hidden in my purse.

The shorts were light as I lifted them, and my brows narrowed. My vision darted around the rest of the clothes.

My purse wasn't there.

I ran to the spot in the living room I had laid on and frantically searched.

Nothing.

My eyes clamped shut and I dug my fingers into my temples. Fear began prodding my chest, and oxygen teased my lungs. I'd had it at the Carnival, where could it have—

Seb.

When he'd caged me against the pool table, he must have swiped it from my pocket. Blind rage, mixed with burning tears blurred my vision.

That piece of shit trash.

To think I'd just allowed my weaknesses to get the better of me.

I needed to go back to the Carnival and confront him, but it was too late to do that now, everything would be closed up and there was no way I would get back in.

Deciding I would go back tomorrow and demand he return my most treasured possession, I moved back to my bedroom and climbed under the duvet barrelling myself in its feathery weight. I allowed the sadness to swallow me as I curled myself into a ball, and the tears drowned me.

I was alone, lost, confused, and all I wanted was my mom.

My entire body felt like it had been on a five-day bender, every muscle screamed with aches, and my head felt as though someone had submerged it in water and then run it over with a car.

To say I had had a bad night's sleep was an understatement.

As my eyes focused, I played through the events of yesterday, bringing me right up to the moment I realised my purse was missing.

The pit in my stomach returned, and raging butterflies began cannonballing themselves around. I tried to swallow the lump in my throat, but it wouldn't budge, forcing me to take responsibility for how careless I'd been.

I'd put myself in that position, I'd allowed someone to take the purse right from under my nose.

The anger had vanished, but in its place, a stream of uneasiness was left jiving under my skin. Seb had been intimidating last night, I could only imagine what he would be like when someone was accusing him of being a thief.

I couldn't think about that though, it didn't matter.

That heartless arsehole had stolen from me, and I intended to retrieve my lost belongings.

I opted for another oversized shirt today, paired with a pair of ripped black jeans. I needed to be comfortable if I was going to be able to fake confidence. Alarm bells roared in my head. I had a scratch, a niggle, I couldn't tranquilise.

It was as though my body was begging me to reconsider my choices—but my heart would never let it win.

For once I was grateful for the stubborn trait I had inherited from my mother. My chest pounded statically as her beautiful face skated through my head.

Leaving the bedroom I stomped into the living room and froze when I spotted the figure in the corner.

Delilah sat with her head leaning on the edge of the table, her raven hair sprawled in a matted mess. I cocked my head for a moment and watched her, a small tingle of panic rising in me when I couldn't see her moving, my instincts suddenly kicking in.

Compressions for thirty, breaths for two.

But then her head turned, and her eyes sprang open when she spotted me. Quickly wiping the drawl from her mouth, she sat upright in the chair.

"Good night?" I laughed as I walked to the fridge and pulled out a bottle of water. Loosening the cap I chugged half of it, desperately trying to dampen my desert dry mouth.

"I think so?" Delilah wiped at her face, and the last of her makeup spread itself around her skin, giving her horrendous panda eyes. That only fanned my laugh more.

"I'll pick you up some painkillers." I dropped another bottle of water onto the table, and she snatched it gratefully.

After swallowing a mouthful, she raised her eyebrow. "Where are you headed?"

"The community garden, I told them I'd help out. I'm going to run and grab some bits for my room as well, some new clothes. Need anything?" With a groan and a thump, Delilah's head slammed against the table as she shook it.

"No, I'll just die quietly here. Hey, before you go. About last night, I'm sorry about Seb, he's normally not that much of an arsehole."

The butterflies stirred at the mention of the man's name.

Great. That meant he had taken a personal dislike to *me*. That was okay, I was about to give him a reason to dislike me.

"Don't worry about it. I've dealt with men like him before."

Delilah lifted her head, "Harriet. Trust me when I say you've *never* met a man like Seb." I raised my eyebrow, waiting for her to elaborate. "Just be careful, you shouldn't ignore him."

I folded my arms, "the guy told me to leave town."

Delilah waved her hand dismissively.

"Ignore that part, but the Carnival. It might be a wise idea to stay clear of it for the time being. Let him get used to you being around." I rolled my eyes.

That wasn't going to happen. What kind of person needed time to get used to someone else being in their town?

Closing the door gently behind me, I skipped down the stairs taking two steps at a time, and out of the building's front door. Immediately I was hit by the sun's penetrating rays.

The heat was strange for October, but I let it warm my body. I was reconsidering my choice of clothing. I made a mental note to go back up and change before I headed to the garden.

My car sat at the side of the road, tempting me. But it was a nice day out, I couldn't give up the opportunity for a walk, especially as it would help to clear my head before I got to the viper's den.

I took my headphones from my bag and turned my music up as high as I could stand. I needed to settle the murmuring voices in my head and sedate them a little before they persuaded me to turn back.

On my walk, I passed two bakeries, a diner, four automotive shops, and an ominous looking bar. No one could argue that Bromlin didn't have the necessities to make it a convenient place to live. It offered everything that a person would need, even those used to life's lavish side.

Turning the corner, the enormous metal gates ahead came into view and my breath lodged in my throat.

It's not too late to turn back.

I scolded the voices in my head, they didn't understand what I had to lose. My heart though, she understood well. But even she couldn't help but plummet when I spotted the metal chains and padlock wrapped around the gate's bars, there was no way to get inside.

I followed around the perimeter, looking for any sign of an opening when part of the fencing dipped lower than the rest.

I stood, my hands firmly planted on my hips as I assessed it, and on deciding that getting the photo back was absolutely worth it, I threw my bag over and began heaving myself up with the bar at the top.

My arms burned, igniting my muscles as I pulled. I needed to go to the gym.

A small victory smile curled on my lips as I bent over the top, but it was short lived.

Suddenly I was falling forward, my face heading straight for the muddy ground below. With a thud and a sudden shooting pain down my leg, I fell onto the field. The pain intensified, and I had to blink to stop stinging tears crashing from my eyes.

Looking at my leg, the fabric of Delilah's jeans had been torn from my hip all the way to my knee, leaving a furious gash in its place that had ripped apart the newest injury on my thigh.

There wasn't any blood yet, but I knew it would come. This is how they always started.

Not wanting to waste any time, I quickly scrambled to my feet, collecting the spilt contents of my bag as I did. The Carnival at night was a riot of people and music, chatter and chaos. The scene in front of me couldn't have been more different.

The ground had been trampled so thoroughly that it no longer resembled grass, the earth underneath covering the green field, and the stalls that were alive with colours and lights were now closed down, covered in stripey sheets of plastic fabric. An eery cloud of fog weaved around each of the small tents and a burning smell hung heavy in the air.

I tread in the direction of the performer's tent, the memory of the steps I'd taken last night guiding me in the direction I hoped was right. Each movement was a losing battle with my legs.

Resistant weight was driving them down, making each footstep heavy and uneven, and the thumping in my chest was so powerful I thought my rib cage might combust. The closer I got to the tent, the clearer the bellowing music that was coming from inside was, and my pounding anxiety intensified.

I desperately wanted to crawl away, but I refused to be a coward. I needed to do this for myself, I needed to do it for my *mom.*

As I reached the tent's opening, a dampness on my thigh distracted me. Peering down my eyes widened at the sight of my leg dripping scarlet and mixing with the sludgy mud.

My face wrinkled; this one was probably going to need stitches.

Shifting the edge of the fabric to the side I spied through the gap; the music wasn't an accurate reflection of the scene in front of me.

Female performers were sprawled around the sofas, their bodies hanging over the edges lifeless and rigid. Other women were sat around in quiet conversation. As well as them, I counted six males, who all looked about the same age as me. They sauntered around the room, but their movements seemed forced as if they weren't controlling their bodies.

As if they were high.

I did another swipe of the room, and chewed on the inside of my mouth, debating my next move. Seb was nowhere to be seen.

"Who are you?" A man's voice from behind startled me, and I let out a little squeal at the intrusion. Spinning around, I hugged my bag closer to my side and rattled my head for an excuse.

The man in front of me looked a little older than the ones inside the tent, and he had curly red hair that fell in ribbons around his face.

At my silence, a boyish grin rose on his face, and I willingly mirrored it back, my cheeks turning rosy. Something about him was charming, and when he held his hand out, I easily took hold of it.

"I'm Tony. Are you looking for someone?" He removed his hand from mine and stashed both into his pockets, rocking on his heels as he did. He appeared almost as though he was nervous, and his head looked over his shoulders several times.

I coughed clearing my throat. "I'm looking for Seb, do you know where I might find him?" I tried to look as innocent as possible, but the daggers protruding from my eyes were sure to give me away.

Tony didn't seem to notice and walked past, holding the tent opening to the side and motioning for me to enter.

"He shouldn't be a minute; do you want a coffee while you wait?" My throat let out a hum. The idea of having a coffee sent a thread of bliss dancing over my tongue. A red flag that I needed to kick the caffeine addiction.

I smiled up at Tony and gently nodded my head.

Following him over to the kitchenette at the back of the room I became very aware of several pairs of eyes inspecting me on my travels, some coming from the men circling around the room, and some from the women sitting in clusters.

It was clear I wasn't welcome here.

I tried to ignore them and kept my eyes firmly fixed ahead of me, but it was hard when I was being looked at by circling vultures.

The space had a strong scent, but I couldn't pinpoint it. Alcohol mixed with marijuana and something muskier, but as Tony poured a cup of black coffee and slid it in my direction, my senses were taken over by the scent of nuts that winded in the air.

Bringing the mug to my mouth, I inhaled the liquid and closed my eyes as the scent calmed my jittery nerves.

"What happened to your leg?" Tony's eyebrow rose as I opened my eyes and looked down at the gash in my thigh. Even though the pain was getting worse, I was somewhat glad that the blood hid the rest of the ugly marks that were carved underneath.

"I jumped the fence. You have a chain around the gate." I shrugged; I didn't have the energy to lie. I expected Tony to be shocked or angry, but he just laughed, the gesture causing his whole body to shake as his head fell back.

Tony gave off such light-hearted positive energy that it was impossible not to immediately warm to him. It was a strange contrast to the frosty introduction I'd had with Seb.

"Next time, just go around the back, there's another entrance by the parking lot." I nodded and took another sip from the burning liquid in my fingers. Tony didn't need to know, but there wouldn't be a next time. There was no way I was stepping foot in this dingy Carnival again.

"Who the *fuck* saw Greyson last night." A demanding voice bellowed as it came from one of the doors on the side of the tent, and the sudden interruption to the quiet startled me.

Seb.

As if on instinct the throb between my legs ignited, and I mentally berated the reaction my body had to the devil. I needed to find a way to keep her preoccupied, apparently fantasising in the shower wasn't going to cut it.

One of the men tailing the room froze, and his voice was low as he spoke.

"He was causing problems."

I thought it couldn't get any more reticent. I was wrong.

Thick tension enveloped the room, everyone's attention on Seb as he stalked towards the man.

The pair stood face to face for a moment, and the throb grew tenfold. Seb had intimidated me last night with his glare, but watching him unleash that on someone else and exert so much dominance had me crumbling.

Stupid woman. You see danger and you get weak at the knees.

Suddenly, Seb's arm swung back and crashed into the man's face. As he fell to the ground Seb clutched the collar of his shirt and yanked him upwards, blood pouring from his now broken nose.

His voice was quiet, but I could still hear the grind of his words as he spoke down at the man.

"Pull a stunt like that again, and it'll be the last you do." He let go, and the man fell back to the ground, his hand swiping at his nose as he went. "You're a fucking mule. You don't make decisions."

The confidence I was so desperately holding onto was crumbling away rapidly.

I wanted the ground to swallow me.

When Seb's glare circled the room and narrowed on me, I nearly begged it to.

"What the fuck is she doing here?" He quickly raced in my direction, and I had to force my legs not to run straight to the exit. Dark emotionless eyes were consuming mine, and as he got closer my body desperately ached to move, but I was paralysed into stillness.

He stood glaring at me and I shuffled on my feet, the movement causing me to wince from the pain in my thigh. Seb looked down and spotted the blood drying against my jeans, but he didn't show an ounce of concern, instead, his attention turned to the man standing at my side.

"Tony. *What* is she doing here?" Seb's voice hissed, and a pang of guilt hit my chest. I'd just watched what Seb was capable of, and knowing that I might be responsible for the same fate being handed to Tony caused my fists to clench.

"He tried to make me leave, but I needed to see you." My voice was quiet, but it still had a level of firmness to it. Seb looked between us both, and then at the coffee steaming in my hands.

"Yeah. Sure looks like he was trying to get you out." He folded his arms, and I couldn't stop my tongue from darting out and dampening my bottom lip at the way his muscles sprung to life. The ink covering every inch of his skin was both attractive and intimidating, and I imagined the fangs of the snake wrapped around my throat puncturing my delicate flesh.

Snap out of it Harriet.

I laid my cup on the counter behind me and mirrored his stance, folding my own arms across my chest. I was thankful for the fabric that was covering my cleavage, I had the upper hand when my body wasn't exposed.

"I've come to get my purse back."

I lifted my chin and refused to separate our eye contact. Looking past Seb I noticed the rest of the room's occupants retreating, leaving the three of us in a stare-off.

Seb was the first one to crack. The corner of his mouth rose into a smirk and a snigger left his lips.

"And what makes you think I have your purse princess." He raised his brow at me.

I hated the nickname; it made me seem delicate and weak. He knew nothing about me, I wasn't a princess.

I was the goddamn kraken.

"I had it last night before I left here, and now it's gone. You were the only person I saw." He pursed his lips together, but the smirk remained. "I know it was you."

"Couldn't resist could you? Stop lying Harriet. I know you came here for me." The words were low, danger coating each one. "Tell me, how wet do you get when we're this close?" He took a step closer, bursting my imaginary bubble. "Or maybe you *want* me this close. I can practically hear the throb between your legs."

I— *What.*

Seb sniggered at my widened eyes and took a step backwards.

"I don't have your purse little siren."

Seriously, how many nicknames did this man have for me?

Breath finally re-entered my lungs.

Seb turned away from me and began walking towards the entrance, but I refused to let him leave. Running from my stunned position I threw my body in front of him, blocking his path and forcing him to stop.

"I *know* it was you. I don't want the purse back, but there's a photo inside I need. Please." I didn't want to seem vulnerable in front of this man, but if it was my only option to get my possessions back I would ignore my pride.

Hell, I would get on my knees if it meant I had that Polaroid.

"Your voice is so sweet when you beg." He edged closer, his words sliding against my ear. "I wonder how you would sound begging on your knees." A lethal grin sparked to life on his face.

It was like he could read my mind.

I wanted to splutter but I choked back my surprise, refusing to give him any indication of the fluster building up inside my chest, though I'm sure the redness smothering my face was enough of a hint.

This man was full of himself.

Seb's eyes narrowed, and he looked thoughtful for a moment before he let out a heavy sigh.

Taking a step back, his fingers ran through his hair, and he turned to face Tony, who was silently stood watching us in the kitchenette. "Get Cherry." A frantic nod came from the redhead, and he hurried off through one of the doors. I didn't take my eyes off Seb, I didn't trust him not to try and steal something else from me.

Like my sanity with the carnage he was causing inside my head.

"I told you, you don't belong here. Why are you here?" His words caught me off guard, but I kept a firm stance.

"My purse, you know that's why—"

"Not here. *Bromlin.* Why did you come to Bromlin?"

That I definitely wasn't getting into with him. I broke our eye contact and peered around the room, my chest thudding from his penetrating gaze. "Change of scenery."

He let out a low chuckle. "People don't come here for a change of scenery, they come here to escape."

"That's the same thing."

"No princess, they come to escape their sins. What they don't realise is they're walking straight through the gates of hell."

Seb stepped forward, invading my personal space again as his hand trailed up my face and he wrapped a strand of hair around his fingers. His eyes were molten cores overpowering my lungs.

I wanted to suffocate.

"I bet you have some sins you'd like to beg forgiveness for."

I didn't ignore the twinkle in his dark eyes as I stared at him, but before I could argue, Tony reappeared in the room, followed by Cherry who, in her hand, held my bright yellow daisy-covered purse.

My eyes dampened at seeing it, and I nearly dissolved to the floor.

"You found it, thank you." Cherry folded her arms, a snarky grin itching on her mouth.

"No, I stole it. Now I'm returning it." The air was knocked from my chest. I opened my mouth but quickly closed it, accepting I didn't need to know why.

I turned, the guilt forcing me to acknowledge I needed to apologise to Seb, but when I turned he was gone.

I quickly unzipped it; the money was gone but at least the photo was still in there. Stashing it into my bag, and after sheepishly smiling at Cherry, I swiftly walked towards the tent's exit.

"I'll come let you out," Tony called behind me, and I slowed, allowing him to walk beside me.

We stayed in comfortable silence as we headed towards the padlocked gate, and as promised Tony let me out and relocked the chains after. "Thank you." His voice was quiet, so quiet I barely heard it. Narrowing my eyes I gave him a questioning look.

"Seb's a good guy really. He's just protective of the Carnival. He doesn't like outsiders." That much was obvious.

"It was nice meeting you, Tony." I smiled at him and surprised myself at the lack of force behind it. He was a gentle giant, and it saddened me a little that he was probably treated like the man inside the tent had been. But I shook the thought from my head. It was none of my business.

Clutching my bag tightly, and throwing my headphones back into my ears, I headed in the direction of the community garden, blissfully ignoring the raging pain evolving in my thigh.

Chapter Eight

Seb

I leant on the sofa, one arm stretched outwards, and used the other to satisfy the hungry need eating at me with a glass of whiskey. When the liquid poured down my throat I closed my eyes, savouring the taste on my tongue.

The scent of vanilla dragged through my senses, along with the memory of Harriet and those startling brown eyes. Like shining opals, they glittered and dazzled.

A trap if there ever was one.

I knew she had been there, the second I walked through the tent I'd been attacked by that intoxicating vanilla signature that belonged only to her. I was so used to the musky scents that littered the air after the opening of the Carnival, that the sweet Madagascan intrusion threw me off. It was the same one that clouded her bathroom when I'd snuck in.

When I'd watched her touch herself to me.

She was fucking delicious, the way her body quivered with each movement of her gentle fingers, the way her pale skin was coated by the lengths of her brunette hair. Her voice was like a line of ecstasy floating against the walls.

And when she said my name. *Fuck.*

She was making it impossible to stay away, and after that, I knew I wouldn't.

But I needed her to see what I was capable of, needed to scare her, find a way to keep *her* away from *me.* I couldn't control myself, but she could control what *she* did.

And what I needed her to do was run fucking miles.

Though I knew that would be pointless. If I had to chase her to the ends of the earth, I would. The chase was the best part.

This had become a game, like a vulture circling its prey, I would circle her until I got what I wanted, *what I craved.*

And what I wanted, was *her.*

Harriet's doe eyes were engraved into my head. Like an addiction, she called to me. When I'd hit Jimmy for the shit he had pulled with Greyson I could have gone easier on him, but I wanted Harriet to fear me, wanted her to see firsthand the chaos I could cause, it was the only way I could stop her magnetising towards me. That wasn't how this worked.

I needed to make sure the other performers didn't try and challenge my decisions as well, the need to be feared was partially responsible for the broken nose I'd inflicted on him.

I had appearances to uphold.

Tony appeared at the tent's entrance, and when he came closer, vanilla followed him. He'd been with *her.* He threw himself down on the sofa and leant his head backwards, his curly red mop flopping around.

"Harriet Wolston. Aged twenty-three. Originally from Callie Bay. She's engaged to high profile businessman Felix Dremorton, met when they were eighteen. Her father is Richard Wolston, of Wolston Enterprises."

My silence encourages Tony to continue. "Her mom, Angie, passed away from an overdose six years ago. She has no siblings or any other relatives."

I nodded, and Tony rose from the sofa.

"I want to know about Felix—why he's not with her." There was a reason why the siren had wound up here, and I intended to find out what it was.

Speaking of, I'd given her long enough to get home. It was time I paid her a visit. See whether she was taking my warning seriously.

If she had, she should be packing her bags by now.

The idea of her running, trying to escape me, caused a frenzy in my head, but the idea of her suddenly hiding with another man had my fists tightening, and anger waived in a tsunami over me.

The need to own her, brand her innocent body and force her to bend to me battled with the chaos to keep her away from this illusive world. I couldn't have her turning up here, she would easily be mistaken for a performer, and I couldn't let that happen.

No one would fucking touch what was mine.

Rising from the sofa, I grabbed the motorbike helmet from the pool table and quickly ran to my bike. The moment I was close enough I threw a leg over and revved the engine.

I needed to feel her porcelain skin in my hands, needed to bathe in her toxic vanilla scent, let it drown me.

I needed her.

Slowing down to a stop outside the back entrance to Harriet's building I leant back for a moment, deciding whether to risk entering through the window again like last night, or whether I should be more chivalrous and enter through the front door.

It would have to be the window, she might not answer the door if she knew I was there. If she didn't let me in I would take the door off its hinges, and I don't think Lilah would be too pleased with me if I did that.

Movement from the corner of my visor caught my attention, and I became distracted by busying bodies in the community garden.

I never understood people's need to plant things, I'm sure there was some philosophical bullshit about letting things grow and blossom, but I wasn't interested in that.

In the centre, beautiful chocolate hair wrapped around Harriet's face, and she wiped her gloved hand against her cheek smearing dry soil over her delicate skin.

She was laughing with an older woman, and she looked so…happy, *carefree*. I narrowed my eyes, observing her, when a man joined the pair. He smiled at my girl and laid his hand on her back, guiding her towards another area of the park.

Every muscle in my body tightened at his contact.

Who the fuck did he think he was?

Throwing myself from the bike, I pulled the gloves from my hand and stalked towards the gate. As soon as I reached the barrier separating us, I folded my arms over the bars and peered across.

"Can I help you?" My presence caught the attention of the woman Harriet had been speaking to, but it wasn't hers I wanted.

At the far back, Harriet and the man leisurely strolled together, his hand never leaving her back.

I was going to cut his fucking hands off.

As if my mind was already anticipating my next move, I reached into the front of my jeans and flipped out a small pocketknife. Flicking it open and closed, the movement distracted me from using my fists. Luckily the woman didn't notice the shining piece of metal in my fingertips.

"I'm here to speak to Harriet." I kept my voice low, and I was grateful that the helmet prevented it from being recognisable.

Not that it was likely this woman knew who I was but I needed to make sure my identity remained safely hidden away.

The woman waved at Harriet, and she began walking towards us, her eyebrows furrowed together.

"This person says they're here for you."

This fucking person. I was more than a person; I was hell itself.

The puzzled expression didn't leave Harriet as we were left alone, and she folded her arms across her chest, her defences immediately being thrown up.

"Can I help you?" Oh sweet princess, you have no idea.

"If he touches you again, he won't have hands left." Her eyes went wide, and she stepped back, but I caught her arm before she could move too far away. "I don't share very well."

Harriet's eyes blinked at my hand on her, and that was when I remembered I'd taken my gloves off revealing my unmistakable ink. Brown eyes pivoted to my other hand where the blade was still being flicked open and closed, and they widened. Horror painted her innocent features.

"And I don't fucking bluff either Harriet. That's your only warning."

I loosened my hold and stalked away from the gate back to my bike. Sitting there for a moment I watched her interactions as she returned to the group of people.

A smirk lifted at my lips when I noticed the man attempt to put his hand back on her again, but she moved, dodging his touch, and sheepishly peered in my direction over her shoulder.

Reving the handlebar of my bike, the loud roar caught the attention of the pair, and as I sped off, I couldn't help the satisfaction that wrapped up my body.

Good, little siren. You're learning to play.

Chapter Nine

Harriet

I was beginning to forget what a good night's sleep felt like. Today was the fifth day I'd laid on my mattress and had to snap myself out of a staring competition with the ceiling.

After my encounter with Seb at the tent, and then with the confrontation at the community garden, I'd settled into becoming a recluse and only leaving the apartment for work. My first couple of shifts at the tech store had gone well, and by well I mean Smithy had only attempted to try and grope me once.

Back in Callie Bay, I'd worked because I wanted to, not that I needed to. Felix brought home enough to support both of us, but I had never been one to rely on the charity of another to survive.

I'd learnt a long time ago that no one can save you apart from yourself.

Blinking my eyes rapidly to soothe the pricking from my stare off, I shunted myself upwards and leaned against the wall. The positive of being a recluse was that my room was finally beginning to take shape.

I'd painted the walls in chaotic purples and blues, and hung abstract prints around the walls. I found it hard to talk about how I was feeling, but the colours and the mixtures of shapes in the frames helped to isolate the hectic riots that stormed around in my mind.

I liked using art to show my feelings, it was as though they told a secret story only I knew the ending to.

As well as the paint, I'd bought myself a dark brown set of drawers that now housed my own new clothes and a neon light that I'd hung above the bed. When turned on it lit up with the words 'Once your own, twice alone.'

A depressing statement to most, but it brought a sense of familiarity to me, something I was desperately trying to hold on to after each night of agitated sleep.

I was clasping on to the idea of freedom and a fresh start that Bromlin promised me, but with each interaction I had outside the confines of the apartment, my heart was struggling to tame the storm brewing in my head.

Seb's words constantly haunted me, and I was beginning to reconsider why I had actually come here. Would it even be worth it if all I did was stay in the apartment?

It was too early to be making decisions, I would have my ritualistic morning coffee and go back to trying to right the world afterwards. Rising slowly, I untangled myself from the comfort of my duvet and began padding towards the door.

The gash on my leg was healing well, but I'd had to give myself stitches to help it along the way. When Delilah had seen it, she was adamant that I went to the emergency room. I'd made that mistake once before.

Go for help with a minor cut, end up being evaluated for saneness.

It wasn't me that was insane, it was everyone else.

After that, I learnt how to sew together my own injuries. Luckily I had a still hand, at least it helped to make them look less grotesque than they eventually would.

Entering the living room, I peered around the space but only a humble silence greeted me. Normally Delilah was up and about before me, hell I didn't think she slept most of the time, but it seemed today was the day she was gifting herself a lie in.

God knew she needed it.

Nearly every day this week I'd heard her stumbling through the doors at unearthly hours. How she was still standing after all her late-night escapades was beyond me.

Whilst I waited for the coffee to brew, I opened up the window above the dining bench and lit a cigarette. Another negative to being an introvert putting herself on house arrest was that the smoking was getting worse, I needed to find a way to sedate the devilled talons sticking in my head and making me weak.

I wasn't weak. I was using my addiction as a distraction, and a distraction was exactly what I needed.

Like mother like daughter.

My phone's cheery ringtone played from my bedroom, and I squinted my eyes at the oven's clock, seven. Who would be calling me at this ungodly hour?

Throwing the remainder of the cigarette out of the window, my feet padded the wooden floorboards to my room, dancing when they hit the plush bobbles of the rug.

It was useless trying to work out who was responsible for the bleating call. After I'd broken the screen a week ago, I'd kept reminding myself to get it replaced, but that was a little tricky when you were attempting to only leave the house for work and emergencies.

Smithy had told me he could get it fixed for a charge, but I didn't like the way he purred the word *charge* and followed it with a wink. The man gave me the creeps, but he also offered me a good cash in hand job. I had to pick my battles.

Clicking the bottom of the phone, I accepted the call and held it up to my mouth. Unfortunately, the volume had also broken during the assault, and each of my calls now had to be taken on loudspeaker.

So when my Dad's voice chalked through it, I was glad I had privacy.

"Happy birthday sweetheart!" His voice sang through the phone, and I nearly threw it again. Of course he would get the date of my birth wrong, but I didn't have the energy to correct him.

"Thanks," I mumbled. I didn't hold much hope for why he was calling me. The only conversation we'd exchanged since I'd left Callie Bay was him telling me what my actions were doing to poor Felix, and I wasn't in the mood for another lecture today.

"What are your plans?" I moved towards the patchwork sofa and collapsed into the cushion, resting my head against the wall behind it.

"Nothing. I have work." There was a long silence on the phone, but I knew he was still there, I heard his sharp inhale when I mentioned my new job.

"So you're staying there then?"

"That's the plan." I didn't hide the bite in my tone well, but that was on purpose. I wanted him to hear the edge in my voice, at least attempt to take me seriously.

"You know Felix is—"

"I don't want to hear about Felix!" I yelled into the speaker, "you don't *know* him Dad. You hold him on a bloody pedestal that he hasn't earned." Again the line went silent, but this time I couldn't hear his shallow breaths. There was a scuffle, and then a low sultry voice flowed into my ear.

"Harriet, *baby*, please. Come home." I ground my teeth, "I just want to know you're okay." I closed my eyes, trying to calm the butterflies itching in my chest, raging with the lie that leaked through the phone.

"Tell us where you are, we'll come get you. Things can go back to normal."

A scoff snuck from my mouth and I shook my head, disbelief coiling behind my eyelids.

"Felix. I am not telling you where I am, you're not my home. *This* is my home." Before he had the opportunity to argue, I firmly pushed my finger into the end call button. Along with a new phone, I was going to need a new number.

How long would it take for him to get it into his head that I wasn't going back?

How long would it take me to realise I *wasn't going back?*

A door closing to my left caught my attention, and Delilah appeared, her body covered in Superman pyjamas and her hair neatly braided behind her head.

"It's your birthday?"

I dropped the phone onto the cushion beside me and shook my head, "no. My Dad never could remember when it was. 31st October, Saturday."

At least he didn't get the month wrong, not that my dad needed a defence, but he was only two days off.

Delilah's face brightened. "Your birthday is Halloween?" Nodding my head, I rose from the sofa and moved towards my bedroom.

"Yep, some say that makes me the devil reincarnated." I gave her a mischievous grin as I entered the room.

I couldn't stop the comfort that swept me up when I was with Delilah, there was just something about her that forced all of my anxiety to evaporate, and I liked her company.

Despite the early morning wake ups I couldn't imagine being in anyone else's apartment. Every morning, regardless of how close to death she felt, Delilah had coffee brewing and some assortment of pastry cooking. Her waffles were my favourite.

Pulling on a pair of washed-out blue jeans, and a white shirt that read *'Not in the mood to talk'* I pulled my hair into a pony on top of my head, grabbed my phone, bag and purse, and headed towards the apartment exit.

"I have work, need anything?" Delilah shook her head, as she threw her cigarette out the window and dragged her feet across the room.

"No, but if you happen to pass a pretty woman on your way home, feel free to tell her where I live." She dramatically flung herself onto the sofa and sank into the cushions.

I laughed, "you already have a pretty woman." I blew her a kiss and jogged down the stairwell, my hair swaying behind me with each step.

"There has to be something you can do man. Everything I need is on here." Tony's voice was desperate as he shoved his laptop back in the direction of Smithy across the counter.

Since I'd started, and since the groping of my arse situation, I'd tried to stay far away from Smithy and the counter, choosing to restock and clean displays rather than actually help anyone.

As much as I wanted to be helpful, most of the customers who came in were suspicious and seedy looking. I would rather be swallowed by the dust mites living under the tables, than get involved in whatever side business Smithy was clearly operating from his shop.

"I don't know what to tell you bud. She's dead." A groan came from Tony, and I peeked over one of the displays, catching a glimpse of his laptop and the accused dead screen.

"Have you tried removing the memory? Or hooking it up to an external monitor?" I asked, my need to provide some kind of intellectual offering winning the fight against my desire to remain hidden.

"Harriet? I didn't know you worked here?"

He looked genuinely surprised. Smithy obviously didn't have a habit of hiring young women, either that or they all walked out before they actually met his customers.

More than likely the latter.

"Can I take a look?" Tony motioned his hands in the direction of the laptop, and I moved closer. On the other side of the counter, Smithy raised an eyebrow and leant back in his squeaking chair. This would be the moment I would prove I was worth the money he was paying me.

"Someone knocked a drink over the screen, it's had this molten lava effect since." I gently tapped my fingers on the keyboard, the screen flinched as if it recognised the movement but the heated swirls stayed firmly on the screen.

"Yeah… your screen is buggered. But the memory still works. Do you have a standing monitor?"

Tony nodded, "yeah I'm sure I have one in storage somewhere." I walked behind the counter and towards the shelving lining the corridor at the back. Fumbling around a few of the boxes labelled 'wires', a large grin spread over my face when I uncovered what I was looking for.

Proudly returning to the floor I held the cable out, a smile stretching from ear to ear across my face.

"Use this HDMI cable, it'll link your laptop up to a new screen so it's functional. Once you've finished with it, bring it back and I'll get a new screen fitted. Try and avoid any more spilt drinks." Tony looked between the cable in my hand and my face, his expression shining brightly as he took the wires from my hand.

"Honestly you have no idea how grateful I am for this,"

"Oh I've met your boss; I think I know what it means." Tony's bright smile turned sour at the mention of Seb, and he stashed the wires inside his jacket.

"We're having a party tonight, not anything big just a couple of friends. You should come."

Tony was too sweet for his own good, after he had heard the conversation between me and Seb he still thought I wanted to be in the same vicinity as the uptight arsehole.

Oh Tony. How incredibly mistaken you are.

"I can't, I actually have plans." It wasn't a complete lie, last week Josie mentioned that she and the rest of the volunteers met for a few drinks at a local bar every Thursday night. I had told her I wasn't going to go, but I figured with this place more than likely becoming my new home for at least the next six months, I needed to make more of an effort with those being so welcoming to me.

Tony nodded his head and tightly squeezed my shoulder before turning and leaving the store, the bell above the door ringing with its familiar jingle when the metal bounced underneath it.

Once again I was left in silence and alone with Smithy.

"Where you headed tonight then?" I couldn't ignore the purr in Smithy's voice, and hearing it parading into my ears triggered my body to stiffen. Still, when I faced him I gave him the boldest smile I could fathom, not letting him know he was bothering me.

"A couple of the volunteers I work with in the community garden invited me for some drinks. I think it was at the Casamere Bar?"

"Ah. Casamere's. Nice place, very secluded, nice ambience. You'll have a great time."

There was something about the way he spoke that set alarm bells off in my head, but I tried to ignore them. For the first time this week, I was looking forward to leaving the colourful confines of my bedroom's four walls, and I intended to make the most of the long weekend I had ahead of me.

I busied myself cleaning more of the display screens, not wanting Smithy to ask more questions about my plans or misinterpret my politeness for something else.

As soon as my shift was over I could look forward to spending time with the friendly group, hopefully they could distract me from thoughts of my handsy boss.

Chapter Ten

Harriet

I ran my hands through my hair loosening the curls I had created and patted down the front of my dress. I wasn't sure what to expect in the bar, but I wanted to make sure I'd made an effort, just in case it was an upmarket place.

I'd chosen a deep red dress that fitted tightly to my body, paired with thick black tights and my very worn, but favourite pair of white high tops. I wasn't a heels kind of girl; comfort was always my number one priority.

Much to Felix's disgust.

The dress had thin spaghetti straps that loosely sat on my bare shoulders, and the edge of the corset-style top dipped slightly down my chest.

I felt sexy, and it had been a long time since I'd had genuine confidence. Maybe this place had something to do with that. Grabbing a black button up shirt I slipped my arms into the fabric. It wasn't cold outside, but I wasn't planning on an early night, and I didn't want to risk the freezing temperatures that would probably be floating in the air by the time I left the bar.

I'd opted for a clutch bag tonight that had a delicate chain handle, and as I filled it with my phone, purse and cigarettes, a whistle came from the doorway.

"Wow. Who's the lucky man?" Delilah leant against the doorway, her arms folded as she raked over my outfit, not attempting to hide the desire twinkling against her pupils.

"No man. I'm going for a drink with some friends from the garden project. You're welcome to join us."

Delilah looked as though she was considering my invitation for a moment, but then let out a heavy sigh.

"I can't, I promised Cherry I'd go to this party at the Carnival tonight. You sure you'd rather hang with the oldies?" I laughed; Delilah had no idea how unappealing being at the Carnival sounded.

How unappealing being near Seb sounded.

"I'm sure, thanks though. Believe it or not, those oldies sound like they know how to have a good time." I walked past her in the doorway and took a bottle of water from the fridge. Loosening the cap, I gulped a few sips before placing it back.

"Which bar are you going to? Maybe I'll pop along later."

"The Casamere? It's just around the corner. But let's not kid ourselves, there's no way you'll be home before me." Delilah's body visibly stiffened, and I wondered if my joke had offended her.

"Make sure you text me when you're on your way home."

Pulling my phone from my bag I shook it in her face, "broken screen remember. I won't be late. Like I said, it's only around the corner. I'll be fine." I gave her a gentle hug and strolled towards the door, "have fun with Cherry."

With a mischievous wink, I disappeared through the doorway.

It took me exactly eight minutes and thirty-one seconds to get to the bar. I knew that because I'd set a timer on my phone, it gave me a good idea of how long it would take me to get home.

The bar was alive with lights and music, and as I got closer excitement escaped into my legs, and I was nearly skipping in eagerness to get inside.

It had been forever since I'd had fun, and I was desperate to balance the numbness with some exhilaration. The security man at the door smiled as I approached.

"Have a great night." I mirrored his expression and pushed against the heavy frosted glass door.

Inside it was more like a club than a bar. A huge mosaic dance floor sat on the far right. Lights in a mixture of pink, white and yellow darted across it, and bodies were writhing together in unison with the music blaring from the DJ's booth.

In front of me, a large bar spanned the entire width and was crowded with more bodies shoving to get to the front and quench their thirst. To the left side of the room booths and single tables were littered around, and it didn't take long for me to spot Josie at the back seated with three other bodies.

Squeezing around the hordes of people creating obstacles in my path I etched closer to the familiar faces, and when I hovered less than a metre away Josie finally noticed me, her hand waving frantically in the air as she stood.

"Harriet! You came!" I smiled back at her and noticed the slight wobble as she stood on her feet. Her arm flew up and motioned around the table.

"This is, Judis and Claire. You already know Daniel." Daniel gave me a small wave and I slid into the booth next to him. He smelt like cucumber and mint, and my nose twitched at the scent.

"Hey you. I'm glad you could make it; the ladies were just trying to find a nice woman to set me up with."

I gleamed in entertainment at the three grey-haired women commandeering the other side of the bench.

"What about you Harriet? A beautiful young woman like you must have a man waiting at home?" I blushed at Josie's compliment and looked down at my bare fingers. I'd taken my ring off a few days ago, my feelings about Felix remaining a messy internal conflict.

"I have a raging roommate at home who prefers the company of females. Does that count?"

Judis leant across the table, and the other two women copied her movements as she kept her voice low.

"When I was your age, I dabbled with other women. You know it's always worth exploring. One of the best lays I ever had was with a woman named—"

"Judis! At least give Harriet a chance to have a drink before she hears the scandals of your sexual conquests." I laughed along with the rest of the table, and Daniel began scooting me from the bench.

"Let's get a drink, by the time we're back they'll have moved on to the next hot topic." Daniel whispered in my ear, and when he rose from the booth and held his hand out to help me, I took it, ignoring the warning bells ringing in my head.

As soon as we stood, his hand laid against the fabric on my back and my muscles tensed. I recalled the threat from the hidden man, who I was certain was Seb, at the garden last week.

I'd seen no sign of him on my travels to and from work and I was praying that the idle warning had been a mistake, one he was now guiltily regretting.

Why do you even care? He doesn't own you.

"You okay?" Daniel's voice shouted over the thumping music bouncing around the room.

"Yeah, sorry. I've not been here before. It's a little disorientating."

We strode closer to the overwhelmingly busy bar, Daniel's hand refusing to break contact as we edged further forward. My anxiety began to scratch under my skin, but I ignored it, focusing on the delicate fingers tickling my back.

After several minutes, and a couple of gentle shoves, we made it to the front and Daniel waved his arm catching the attention of the member of staff running around wildly. She came towards us, flinging a towel over her shoulder.

"What can I get you?" Despite the chaos that was unfolding her smile was warm and friendly, and I almost felt a little guilty for adding to her hectic workload.

"I'll have a beer, Harriet?" Daniel knocked me from my trance.

"I'll have a vodka soda please." I offered her a sympathetic smile as she crafted our drinks.

"How are you liking Bromlin?" I contemplated Daniel's question for a moment, deliberating on how much truth I should tell.

"It's different to what I'm used to, I'm sure I'll settle soon."

"Different how?" He thanked the server when she passed our drinks over the counter, and gave her a twenty from his pocket.

"Busier, louder. Even though I was in the centre of a city my home was calmer, but I like the chaos here. It's just taking me some time to get used to it." Daniel nodded and I was thankful his interrogation had come to an end.

Back at the table, the three women we had left behind were now lying in a bundle over each other, ribbons of laughter shaking their bodies.

They were too distracted by whatever it was that had entertained them to notice us as we returned, and incoherent words streamed from their lips. Josie was the first to realise they had company, and when her hysterical laughter stopped our eyes narrowed in confusion.

"You're back! We were just reliving our college days. Did you know Judis and Claire here dated the same man without knowing for a whole year?"

Her words trailed off as she fell back in strings of laughter again, and my own chest vibrated as I looked between the three of them. They filled me with an envy I was trying to disguise. I wanted so badly to have a friendship like theirs.

Even back home, I'd always struggled to make friends, I was a self-proclaimed hermit. So much of my life had been spent looking out for my mom that I'd never had the time to make friends, and those that I did make soon ran a mile when they came to my home.

I shouldn't have been surprised, but with every friendly face I lost I became more and more alone, eventually preferring my own company over anyone else's.

Sitting here though, surrounded by laughter and joy, made me realise what I had lost out on.

Even Delilah had welcomed me with open arms. Before she had even met me she'd decided I was worthy of her time. Maybe this corrupt little town wasn't so bad after all, maybe I just needed to be more selective with whom I interacted with, and avoid the Carnival like the plague.

Thinking about the Carnival brought images of Seb's wickedly handsome face, and mouthwatering muscular body to the forefront of my mind, and I had to clench my thighs in hope of appeasing the throb that was starting to stir between my legs.

I scolded my body for its lack of control, and the hysterical need that it felt when I thought about the dark-eyed devil.

"Let's toast. To new friendships and a new garden!" Josie's words slurred but as she raised her hand in the air, a shot glass clasped between her fingers, we all copied her movements. Following her one by one we chucked the liquid back and let the metallic burning coat our tongues and throats.

I welcomed the liquid, the furnace caressing my tastebuds, and my eyes closed as the familiar numbness soothed my rioting head.

"I should head out. Can you make sure these three get home okay!" I shouted at Daniel, my voice quiet under the roar of the music.

We hadn't moved from the booth all night, and empty glasses were piled over every inch of the table's sticky surface. After several toasts to whatever the three women could think of, and bets about who could drink who under the table, my eyes were heavy and desperately trying to close.

Shuffling from the bench I stumbled slightly when I got to my feet, and I had to grab onto the table's edge to stay balanced. I was a lightweight at the best of times, but after the new meds the doctor had prescribed me I knew I had them to blame for this particularly inebriated episode.

Daniel reached a shaky hand towards me, attempting to help stabilise my clumsy movements.

"I'm fine, just get them home." I drunkenly smiled at him and began my saunter to the entrance of the bar, keeping my eyes strictly ahead in an attempt to walk in a straight line.

Eight minutes and thirty-one seconds, that's all it would take for me to get home and drown in the comfort of my feathery duvet. I could already feel the relaxing sheet touching my body and a sweet hum left my lips.

Outside the bar the street was quiet. There were a couple of people walking on the other side of the road, and a few cars passed as I tackled the sidewalk, but otherwise it was deserted.

My steps were small and concentrated. I was grateful I'd worn my high tops, but even those couldn't control my uneven footsteps, and I had to pause several times to stop myself from tumbling to the ground.

"Harriet!"

My eyes narrowed. Great, my imagination picked *now* to hallucinate. Like the bloody alcohol wasn't doing a good enough job on its own.

"Harriet! Wait up!" I came to a stop and turned to find the source of the voice yelling my name.

A hooded figure began getting closer, but I couldn't focus my eyes, the alcohol was blurring my vision and my gentle rock from side to side encouraged the disorientation.

"Who are you?" How did he know my name? I folded my arms in an attempt to make myself appear stern, but I couldn't see the features of the man, the hood pulled low over his face concealing himself.

He stepped closer, looking from side to side as he did, and then leant down, his face barely inches from mine. "A friend."

His sudden hand against my throat forced me to stumble backwards and I was dragged into a dark alleyway around the side of a building. I reached up and hysterically clawed my nails in the direction of the man's face, attempting to loosen the hold he had on me. But it was no good. With barely any force the man slammed me backwards against a wall and all of the air dissolved from my lungs.

I didn't have time to take a breath before the man's body was shoved against mine, his hands gripping the fabric of my dress and tearing at my tights. My head was whirling, and for a moment I thought I was going to be sick.

My mind caught up with what was happening, and I let out an earth-shattering scream, my eyes immediately filling with tears. A gloved hand came up and held itself tightly over my mouth and my eyes slammed shut in fear as stale, beer-fumed breath fanned over my face.

"When someone says you don't belong here, you really should listen."

His gruff hands tugged at my tights, and the elastic snapped as the material laddered further apart.

Did Seb have something to do with this? The man's words mimicked his exactly. I knew what he was capable of, I'd watched him with the man in the tent, but I never thought he could resort to this.

I threw my hands up again and slammed them against the man's face, but his heavy weight held me cemented in place. My mind was doing somersaults, the voices rattling around dying to break free.

"Vanilla's my favourite scent." The words were quiet against my ear and I trembled at the sadistic tone. Desperate fingers assaulted my skin as he squeezed my thigh attempting to shove my legs apart, each one growing more forceful the higher they climbed.

He moved his hand for a moment, and In between the tears, I could see him fumbling with the belt on his jeans.

This was not happening.

Using his distraction as an opportunity, I quickly raised my leg and rammed my knee into his groin.

"You fucking bitch." The man wheezed.

That got me a reaction. He stumbled back, and my frozen legs followed my brain's command to run.

Turning the corner of the alley I ran face first into a muscular chest, and a tight grip on my arms stopped me from tumbling to the ground.

"Harriet?" My body broke like a dam. "Look at me. What's going on? Are you hurt?"

Streams of tears began caking my face, and the air lodged in my throat attacked, causing shallow breaths to weave from my mouth in raspy spurts.

"He—"

I threw my arms behind me, but Seb's grip didn't loosen, if anything it tightened as he dragged my body closer to his.

"There was a man, he… he ripped my tights."

It was as though the adrenaline hidden in my body had finally decided to sneak out from the crevices, and I pushed away from Seb, my arms running aggressively through my hair.

"He tried… he tried too…"

"I'll fucking kill him."

"No! Please. Don't leave me."

I was beginning to hyperventilate, the familiar panicked motions flittered from my mouth and I struggled to gain enough air to take full breaths.

One. Two. Three. Four.

Seb's body was immediately on top of mine, one of his hands smoothing down my hair as the other held me in a vice against his body.

"Princess, it's okay. I'm here now. He can't touch you." Trembles violently shook my body and I held onto his shirt, letting the tears soak into the fabric.

My vision stayed blurry, my eyes refusing to open right up until the moment I walked through the apartment's front door.

Chapter Eleven

Seb

The party was in full swing, and I welcomed the calmness that came with the flowing drinks and boozy atmosphere. Most people probably thought it unusual to refer to a raging party as calm, but for me, it was familiar, comfortable. No masks, no costumes.

A moment when I could just *be*.

The Carnival itself was one thing, but the performers deserved credit, they knew how to throw a successful party.

Carnival events included all of the shady business we dipped our toes in, the performer's party was something entirely different. No drugs, no illegal activity or illicit scenes playing out in locked rooms, just friends sharing an enjoyment for cheap beer and corny music.

In the corner I spotted Cherry, Delilah, and Tony, all flicking their eyes intensely between each other, their emotions unreadable. I grabbed another plastic cup from the counter of the kitchenette and pursued in their direction.

"I'm telling you; *Superman* trumps all others." A grin appeared on my face as I got closer, trust Lilah to be arguing about superheroes.

"What proof do you have?" Tony challenged at the same time I arrived in front of them. Each of them gave me their own version of a welcome, Cherry's being the most enthusiastic with a beaming smile and a wave of her hand.

"Where's Haribo?" I couldn't help myself. I'd thought of hundreds of nicknames to get under her skin.

I wanted Harriet to stay as far away from me as possible, but the primal obsession that was wrapping around my muscles itched to have her here, sitting on my lap, claiming her so everyone knew who she belonged to.

"Don't let her hear you call her that. She may look innocent but I'm pretty sure she's a spitfire underneath it all."

It was the spitfire I was trying to lure out.

"She's off with some volunteers from the community garden. They're at a bar tonight." I was torn between the idea of letting her enjoy her night, and heading to the bar and bringing her back to where the real party was.

Where I could show her off and worship her like the queen she was.

"What bar?"

I took a long gulp from my cup, turning my nose up at the stale tasting beer.

"Casamere's?"

My body stilled. The Carnival had good connections within Casamere's, but all for the wrong reasons.

It was known for serving the criminal underworld of Bromlin. A hub where the vilest of creatures could prey on the vulnerable.

Some of the performers had gone in there a few times but now refused. Knowing the type of clientele that lurked in its shadows, and took advantage of the women who had had one too many drinks, had my fists clenching.

It could have been any bar. Why the fuck did it have to be that one?

I leant my head back at Tony, signalling that I wanted a private conversation with him, and he scurried behind me as I walked towards the tent's opening.

"Keep them busy. I'm going to find her." Tony nodded, and as I left I watched him settle back on the sofa and continue to entertain the two women. Guy had more patience than me when it came to those two.

My motorbike roared to life under my fingertips, and within minutes I was pulling up outside the bar.

The air was filled with chaotic noise, and the darkness made the place appear even more dingy than I remembered. Patrons spilt from the entranceway, and I spotted the man from the community garden helping three stumbling women into the back of a cab.

But no Harriet.

Lifting myself from the seat I started walking towards the entrance door when the sound of a curdling high-pitched scream pierced my senses. All of the hairs on my body stood up.

Running in the direction of the sound I rounded a corner, and was slammed straight into by none other than my doe eyed girl.

My brows pulled together when I took in the panic on her face. Black ink fell in streaks down her cheeks, and what had been scarlet red lipstick was now smeared across her face. When I noticed the tear in her tights, my vision turned red.

"Harriet? Look at me. Are you hurt?"

She looked everywhere but at me, her frantic eyes darting in terror. She tried to battle against my hold, but I wasn't letting her go, if I did she'd fall to the ground from the shake in her legs.

She was close to falling apart.

"He tried to…he tried to…" I couldn't listen to this, and I wasn't about to make her relive what it was obvious she had just been through.

"I'm going to fucking kill him." Aggressive vibrations shook my body.

"No! Please. Don't leave me."

Pulling her head against my chest, I smoothed down her hair, attempting to offer some comfort. After a few minutes, her rigid muscles loosened and I pulled away slightly, swiping her wild hair from her face.

"Princess, it's okay. I'm here now." My words opened the dam that was holding her together, and her tears fell in a tsunami over her face. I needed to get her somewhere safe, somewhere warm. She would go into shock soon.

"I'm going to take you home." Her head nodded against my chest, but she didn't remove the vice she had on my shirt. Her apartment was only around the corner from here, it wouldn't take long to walk.

Choosing to abandon my bike at the front of the bar I pulled her to my side and began walking to the apartment, her fingers refusing to unlock from the material of my shirt.

She was counting under her breath, scaling from one to five and then starting over again. It was obviously a coping mechanism she had learnt.

I hated that she had ever had to *use* a coping mechanism.

What happened to her?

When we reached the door I flipped up the mat and Harriet raised her eyebrow at me.

"Lilah keeps a spare key here. Emergencies." I didn't see a bag hanging from Harriet, and assuming she had lost hers when the man grabbed her, we had no other option but to use the key stashed in the hiding spot.

"Why do you call her Lilah?" Her voice was quiet and wobbly.

"Little Lilah sounds better than Little Delilah." I curled the corner of my lips, but only a small, sad smile of her own returned.

I shoved the door open, and she quietly walked ahead, her arms wrapped tightly around her body as she stumbled into the room and immediately towards the window over the bench.

Harriet sat upright, her chest rising heavily as she took in a deep breath.

"Thank you."

I pulled out one of the dining chairs and slumped back on it, kicking my legs out in front.

"You have nothing to thank me for."

"If you hadn't shown up, he would of…"

Her voice trailed off and she picked a cigarette out of a stray packet on the sill, bringing it to life with the flick of a silver lighter.

"He would have gone further." Her head dropped, and she fumbled with the hem of her dress.

I scraped my seat closer to her and squeezed one of her hands, the contact sending an electrical current hurling to my fingertips.

"There's no way that would have happened, you fought him off before I even got there."

A tight smile played at her mouth, and she bit down on her lower lip. "You keep telling me I don't belong here. I think you're right."

I was frustrated that she chose now to use my words against me, but she was right. I had told her she didn't belong here, and I'd wanted nothing more than for her to get in her car and drive far away from this hell hole.

But everything had changed. I knew no matter how far she tried to run, I would hunt her and bring her back.

Kicking and screaming, bound and gagged. It didn't matter. Eventually I would own her, and tease out the powerful siren that I knew was begging to come out and play.

"I need to shower, I can feel his hands on me." My teeth ground together, and I tightened my fists, attempting to sedate the voice in my head taunting me to snap.

"You should get your leg checked on."

Harriet's head immediately whipped to her thigh, where the split fabric of her tights revealed a painting of scars and tiny burn marks.

Now I could see her legs in the light, my eyes narrowed.

Some of the marks were buried into her skin, as though they had been there for years, others were raised with purple bruises outlining them. She desperately pulled at her dress, attempting to hide them with the fabric.

But it was too late, I'd already seen them.

"Why?"

There were a couple of dried marks from where the man's dirty hands had groped at her, but none of the cuts were fresh enough to have been caused tonight, though there were a couple that couldn't have been more than a few days old.

I tilted my head and pulled her tight hand away from its poor attempt at creating a shield.

"I don't know."

"Don't lie to me." I needed to calm down, but knowing it was her own hands inflicting the scattered injuries had me boiling.

I knew what it was like to feel like there was no choice, no way of escaping the shackles. But I also knew it was a hole that would swallow you up if you gave it a chance.

"Don't do this Seb. Not now." She was broken, and I was deepening the cracks. "You should go."

Harriet jumped from the ledge and quickly pushed past me. Heading straight for the door she swung it open, keeping her head low when I approached. I stopped in front of her, waiting for her challenging glare to appear, but it never did.

Hooking a finger under her chin, I raised her eyes to meet mine, and I looked between both of them, searching for an answer that was locked tightly away inside her.

"Harriet—" She shook her head from my hold and resumed her stare with the floor.

"Please go Seb." I wasn't going to push her tonight, not when she was so fragile. But at some point, I would find out who caused her to feel so much pain, so much loss that she thought hurting herself was the only way to dull the feelings.

I turned as I walked through the door, but Harriet didn't look up, her eyes still firmly fixed on the ground.

An unfamiliar ache rocked through my chest, and after she closed the door I stood there frozen, my ears pricking at the sound of her cries behind the metal frame guarding her.

I didn't stop to respond to pleasantries as I walked back through the opening in the tent, my vision firmly fixed on the trio still seated on the sofas.

I shook with rage, and as I approached, Cherry's eyes narrowed, and Tony's body stiffened.

Delilah, however, was immune to the reactions happening around her and smiled brightly. That smile quickly dissipated when she saw the rage melting from my skin.

"You need to go home Lilah."

I tried not to aim my furnace of rage at her but each word dripped in venom, and her body cowered as it rose from the sofa.

"Why? What's wrong?"

I chewed on the side of my mouth, images of Harriet's trembling body in my arms violently knocking around behind my eyelids.

I needed to find a way to get the anger out, find a way to calm the riots. Without thinking I slammed my fist onto a nearby table, splintering the wood and forcing the empty plastic cups to spill to the ground.

"Some *scumbag* attacked Harriet. She needs you." I hissed, the violent shakes attacking every one of my muscles.

I wanted her to need me.

"Is she okay?"

"Some slimy fucking greaseball tried to *rape* her, and you're asking me if she's okay?!"

My voice rose, and the whole tent went silent. Turning my attention, I glared at Tony. "You find out everything you can about that dive bar, get their CCTV from tonight, threaten them. I don't care what you have to do. But if I don't have the name of the man responsible in my hands by the morning, I swear to god I will rain fucking hell on this pathetic excuse for a town!"

I didn't wait for an answer, I knew he would find out everything I needed to know. Storming away, I crashed into one of the doors leading to my bedroom, my sanctuary.

Here I could drop the mask, remove myself from a position of authority and be myself.

But I couldn't escape the carnage that was bouncing around in my head, or the primal need to draw blood. I would hunt the man who had broken my girl, and every one before him.

After I was done with them, they'd wish they had never met Harriet Wolston.

Chapter Twelve

Harriet

The saying goes, what doesn't kill you makes you stronger. I didn't feel stronger.

I felt like I was slowly dying, being forced to suffer the same heartbreaking death as my mother. I was starting to understand why she had turned to drugs after my father had left her, why she had resorted to something so extreme to help her live through life.

Drugs were her addiction, pain was mine.

My fingers danced over my leg, and I admired the two new marks I had engraved into my skin. I needed to cut away the feel of that man's hands on me, stop the scratch that was eating away at me piece by piece.

Today, more than any other day, I was reminded of the little I had to show for my life, and how insignificant my presence on this earth was. The idea that my life held so little value to the world around it ached my chest, but it was a feeling I was familiar with, even welcomed with open arms.

I'd spent the whole of yesterday locked in my room. Delilah had come in a couple of times to check on me, but every time I heard the gentle creak of the door's hinges I pulled my duvet tighter over my head. I didn't want to face her, I didn't want to face the world.

She sat with me, tried to soothe me with her voice whilst her fingers swept through my hair. But her words of reassurance did little to calm me, my tears stinging against my eyes like tiny pins.

This morning I was feeling a little better.

Despite knowing my attacker was still out there, lurking in the shadows, I was optimistic that I would make today a good day and at least I had the energy to get out of bed.

Once I was up I slipped on a pair of dark leggings and a tank top and headed for the front room.

"HAPPY BIRTHDAY!" I wasn't expecting the concord of voices to hammer me as soon as I left the room, nor was I expecting three beaming smiles to be shining at me either.

The living room's plain walls had been camouflaged by a kaleidoscope of colours hanging in triangular bunting around the room. A multitude of colourful balloons were scattered around every inch of the floor, and taped to the cabinets in the kitchen were sparkling banners that read Happy Birthday in bold golden letters.

A sleepy smile grew on my face as Josie stepped forward and wrapped me tightly in her arms. She smelt of jasmine and lavender, the floral smells tickling my nose as I inhaled the freshness. Tony and Delilah followed her movements, and soon we were a bundled mess of embraces, standing in the middle of the balloons.

A stray tear fell from my eye and as Josie took a step back, separating us all, she swiped it away with her thumb.

"Harriet. I'm so sorry. I shouldn't have gotten myself into such a state. Dan, he should have been with you." I couldn't listen to other people take the blame for what one sick person had attempted to do to me.

I refused to allow others to carry that kind of burden.

Taking Josie's hands in mine, I gave her a warm smile. It was genuine. Josie had welcomed me with open arms, and I was grateful that she was becoming a part of my life.

Even if it wouldn't be for much longer.

After the events that had unravelled, I was beginning to realise that I couldn't stay. After today was over, I would call Felix and have him come get me. As much as I didn't want to leave my new friends, I didn't want to stay either.

I was ready to admit that life with Felix was calm. Boring, but calm. I needed that.

You should be grateful for that.

There was only one thing that had me holding off, and that was the haunting eyes of the man who had been the first to warn me away.

Despite Seb's words, his actions had me recoiling. He had warned me that I didn't belong here, yet he'd jumped to my side when I needed him. He'd given me severe whiplash, and before I left I wanted to get some explanations from him, understand why he was behaving the way he was around me.

"We're going to do something fun for your birthday." Delilah was hopping on the spot, and I wondered whether whatever she had planned was her idea of fun or mine. Tony crossed the front room back towards us, a steaming hot cup of coffee in his hands. I gratefully took the mug, and immediately began devouring the sugary nectar, each swallow burning my throat with sweet ecstasy.

I silently mouthed a thank you, and he broadly smiled, the dimples I'd not noticed before appearing on his cheeks.

Tony was handsome, in a mischievous kind of way.

"What did you have planned?"

I took a breath from the drink and waited to find out what the day had in store for me.

"I'm taking you to the new mall that's opened a town away, we'll get lunch, have our hair done. Tonight's Fright Night at The Carnival, Tony got us tickets."

A pit formed in my stomach. Spending my birthday night at the Carnival sounded like the last thing I wanted to do, but knowing it would be the last time I saw Seb had me arguing with the ruckuses in my head.

I disguised my concern with a smile, not wanting to give her any indication of my reluctance. "Give me a minute to change and I'll be right with you." I forced my voice to sound as upbeat as I could muster, and Delilah didn't seem to notice the force behind it as she skipped off towards the window and planted herself on the bench.

I thanked Tony again for the coffee and he nodded his head, following behind me as I walked towards my bedroom.

"Seb's taken care of it. The guy that attacked you, he won't do it again. Not to anybody." I stopped in my tracks and turned to face him, his eyes were a scorching emerald, and it looked as though flicks of silver splashed around in their depths.

"What do you mean *taken care of it*?" I should have been concerned with how he had said the words, but all I felt was satisfaction.

Seb wasn't scared to throw his weight around with his own friends, I could only imagine what he was like when someone committed such a vile act. A strange, almost euphoric thrill danced around behind my ribcage, and as Tony walked away, that feeling remained.

Quickly swapping my leggings for a pair of black jeans, and throwing a jumper over my head, I re-entered the living room. Tony and Josie had gone, leaving me and Delilah standing in the colourful space.

"I hope this is okay. I know you've been having a rough time since you got here. I just wanted you to have some fun."

Without thinking, I wrapped my arms around her small frame, squeezing her tightly, "thank you."

I would miss Delilah when I left. She was chaotic and unpredictable, but she was also incredibly loyal and had shown me nothing but kindness since I'd got here. I was grateful I'd at least had the chance to meet her.

As she pulled away, she dug into her pocket and pulled out a phone. "I know you don't have one. It's an old model, something I found in a drawer, but you should have it. I've charged it, added a SIM card and some contacts. It's good to go." I was really going to miss having this woman around, she'd become the fairy godmother I had no idea I needed.

I tapped the screen, and it came to life. Delilah had already added a selection of names, and when I spotted Seb's the pit in my stomach dropped.

"Seb has this number?" She nodded, "Why?"

"He didn't give me much choice."

I hovered my finger over his name, the temptation to block it sitting in my fingertips. It didn't matter what he had done for me, the man was still hell, and I had no intention of entertaining his erratic behaviour.

"Cab's here." Delilah snapped me from my thoughts, and I locked the phone's screen, making a mental note to go back later and wipe the man from the small list of names.

Ignoring the voices, I solidified my decision. I had no reason to keep it.

The shopping mall was every bit as impressive as Delilah had made it out to be, and after following her around for hours we finally settled on some seats outside a busy café. She began tapping away on her phone, and then suddenly stuck it out and right into my face.

"I'm thinking of this for a costume tonight. I have something similar in my closet."

The woman in the photo was wearing a half zipped up nurses' outfit, paired with red stockings and a small cap with a red cross on it. The outfit was covered in splashes of fake blood and even came with a stethoscope.

I peered around the phone at her, "I think that would look great on you." Delilah pouted at the image again and then peered down at her chest.

"I don't know if I have the tits for it." I half-heartedly laughed at her comment, but I was distracted by the passersby. I liked people watching, I created stories in my head about who they were and what lives they led.

My shrink used to tell me it was a distraction mechanism to pull the focus off of my own life by determining others. Though I wasn't entirely sure how accurate that was. Even if it was, who could blame me for wanting to imagine a better world.

"Any idea what you'll go as?" Delilah's voice snapped me from my daydream.

I hadn't even thought about costumes. I had no idea about the fright night until this morning, and that wasn't enough time to find something. "I think I'll just wear black jeans and whatever shirt doesn't need washing."

Delilah leant back in her chair, her arms firmly folded over her chest whilst another pout formed on her mouth. The nickname Little Lilah was sitting on the tip of my tongue, as was a heated desire to taste Seb's skin under it.

Stop it woman. In twenty-four hours he will have forgotten all about you.

"You can't go as yourself. It's your *birthday*. Besides, it's fancy dress to enter." She looked thoughtful for a moment, and as if a lightbulb had come alive above her head, a contagious smile stretched the width of her face. "I have the perfect costume for you!"

I groaned, not realising how loud I had been until the smile on Delilah's face shrank and a look of disappointment stole its place.

"Sorry Delilah, I didn't mean to sound ungrateful." I forced my voice to pick up, attempting to recreate the cheerful tone that had come from her, "what is it?"

Delilah raised her eyebrow and the corner of her mouth curled in a mischievous smirk. "You'll have to wait and see." Her tone was light and playful, and I couldn't help but absorb some of her energy. My own body loosening against the aura shining from her.

Accepting that she wasn't going to budge, I let myself relax into the chair and began watching the crowds of people hurrying around us again. Frantic bodies darted in every direction, the whispers of voices echoing in the air. In the middle of the dining hall, an impressively large fountain stood monumental, the water spouting from it in rhythm to the mall's musical sounds.

An involuntary tune slipped from my mouth, recognising the music that was flowing in the air. But my hum sharply stopped, and the oxygen dispersed from my lungs when I spotted a man barrelling towards us, his blonde hair firmly stuck in place on his head, and his glaring crystal blue eyes throwing daggers in my direction.

As he got closer I shoved my seat back, my body ready to go into flight mode, but my legs froze in place. Standing inches away from me, he looked between me and Delilah, who was now also standing, looking like a ferocious pixie ready to come to my aid.

No one could argue that Delilah wasn't loyal.

"Time to go Harriet," Felix gripped my forearm, and the sudden contact knocked me back. But I had enough stability to pull away from his razor-sharp nails digging into my skin.

"I'm not doing this here Felix." I kept my voice low, but at the mention of his name Delilah perked up, and she rounded the table to stand beside me.

"Who's your pet?" I scowled at him.

"Go fuck yourself Felix." No matter what my intentions were after tonight, I refused to allow him to make a scene here.

Passersby were already walking slower, trying to eavesdrop on the commotion, and my cheeks burned hot with embarrassment.

"Someone grew a pair of balls whilst they've been on their holiday." Felix moved closer to me, his face barely inches away from mine. "Harriet. Whatever point it was you were trying to make, you've made it. We're going home."

"She's not going anywhere with you." Delilah's words were laced with bite, but Felix just raised his eyebrow and smirked at her.

"And you're going to be the one to stop me? What are you, like five foot?"

"Don't tempt me. I'll burn your fucking house down if you don't back the fuck up."

"Problem?" Oh dear god, this was the last thing I needed. Felix turned at the sound of another man, and his eyes travelled over Seb's body.

Flinging his arm around my shoulder, Felix steered me past my once again knight in shining armour.

Or maybe wolf in sheep's clothing.

Don't get used to it. He won't care when you leave.

"You've been making friends babe, time to say goodbye." He started to walk us away but before he could, Seb stepped to the side blocking us from leaving. With a frustrated huff, Felix withdrew his arm from my body.

"Harriet isn't going anywhere with you."

"It seems you lot have some delirious notion that you can tell me what will and won't happen with *my* fiancé. I don't know how things work in this grimy little slum but where we're from it's always better not to argue with the future husband."

Future husband. The words made my skin crawl.

Both men stood nose to nose, their chests rising and falling in some kind of power play.

A power play over *me.*

Nope, this was not how my birthday would go.

Shoving past Felix I wedged myself between him and Seb and looked up, forcing his eyes down to me. "Please don't do this here. I can handle it." Seb didn't look convinced, but as I pleaded with him, he raised his hands in defence and took a couple of steps backwards.

I turned to face Felix, forcing his attention away from Seb and onto me. "I'll call you later, just please go."

His mouth rose in a grin, and he lowered his mouth, the words piercing my ear. "I'll be waiting." Felix pulled his shoulders back and walked away, but not before knocking his body against Seb's shoulder as he went.

Next to me, Delilah followed my stare, "*that's* the ex?" I nodded, the red-hot flame still burning my skin. How had he even found me? I shook my head, I wasn't going to think about that right now, not when there was a shaking man made of pure concrete standing in front of me.

"What are you doing here?"

I was beginning to tire of Seb showing up whenever I left the house, feeling as though he had a right to come running to my side. As though he *belonged* at my side.

"We're going for lunch."

It was hard to hide my surprise. "We are?"

A boyish smile curled at his lips, and my shoulders dropped at his charm.

Don't fall for it.

"Yes. It is your birthday after all."

I whipped my head around at Delilah. I'd told her that I didn't like people making a fuss of me, and sharing the details of my birthday seemed the complete opposite of that request. She held her hands up in defence and shot her glare at Seb.

"Nothing to do with me, I didn't tell him."

Seb shrugged and held his arm out, and as I took it I raised my eyebrow at him. "Didn't take you as one for chivalry." That devilish grin bounced around his face, causing my insides to tighten.

"There's a lot you don't know about me princess."

"Why do you call me that?"

"Call you what?" This man was really going to make me drag it from him.

"Princess." He chuckled to himself as we reached the escalators, his body forming a cage around mine against the rubber handrail.

"Because you deserve to be worshipped. Every man here should fall to their knees for you."

His acclimation took me off guard, and for a moment I was stunned for words. Seb had only spoken a few sentences to me before the incident the other night, and all of them were warnings or demands trying to make me leave.

His suddenly kind words pelted me like an iron branding.

This man was tormenting me with his mood swings. One minute he wanted me to leave, the next he was treating me like he wanted me to stay. I was like a dog on a leash being dragged backwards every other day.

"Tony told me you dealt with the man from the other night. What did you do to him?"

Seb's body tightened, his fists clenching at his sides. But as quickly as his uptight posture had been revealed it disappeared again, completely concealed by a boyish mask.

"You don't have to worry about him."

I didn't like that he swerved around my question, but sensing that he wouldn't give me a straightforward answer I chose to change the subject.

"What are you going as tonight?" He continued to hold his hand out for me as we left the escalator and travelled through the busy mall. His hand felt rough in mine, and I couldn't ignore the fireworks catapulting inside me.

I desperately needed to reign it in and remember I was leaving.

I had to leave.

"Haven't decided yet. What about you?"

"Delilah's picked something out for me, I didn't have time to give it much thought." He looked at me from the corner of his eye.

"You're letting Delilah pick out your costume? You're brave."

"Brave or stupid, I haven't quite decided yet." I liked that he didn't bring up the other night, I knew that for the last forty-eight hours, Delilah had walked on eggshells around me. But with Seb, nothing about our conversation felt forced.

We mulled around the shopping mall, settling into a comfortable silence, when I spotted Seb watching me. "What?" I bleated.

He pursed his lips and looked straight out ahead as he spoke. "Is he responsible for you hurting yourself?"

My heart pounded in my chest; it didn't take a genius to know what he was referring to. I'd never shared much from my past, even Felix didn't know all of the details. People only knew what I wanted them to know.

"I have a heavy past Seb, Felix isn't responsible for that."

He continued to look straight out ahead, but his eyes were narrowing, and his jaw ticked. "Then who is?"

"Why do you want to know?"

"So I can gorge their fucking eyes out and put them in a glass jar as a reward."

I gulped. I needed to steer us away from this conversation. Seb was a roller coaster and one I was getting flung around on. He had the ability to save me, but he was constantly choosing to ruin me instead.

"I'm going to head back to Callie tomorrow." Seb suddenly turned in front of my body and I slammed straight into him, my shove doing nothing to stammer his broad frame.

"What."

"I need to go home Seb. You were right, I don't belong here." I kept my head low, not wanting to look into his intimidating eyes.

"This is your home." He grumbled.

"We both know it's not."

"So things get hard, and you split?"

"Hard? You call what happened to me hard? I've lived around Callie my entire life, and no one ever attacked me! Forgive me if I would rather stay somewhere I feel safe."

Seb let out a lethal chuckle. "So you'd rather go back to the scumbag that fucks other women? Be a pawn in some fucking slimeballs game?" A pang hit my chest. I didn't tell him about Felix.

"You've been here less than two weeks Harry."

Harry.

Images of my mother violently stomped through my head, the familiar nickname bouncing around, encouraging the marching band that was building walls behind my eyelids. My skin went cold, and the hairs on my arms stuck up as a chill ran over my skin.

Bile rose in my throat, and I begged my lungs to let me breathe, let me waver the storm.

After a few minutes, it passed and I opened my eyes to see Seb staring at me, his own eyes narrowed as concern swept over his features.

"Harriet." He reached out for my arm, but I pulled it back slightly, not wanting to feel the sparks that would shock me on contact.

"It's the right thing." I couldn't stand here and listen to him; I wouldn't let him intimidate me into staying somewhere that was so desperately trying to push me out.

"I have to go. Delilah will be wondering where I am." I expected him to try and stop me, but as I walked away I knew I was alone, and my racing heart calmed and finally stilled.

Chapter Thirteen

Harriet

Note to self, if I meet Delilah in another life never let her pick a Halloween costume again.

When I saw the smirk on her face and she dangled a bundle of sparkling fabric and two tasselled pom poms out towards me, I knew I was going to regret my lack of choice in this decision.

The cheerleading costume was two sizes too small, causing the dip over the front to push my chest out, the edge of the black bralette underneath noticeable from the edges. The panelled skirt that I was wearing barely covered my arse, and I was sure that more than one person would get an eyeful of my backside tonight.

I'd wrapped bandages around my thighs, partially so I could cover them in red food colouring and at least attempt to give my costume a frightful look, but also to hide the marks on my legs. I'd been careless, allowed too many people to get an eyeful of an addiction I wasn't ready to surrender.

Delilah had pulled my hair into two bunches on either side of my head, looping strands of tinsel through each one and dusting the ends in a glittery spray.

After I'd made the finishing touches to my dark smoky eyes and deep crimson lips, I added a few more splotches of the food colouring and tilted my head in the mirror.

Despite the altercation with the sizing, the costume suited me in some strange way.

The glistening speckles that were scattered around the fabric rainbowed in the light, and my dark hair complemented the washed-out colours of the costume.

Behind me Dlilah spun, her stethoscope nearly falling from her neck as she did. "We look perfect. I knew dead cheerleader would suit you." Was that a compliment?

I was starting to think *dead* suited me. I slammed my eyes closed, warning the intrusive thoughts back into hiding.

When she walked away, I quickly hurried after her, "did you speak to Seb today?" Delilah didn't seem fazed by my question as she stuffed a small first aid bag with her phone and purse, and strapped it around her waist.

"No, should I have?"

"No." I stood at her side, began packing my own belongings into a bag, and clasped it around my body.

"You should probably be careful around him." I paused and turned towards her, but she didn't look at me. "Seb's great don't get me wrong. But the guy… well he's…"

"Whatever you're trying to say it doesn't matter. Nothing is going on between us." Delilah nodded her head and finally turned to look in my direction.

"Maybe not according to you, but I've seen the way he looks at you whenever you're around. Hell even when you're on the other side of the room he finds you."

She plastered her hands to her hips, and I was struggling to take her seriously in her costume. "It doesn't take a genius to work out the man's *obsessed* with you."

Silence settled between us, and for a moment we stood staring at each other, until a hysterical laugh vibrated through my entire body and I roared in fits of laughter.

"I don't think we know the same Seb." I calmed the string tickling me. "The guy literally told me to leave town Delilah, you couldn't be any further from the truth,"

A swarm of rioting butterflies circled around in my stomach; I knew how Seb felt about me.

Granted, he had soothed me when I needed it and today his words had been mostly soft and caring. But otherwise, he was brash, rude, and made it very clear he had no interest in me loitering around his little town.

But still, I couldn't help the twinkle of warmth that was spreading over my skin and the ache that was beginning to form between my legs.

I would never admit it, but there was something about Seb that drew me to him. His devilish smirk, his mysterious bravado. He piqued my intrigue, and the idea that he might have some subtle interest in me had my head spinning for a moment before the thoughts were quickly squashed by the remembrance that tonight was my last night here.

A sudden sadness began to engulf me. I had become attached to this tiny, isolated town and its inhabitants so quickly. I didn't want to give it up.

Even with everything that had happened there was something about it that argued with me to stay, make it my permanent home. A small tear fell down my cheek, and before Delilah had a chance to see it, I pulled her into my arms, her body freezing under my abrupt contact.

"Thank you. For everything you've done for me."

Delilah laughed against my shoulder, "don't thank me yet, we have to get through tonight first." I released her and she walked towards the kitchen, pulling two shot glasses and a bottle of vodka from the top shelf.

Quickly tipping the clear liquid into the two glasses, she glided one across the counter towards me. I didn't wait for her to count before I threw the burning liquid down my throat.

As soon as I slammed the glass back on the table, she was refilling it and we quickly gulped back four shots of the scorching liquid. With each one, my muscles slackened and the tension weaving underneath my skin calmed, morphing into a gentle stroke.

Giving ourselves a once over we were a bundle of excited nerves, and as we took another swig from the bottle of fire we eagerly left the apartment and began our stagger to the Carnival.

The Carnival was alive with people, every inch of the muddy floor was covered in storming feet. I thought the opening night was busy, but this was something entirely different.

We were tightly packed between bodies as Delilah and I attempted to shove past the hoards. My eyes were wide, admiring all of the colourful costumes and accentuate characters that were moulding around the space. No matter where I looked the colours transformed and I was captivated.

Every possible creation you could imagine was there. People dressed head to toe in black cloaks with masks covering their faces, women dressed in short flowery dresses with wings on their backs. Even a group beyond the crowds were dressed in pirate gear, with rubber swords sticking out from their waistbands.

We paused just outside a small tent, and hearing a wail of cheers and shouts coming from inside, decided to dip in and join the ambush of people.

The tent was dimly lit with candles scattered around the edges, and in the centre, a young woman stood in a ballerina's costume, her head bowed underneath a spotlight. Light violins started humming from the speakers, and the candlelight flickered as the ballerina jerked her head upwards.

Her face was painted to look like a broken doll, her movements beginning rigid and robotic.

When the violins became frantic, so did she. Her body levitated, and I spotted the knives strapped to her feet. The woman was *literally* walking on daggers.

Her graceful movements held us in a trance, the way her body swung around delicately and chaotically all at the same time.

I envied the way she danced, the way she swung herself around the small tent with such elegance. I wished I had the same grace when I moved.

In comparison, I was an elephant. Especially now I had alcohol in my system.

When the performance ended, we were escorted out of the tent and the cool wind howled as it arched through our bodies.

Despite my birthday, I'd never spent Halloween out with friends.

Each year Felix would take me out for dinner at a fancy restaurant, and we'd end up back home and in bed before ten. Before him, I'd spend it watching romance films with my mom and stuffing my face with buttery popcorn.

My mother's lifeless body began creeping into my vision but I quickly shook myself out of it, refusing to allow the images to hold me hostage tonight.

Delilah's fingers threaded through mine, pulling me out of my daydream, and she shouted above the loud noises encompassing us. "Let's go to the ghost walk! Before the queue gets too long!" I nodded at her and smiled widely.

Delilah pulled us through the crowds, and carefree winds knocked against me. I welcomed the air. The queue for the Ghost Walk wasn't long, and we only waited for thirty minutes before we were next in line to journey through the haunted ride.

At the front of the line, four cloaked and masked figures stood. I'd expected them to interact with the crowds as they waited but they just stood there. Maybe they *were* statues, it was getting darker, so it was difficult to tell what was real and what wasn't.

The security announcement bellowed over the speaker as the two of us, along with eight others, were squished into a small room. At the end of the announcement a loud high-pitched ring squeezed through the air, and we all covered our ears to block out the sound. It was obviously a tactic to disorientate us. But it worked.

The door in front of us creaked open, and my mind became clouded and dizzy. After several moments we were silently ushered through by the staff escorting us.

The room we entered was lit up by nothing more than a singular red bulb sitting bright in the middle. I couldn't see any of the other people, and I'd lost Delilah's hand in the barrage through the door.

A strange mixture of fear, adrenaline and excitement caressed my skin as my eyes squinted against the darkness.

I suddenly became aware of how incredibly silent it was.

"Maybe we need to find an exit?" I uttered.

Silence.

No one answered and I edged closer to the red bulb, hoping it would offer some guidance to where everyone else had disappeared to. "Hello?"

I wasn't one to scare easily, but the silence was making me feel uneasy.

"There's only one way to escape."

A cool wind whipped over my shoulder, and my senses were abruptly overwhelmed by a smoky scent twisting straight through me and melting into my mind.

I knew who that scent belonged to, even without being able to see him.

If danger had a smell, that was it.

A pressure against my back had my body tensing, and a rough finger began trailing the length of my arm.

"It's dangerous to be alone in dark places. You never know who could be lurking in the shadows."

My eyes closed, the words sending a violent wave of desire through my ears.

"You lost princess?" Every hair on my body pricked.

The voice was husky and low, his tone stroking every corner of my psyche. I didn't know if it was the alcohol that was causing me to lose my inhibitions, but that was what I was going to blame it on.

Any excuse.

His body was firmly pressed into mine now, restricting my movements, and his breaths whispered against my neck. An inaudible hum escaped my lips and euphoria swarmed my head.

Unruly fantasies that had been hidden away, the ones I harboured an absolute secret, barrelled around in my head, each one making me more and more desperate to let this man soothe the hurricane.

I wanted his ghosts to creep over my skin, allow his darkness to swallow me up.

I couldn't deny how Seb made me feel, the throb dancing between my legs was evident enough of that, and right now I wanted nothing more than to feel his fingers on my bare skin, allow them to quiet the flame that was branding a furnace beneath my costume.

Fuck it. I was leaving tomorrow morning anyway. What did I have to lose?

"Seb, please." I pushed my arse into him, and he vibrated with a growl as one of his hands snaked up my body and wrapped around my throat, holding me firmly in place.

"Did you think you could hide from me? Think I wouldn't hunt you down."

The air fighting to be released sent twinkling speckles into my eyes, and my body caved against his firm hold. I wrapped my hand around his forearm to keep myself steady.

"I'll never let you escape me."

More inaudible sounds trickled from my mouth, his promising words tightening the throb between my legs.

"Use your words, what do you want?" His left hand began trailing up my bare leg, playing with the frayed edges of the bandages wrapped around my thighs.

I held my breath as his fingers travelled higher until they were brushing against the edge of my skirt.

"You," I whispered.

A low rumble sounded from behind me, and his voice hissed into my ear. "You have no idea how long I've waited for you to say that."

His tongue darted out and swiped across my shoulder. "You make me fucking desperate Harriet. If I had known you existed, I would have burnt the fucking world hunting you down."

Need poured between my legs, his words sending sweet shivers over my skin.

His tongue stopped its assault. "But that's not an answer, I'm already here." A subtle frustration climbed through me, urged on by the desperate need pooling at my core.

"Words." I closed my eyes. I'd never been good at giving direction to what I wanted, and the lack of movement from Seb's hand was causing the carnal need to deepen.

"I want you to touch me." My words were quiet, but I knew he'd heard them, I could feel his smirk against my cheek.

"Touch you where?" A hot flush crept up my neck and warmed my face. I wasn't embarrassed, but his low voice mixed with his baiting touch was causing the butterflies to riot around in my stomach.

"Here." I grabbed a hold of his teasing hand and pulled it up my skirt, laying it on top of my sweet spot.

I wished I had this kind of confidence all of the time.

A low laugh shook through him, and he nipped at the bottom of my ear, his teeth delicately biting on my sensitive skin. His finger traced patterns over the lacy material creating a wall between his touch and my bundle of sensitive nerves.

"Eager little thing you are." His fingers edged against the side of the fabric and then dipped below.

"Please—"

"Princess, keep begging me like that and I'll fuck you loud enough for everyone outside to hear."

Holy Shit.

When his fingers made contact with my clit, I nearly fell apart right there.

"So fucking wet. Does the idea of everyone hearing you turn you on little siren?" I tried to move my head in his direction, but his firm hold around my throat was leaving me immobile, and as he began swirling, painting patterns on me, quiet hums of delight trickled from my lips.

"That's it, sing for me." His fingers began to quicken and as my legs quivered, my release building tightly inside of me, Seb suddenly stopped, and my eyes shot open.

"What—"

"Tell me you'll stay." His fingers picked up, and he began attacking my clit again, each movement sending shockwaves through me and drawing out my release.

I was panting, desperate to fall over the edge, "I can't…" Seb's fingers stilled again, and my chest hammered.

"I can do this all night, no one else is coming in here until you agree." Again his fingers worked me, "tell me you'll stay."

I couldn't stay, I knew I couldn't. But the devil behind me was holding me hostage, me *and* my orgasm. Breathy moans left my mouth as Seb's fingers slowed to a stop, and my release ran back into hiding.

"Seb—" Tears pricked the corners of my eyes from the pain his blackmail was creating.

"Yes *you can.*"

I couldn't take another second of torture.

"Fine! Okay! I'll stay." His hold suddenly released from my neck, and he was turning my body to face his.

I stared at his eyes, illuminated red by the bulb behind us.

He looked like the grim reaper ready to steal me into the pits of hell.

He tutted and began lowering to the ground. "No one ever teach you not to make a deal with the devil?"

My eyebrows furrowed, but I didn't have time to think too much about it before Seb was hooking one of my legs over his shoulder, and pulling the fabric covering me to the side exposing my pussy.

"So pretty." He stared at me from below, and lost myself in him for a moment before he disappeared under my skirt and his dangerous tongue landed right on my nerve filled bud.

I nearly folded right there, and as he continued his assault I gripped onto the strands of his hair, using them to keep myself upright whilst my legs threatened to buckle underneath me.

Trails of sweet song left my throat, and I threw my head back with each flittering shudder that embraced my body. My release was finally coming out again, and I mentally begged Seb not to stop, I wouldn't be able to take it again if he did.

"Oh god," My core tightened as I tiptoed the edge. Seb smiled against me and his hungry tongue continued to flick my clit, his fingers holding me open, giving him direct access to my most sensitive spot.

"Call to your god all you like princess, but you're already in hell. No one can save you now."

With his words I plummeted over the edge, my legs shaking beneath me. Seb's hands gripped behind my arse, holding me up and dragging me closer into his mouth. As my body continued to shake, he didn't stop, his tongue drinking in every fragment that was surrendering at his mercy.

Seb rose in front of me whilst my body panted, trying to regain a normal rhythm. I reluctantly opened my eyes, not wanting to leave the heaven I was floating in.

Dark eyes penetrated mine and a dreaded fear began creeping inside of me.

Seb had manipulated me into staying, but was that all I had just agreed to?

Delilah had tried to warn me, and when I looked at him now I could see the danger melting from him, as though his true identity was finally rising to the surface.

He wasn't bothering to wear a mask anymore. He was embracing the darkness.

Seb was smirking, and a crimson flush travelled over my skin as the reality of what we had just done caught up with me. Spotting the horrified expression in my eyes, he leant his head against mine.

"If you run, I'll find you."

The malice in his tone sent goosebumps over my skin, I had just become prey to the devil, and I had the impression his words were a promise he had no intention of breaking.

Though the idea of being chased by the boogie man himself, now that was a gamble I might make.

After I had finished smoothing my skirt down and tightening the bands around my hair, I stood tall, mustering all of my confidence.

"I don't belong to anyone Seb."

I folded my arms over my chest, but he ripped them apart, shrouding my body under his. Gripping his hand around my throat he forced my head upwards and glared at me.

"I dare you Harriet. I *dare* you to try and stop me from owning every surface of your skin, every inch of your soul. You're right. You don't belong to anyone. You *only* belong to me."

Before I could argue he was seizing my hand and pulling me through the darkness that was surrounding us.

As soon as we went through a door cool air slammed into my body, and I stood there for a moment, my skin absorbing each gust of the cool breeze that surrendered itself. My lungs expanded as the air travelled inside my body and I turned, expecting to see Seb standing beside me, but he was gone.

The man was a shadow, lurking in the crevices but always ready to pounce.

"Harriet!" My name was shouted through the crowds of people gathered. "What happened? We were all asked to leave but I couldn't find you." I let out an unconvincing laugh at Delilah in front of me, a look of concern etched across her face.

"I guess I got locked inside, I don't know. How long was I in there for?"

"Nearly an hour, they said no one was inside. We need to put trackers on our phones." She laughed and shook her head, "come on, let's get a beer." I allowed Delilah to lead me through the crowds once again, my mind still reeling against the touch of Seb, his wicked tongue, and his dangerous promises.

After throwing our drinks back one after the other, I was settling back into the tantalising numbness that Seb had dragged me from. Peering around the Carnival I spotted the performer's tent at the far end, lights, and music blaring from the opening.

Feeling brave, and a little risky, I nodded at the tent catching Delilah's attention.

"What's going on in there? It's like they're having their own private party?" She followed my glare, and then quickly looked back at me.

"Yeah, fright nights are their best night. I guess performers in short skirts and fancy lingerie appeals to their private customers."

Private customers?

The illusive words caught my attention and piqued my curiosity, and I raced in the direction of the dazzling kaleidoscope of colours. A tight hand catching my wrist knocked me backwards, and I narrowed my eyes at Delilah.

"I won't stop you if you go in there, but you need to be ready for what you'll see."

Confusion bounced around in my head, and I turned back towards the tent. If Delilah's words were an attempt to keep me away, they were doing the opposite.

I was fed up with people giving me their opinion on where I should and shouldn't go.

I smiled at her brightly, not revealing my frustration. "It takes a lot to shock me." I slipped away from her grip and began descending forward.

Each stride loudened the music, and curiosity fuelled my spiking adrenaline.

I didn't stop outside, I didn't want the chance to reconsider my bold movements.

But when I entered through the fabric's parting, I wished I had.

Men swamped the horseshoe sofas, their bodies hidden by those of the female performers dancing across them in sultry seductive movements. Most were topless, some wearing nothing at all.

Around the table men and women sniffed crushed white powder and smoked cigarettes laced with venom.

Stale groans filtered through the air and my eyes whipped to one of the open doors on the far side of the tent, the doors that were usually closed.

Inside flowing red hair spilled over the edge of a bed, whilst a man's hand gripped around the edge of Cherry's neck, his other holding a small knife against her throat. Above her head, her wrists were bound by a burgundy ribbon. I panicked for a moment, fear that the man was attempting to hurt her, but with every thrust he made her eyes rolled back and she cried with ecstasy.

A stiff hold on my arm pulled me from my daze, and I stared into the eyes of Tony who was already dragging me through the tent's occupants and to the kitchenette.

"You shouldn't be here Harriet." He whispered, but I barely heard it, my mind too preoccupied by the scenes playing out. Illicit groans filtered through the air like music, and I struggled to comprehend the heated chaos unfolding in front of me.

My eyes were filling with moisture, unanswerable confusion sweeping through my body. "What is this?" Anxiety grappled with my throat, my words spitting from my mouth.

Stilettos tapping against the floor caught my attention, and as they loudened I held my breath, my fight or flight beginning to catch up with me. Questions threatened to spill from my lips, but I didn't have time to ask them before Tony grabbed my shoulders and pushed me down, hiding me behind the counter.

"Tony. Where is Seb?"

My chest hitched at his name, surely he didn't know what was going on here. The woman's voice was tight, an undeniable bite rumbling from it as the words left her mouth. Something about the way she spoke evoked an immediate fear in me. She reeked of power and control, and I had no doubt that she was responsible for what was going on here.

I pulled my legs up tight against my body, attempting to make myself smaller as the smell of smoky chaos entered the room.

Danger had arrived, and he had the tongue of a god.

Chapter Fourteen

Seb

I'd gotten caught up by Harriet, I'd been careless. But I needed to make sure she knew she couldn't run, that I would hunt her to the ends of the earth if I needed to.

And fuck me if it wasn't worth it. I could still taste her on my tongue. She was heroine, and I was addicted.

When I entered the tent I was immediately hit by the sweet scent of vanilla, and I quickly scanned around the faces searching for the doe eyes haunting my mind.

My eyes narrowed as I passed each face that wasn't hers, but when they landed on a nervous looking Tony, and Saffron who was standing inches away from him across the kitchen, I knew where I would find her.

I needed to get Saffron away from that counter.

"There you are!" I stalked towards her, and she stood with her hands on her hips. "Where have you been?" My jaw ticked at her aggressive tone and at the tuffs of brunette hair that were sticking out below the other side of the counter.

What the fuck was she doing in here?

"I was checking on the mules." I lied, stopping in front of her and lifting my chin, challenging her glare.

"We're down tonight, the money isn't where it should be."

"What more do you expect to be done, the girls are working, the mules are running."

Saffron suddenly shoved past as three more men entered the tent. Her snidey voice dropped, an innocent, feminine one taking its place. "Gentlemen, how can I help?"

"We want the redhead." My fists tightened at my sides; they hadn't even had the decency to know the name of the girl they were about to hire.

The smile coating Saffron's face was sickening. I knew that look, she was mentally calculating the money she was about to make.

"She's with another client." The men's eyes roamed over my frame at my interruption, and they all pulled their shoulders back attempting to challenge me.

"Afterwards then." They began walking towards the pool table, their eyes hungrily roaming over the rest of the girls in the space.

Saffron faced me, her eyebrow rising, but I was too busy watching the three men to look at her. Something about them felt off. "I don't care whether her body is limp and broken, as soon as her client comes out you send them in." My teeth ground together. "I want the drugs ramped up as well," she continued, "if this whole Carnival isn't high by the end of the night, you'll be held responsible."

I looked down at her, my eyes burning in rage. "Whatever you say."

Her chin lifted before she walked out of the tent, nodding to the three sleazy men as she left.

I needed to get Harriet out of there, but it would be impossible without someone noticing her. Turning to face Tony and pushing my body as far as I could over the counter, I hissed in his direction.

"Get her the fuck out of here now." Tony nodded frantically and looked down next to him. I needed to find a way to distract the three men. The ones who hadn't taken their eyes off of me since they arrived.

Sudden movement caught my attention and two of the men ran to stand behind me whilst the other rounded the corner of the counter, a smirk covering his face when he spotted Harriet on the floor.

He leaned down, gripped the top of her arm and dragged her to stand, her body hanging rigid against his hold.

"What do we have here?"

Harriet was snarling at him. Good, she was learning.

Pulling her body against his, he gripped her chin firmly turning her face to look at me. Black streaks ran down her cheeks, and her tiny body trembled.

This wasn't what was supposed to happen, this wasn't how she was supposed to find out about the Carnival.

About me.

"She seems like she has bite. We like bite."

I stayed silent.

"How much?" One of the other men barked and I whipped my head to look at him. Keeping my voice low I remained as professional as was humanly possible.

"She isn't for hire."

"Pity. She's gorgeous." Leaning back he roamed over her legs and arse. With each inch of her body he crossed I struggled against the raging chaos that wanted to spill out, teach him not to touch what didn't belong to him.

The man next to me smirked, "you sure? We would pay a good price for her."

Didn't I fucking know it. These sleazes reeked of dirty money. The fact they thought there was a price on Harriet was laughable.

Fuck professional.

"Are you deaf? I just told you she's not for fucking hire, and if you don't take your hands off her I'll take them off for you." I looked at Tony, "take her home."

The man loosened his grip on Harriet, and as Tony dragged her from the tent the three men followed hungrily behind.

At the same time, Cherry's client walked out of one of the bedrooms, buckling his belt as he left.

"*The redhead* is ready for you now." I spat.

The three men looked at each other and then stared at me with snarky grins. "I think we've changed our minds. We'll wait for the brunette to become available."

"For the last fucking time, she's not for hire. You'll have to pick one of the other girls to suck your dicks." My voice rose with anger at their dismissiveness.

"We'll see."

They barged past me and exited the tent. I didn't stop staring until they were completely out of sight and as they disappeared the rage settled.

I needed to get to Harriet's. God knows what would be going through that complicated head of hers after what she'd just seen.

Cherry emerged from one of the bedrooms, her body hidden by a silk black robe, "everything okay Seb?" Emerald eyes narrowed on my uptight posture.

"I need to go, can you find Delilah? Let her know I've taken Harriet home."

A mischievous grin crossed Cherry's face, "of course, make sure you behave yourself." With a wink she walked back into the bedroom, closing the door softly behind her.

She had no fucking idea.

Collecting my bike keys from one of the drawers, I left the tent, not bothering to grab my helmet on the way, my mind too preoccupied by what I might walk into at Harriet's apartment.

At whatever carnage I'd just unleashed.

Lifting the doormat, I was pleasantly surprised to see the key gleaming from the ground. Lilah had obviously returned it after I'd used it to get Harriet home, and I was silently thanking the dark-haired cannonball for her organisation.

Though I'm sure that was more for her own benefit than mine.

Quietly pushing the door open, the sound of the TV buzzing filled the room and across from it Tony sat sprawled over the sofa watching the screen intently.

The moment he spotted me he sat up and pushed the power button on the remote cloaking us in silence.

"Where is she?" I didn't need to expand; Tony knew exactly who I was talking about.

"She went straight into the bathroom when we got back, I heard the tap running." I nodded. "She didn't say anything in the car."

"I'll take it from here." Tony collected his stuff before silently exiting the apartment. I turned to the bathroom door sitting slightly ajar, steam evaporating from around the edges. Sneaking closer I spotted her costume littered on the floor, along with her bag and pompoms.

I knocked gently on the door, but I was greeted by quiet.

"Harriet." Still I was met with silence, apart from the gentle splash of water as her body moved around in the tub.

Pushing against the door, it willingly opened and lying peacefully in front of me was the goddess herself.

Her eyes were glued to the ceiling, dry streaks collecting at the edges and staining down her cheeks. She didn't acknowledge me as I entered, and knowing that when she did she would have questions I leaned against the sink, my arms folded, waiting patiently for her to speak.

It didn't take long.

"So, you're like a pimp?" I wanted to laugh at how wrong she was, but I sensed now wasn't the time for humour.

"No."

"No? Then what the hell was that back there?" Harriet tore her glare from the ceiling, her eyes heated pits of questions, all of them dancing over her pupils and aimed at me.

"It was The Carnival."

Harriet let out a breathy laugh and shook her head. "Is this how it's going to be, I ask you questions, and you give me obscure answers? You want me to stay Seb, you need to give me a reason to. *That place* has done the opposite."

She was right. Harriet had heard too much, *seen* too much. The only way to make her understand was to be completely transparent with her, and hope she understood when I was finished.

"At fifteen I was homeless. Saffron, the woman you heard earlier, took me in, gave me a bed, food. She walked into my life pretty much like a guardian angel." I moved across the room and sat on the floor next to the tub, making sure to keep my eyes fixed on Harriet.

"I earned my way by stealing. She would send me around the Carnival with a list of things she needed, and if I wanted to keep my bed and food I had to bring those things to her. That was when I met Cherry. She was the same age as me, kicked out of home. We instantly clicked. I guess we found comfort in each other."

Harriet's chest rose and fell in stutters, "when I turned twenty-one, Saffron made me available to 'hire'. We had a group of high-paying women she was trying to appeal to. I guess I was the appeal."

I thought back to my first encounter with one of the women. I had been told about some of the fantasies she had, about the things she wanted me to do.

"They all had extreme desires, something that they weren't getting from their husbands. But once I had given them what they wanted, it was as though the fascination had worn off. When women pay for sex, it normally only takes once or twice for them to get whatever it is they need from it. Men are different. They like holding onto the power, like *feeling* powerful."

I observed Harriet but she remained emotionless, concealing her feelings in a cage. "When the work dried up, I needed to find a way to earn my place. I suggested to Saffron that I could work as a middleman between everyone. Soon I was organising the drug runs and negotiating with clients. I was basically running everything." I paused. "It wasn't going to be forever. I had a plan with Cherry of how we could finally get out. I thought I'd survived through the worst. But then you showed up."

I tilted my head back, leaning it against the tiles and closed my eyes. "I wanted you to leave desperately so things could go back to normal. But I can't let you go. You're like a poison that's keeping me alive."

Harriet remained silent, her eyes glaring at me and anger radiating off of her.

"Don't use me as a scapegoat for how you have allowed those women to be treated, for the drugs that you cart around and feed people." She stood and stepped over the edge of the bathtub, her body sending water showering over me.

"Drugs murdered my mother, and there is never an excuse for supplying them to people." I followed her out of the bathroom, and she grabbed a towel, wrapping it tightly around her still-dripping body. "I want you to leave."

"You know I won't do that."

"It's not up for negotiation Seb."

I stepped forward, but Harriet moved away from me and perched in front of the window, her head dropping into her hands.

"I can't do this. You're exhausting." She looked up at me between her fingers. "Please, just go." I hated the way her voice broke, the pleading desperation that spilt from her lips.

I needed to give her this. Needed to give her tonight to filter through her thoughts.

Tomorrow. We had tomorrow.

"I don't want to see you again Seb."

Tomorrow.

Walking to the front door, I took one last look at Harriet, but her attention remained distracted by the outside world.

I waited for a moment, waited for her to stop me, but she didn't. When I closed the door I stayed for a few minutes expecting her to come outside, change her mind. But she never did.

I was being cut off.

Tomorrow.

Chapter Fifteen

Harriet

I'd spent most of Sunday curled up in bed, begging the feathery duvet to absorb me into the underworld. My eyes were raw from Seb's turbulent admissions about the Carnival, and my head was a riot of emotions, each hauling me in a different direction.

I couldn't deny that he was addicting. He was mysterious and dark, and I was pretty sure it was my own ghosts that called to him.

I was conflicted.

Seb mentioned that he wanted out of the Carnival, but he was grounded into its cogs so tightly, *so deeply*, that it seemed impossible he would ever get out.

I wanted to know what kept him there, but I wasn't sure I was ready to hear more truths about the corrupt world he lived in.

I was angry. Angry that he had been dragged into that world at sixteen, angry that he had been made to feel that he had to feed into it somehow, and even angrier that he had become part of the mechanisms that kept it running, that kept it surviving.

The sex I could look past. Just. I wasn't naïve enough to not know that things like that were happening all over the country. But the drugs, that was where my mind screamed the loudest.

Since my mother, I'd had a strict rule to never let drugs enter my life again in any capacity. I refused to allow a handsome man to manipulate my values.

But Seb had sunk his nails so deep into me that they were lodged, and it would take more than a few days away from him to loosen them.

I was finally ready to admit he was *my* drug.

Pulling my jeans up my legs, and throwing my new 'SMITHY'S TECH' polo over my head, I dressed for work. I was meant to be off today, but I needed a distraction. Anything was better than sitting around the apartment and allowing last night's escapades to torment my already tired head.

The smell of waffles suddenly pricked my senses, and I hummed as the delightful scent hit my nose.

"Good morning!" a cheery voice called as I entered the room, and Delilah smiled brightly at me.

"Someone's in a good mood." Delilah blushed, and I knew that look. That was the I-just-got-laid look. I rose my eyebrow. "Who is she?" Seconds later, tangled red hair and a naked body appeared at Delilah's side.

Alarm bells immediately rang in my head, "Cherry, sorry I didn't realise you were here." I hid my eyes with my hand, but it was impossible to hide the embarrassment turning my skin crimson.

The redhead kissed the top of Delilah's head and took a bite from the waffle she was about to plate up.

The last time I'd seen her she was being laid over a bed by a man. No wonder she took no issues striding around naked in a place that wasn't hers.

"Don't sweat it. Join us for breakfast." Knowing everything I did now about the Carnival, *about Cherry*, had me stumbling over my words. That and the fact that we hadn't gotten off to the best of starts, something I was now forgiving after learning about her circumstances.

I laughed at my lack of communication when I realised they were both staring at me. "I'd love to, but I have work." I smiled tightly at the pair, and grabbed my phone, stashing it into my back pocket. "I'll see you guys later?" They both waved as I left the room.

The further towards the building's exit I got, The more I hoped the unease would settle, but with each step it grew louder and louder until the noise became unbearable.

Delilah had tried to warn me away from Seb, I wonder if that's because she knew about what went on at the Carnival. If she did, how did she look past that with Cherry? The two were obviously close, and I wished that my own morals would allow me to look past the shady dealings that went on around Seb.

At least I thought I did.

I told him I didn't want to see him again. I needed to remember that.

It was warm outside today, and I relished the sun's kisses on my skin, heating my entire body and melting away some of my nerves. When I stepped into Smithy's I was thankful that the remaining discomfort had scurried away.

He was hunched over the counter and as the bell above the door jingled, announcing my entrance, he looked up and smiled proudly at spotting the new polo.

"Suits you," I did a twirl, and Smithy laughed. "There's someone here to see you." My mood instantly dropped, and a pool of dread came to life behind my ribcage. But when dirty blonde hair came into sight instead of black, my body instantly eased.

"Daniel. what are you doing here?" He looked out of place in the tech store. It was scruffy and cluttered. In comparison, he was the complete opposite. He wore an immaculate branded jumper and jeans, and his trainers looked as though they'd never been worn.

He shuffled on his feet, his hands firmly stashed in his pockets. Daniel looked over at Tony, who was grinning like a Cheshire cat, clearly entertained by his nervousness.

"I was wondering if you wanted to go to dinner?" My eyes widened, the last thing I had expected was for him to be asking me on a date. I leaned on the display cabinet, hoping that it would help him relax. Smiling, I slowly nodded my head.

I needed to give myself the chance to meet someone new.

I needed to give myself the chance to forget about Seb *and* Felix.

"Yeah, I'd like that." He immediately relaxed, and a playful smile scattered over his mouth. "When did you have in mind?"

"I was actually hoping we could get together tonight, there's a new restaurant a friend of mine has opened down the road. We could try it."

"Sounds great." I beamed.

"Great," his smile didn't budge, "I'll pick you up at eight." I waved from the doorway as he walked towards his car. I was pleasantly surprised to see he had a Mustang like me.

"Don't let Seb catch wind of that." I turned to face Smithy, my face contorting into confusion.

"Excuse me?"

"Seb will have a field day if he knows you're going on a date with some stuck-up grad school kid. Bromlin's managed to survive without any limbs being cut off for this long. Best not to provoke the beast now."

"He has nothing to do with this," I said flatly. Smithy shrugged and began busying himself behind the counter, shuffling paperwork and tapping on the register.

"He know that?"

I huffed and folded my arms across my chest. "I don't need permission from a man I barely know, about who I can and can't date." Smithy stopped his fumbling. He looked as though he had something to say, but before he could I held my finger up, "I don't want to hear it."

Hiding amongst the display cabinets, I began wiping them with the cloth that was hanging from my back pocket.

Why would Smithy know anything about what was going on between me and Seb? I let conspiracies dance around in my head as I continued to clean. It didn't matter, I wouldn't be seeing him again.

I'd already allowed my morals to be compromised once, I wouldn't let it happen again.

I refused to become a pawn in his corrupt chess game.

My heart sank a little in disappointment, but I ignored it.

Stupid heart.

The rest of my shift passed quickly in comfortable silence, Smithy quickly realised I didn't want to talk about Seb, and luckily for me, he respected that.

Outside the night was drawing in, and I was surprised by the excitement bubbling at seeing Daniel later. I liked that he came with no strings attached, he had only ever been warm and friendly to me, welcoming my presence with open arms.

He was good for me, *spending time with him would be good for me.*

He was also a distraction from the devil that was haunting my mind, something I was desperate for relief from.

When I got back to the apartment, I paused. Loud thumping music came from inside, the base causing the door to vibrate slightly as I pushed it open.

The living room was commandeered with people, most of whom looked unfamiliar. In the kitchen, Delilah stood between Cherry's legs, a smile bold enough to light up the room spread across her face. I smiled to myself for a moment, her happiness contagious, and when she spotted me she waved.

"I didn't know you were having a party tonight?" I raised my eyebrow but made sure to keep my tone playful so she knew I wasn't mad.

"It's just a few friends…and their friends." She shyly smiled at me, and I shook my head, a gentle laugh spilling from my body.

Cherry's eyes were soft when they landed on mine. "You should join us."

I appreciated her invitation, but I wasn't going to bail on Daniel. "Thanks, but I have a date." I boldly curled my lips, but her smile turned into a frown.

"Does Seb know?"

What the hell was it with everyone assuming the man-child needed to know about my life, a life I was desperately trying to separate him from.

"No." I didn't say anything else as I sulked towards my bedroom and slammed the door behind me. I heard a chorus of noises, and then the music took over again.

I was trying to escape him, but he was making it impossible.

Flicking through my drawers, I decided on a purple and white patchwork dress with puffy sleeves and a matching pair of tights. I wasn't sure how posh this place would be, but I wanted to make sure I dressed up rather than down. I was desperate for Daniel's approval.

Pulling my hair down from its band and running my fingers through the dry ends, I separated the strands before picking up the bag next to my mattress and stuffing the contents with all of the necessities. A roar of intoxicated cheers sounded from the living room when the front door slammed, and I looked at the time on my phone. Daniel would be here any minute.

Taking that as my cue to leave, I walked back into the living room but froze when magnificent coal black eyes stared straight through me. The stubble on his face had darkened, and I had to resist the temptation to run my hand over it.

What is wrong with you?

Seb's hungry gaze roamed over my body and a flush heated my skin when his eyes landed back on mine. A few voices quietened as he stalked closer, and his hand swiped a strand of my hair from my face.

"Going somewhere princess?" I wasn't getting into this with him now.

"Yes. I'm meeting a friend." *Technically not a lie.*

"You always get this dressed up for a friend?" A strange feeling jumped around inside of me.

I didn't like the fact he was starting to create a scene, but the jealousy, the possessiveness that was melting from him stirred a familiar throb between my legs.

I mentally scolded my body's lack of restraint when it came to this man.

Don't let him manipulate you.

"It's none of your business."

"*You're* my business. Stop avoiding the question." He stepped a little closer. "How about you go back into your room, and I'll make you sing the answer." His voice lowered. "You tasted so sweet the first time, I bet you'd be even more delicious the second."

"I'm going to be late." I hurried past him and surprisingly he let me, but when I pulled the door closed the last thing I saw was him, and the daggers he was aiming in my direction.

Daniel was already waiting when I got downstairs. As soon as he saw me, he stepped out of his car and rounded it, opening the passenger side for me to get in. I smiled brightly as I lowered myself into the seat and took a deep inhale.

The car smelt like bubble gum, and I tapped the freshener hanging from the rear-view mirror causing it to frantically spin.

It looked like how my head felt.

"Sorry, the cars a little fruity, thought I had better get it cleaned. Wouldn't want you thinking I'm a slob." Daniel laughed, but it came out as a stutter as if he was nervous. I laid my hand on top of his, stealing his attention.

"It smells great, thank you for making the effort." He mirrored my expression, and when he moved his hand he pulled mine with it, resting it on his leg.

The restaurant wasn't far away. The building was surrounded with floor-to-ceiling windows, and through them, the lighting inside offered a delicate glow. Each of the tables were neatly decorated with white plaster styled trees that hung tiny glass bulbs from the branches.

I was glad I'd dressed up.

Daniel held the door open for me as we walked in, and we were quickly seated by a man wearing a three-piece suit. I'd never been to a restaurant where the waiters wore suits, even the places Felix used to take me weren't this fancy.

You're a fraud. You don't belong here.

"Did you say your friend owned this place?" I shook the intrusive voices from my head.

Daniel smiled and thanked the waiter as he poured two glasses of water into the crystal tumblers on the table. "Yes, it's his second one, though this one is a little more prestigious." I took a sip from the glass and noted the clusters of people seated in various areas of the space.

"I can see. This place is stunning."

"So, how did you end up in Bromlin?"

I considered how to answer for a moment, "a messy breakup. It's complicated. Honestly? I didn't know where I was going to go. I saw Delilah's ad on a leaflet." Daniel rest his elbows on the table and leaned across, giving me his undivided attention.

"Well I would be lying if I said I'm not slightly pleased." I laughed at Daniel's honesty just as a waiter came over and took our orders.

"What about you? How did you end up here?"

"I moved about a year ago, I had some friends that lived here at the time and thought it would be a good move." The waiter brought over two wine glasses and popped the cork on a vintage white Pino Grigio. I practically hummed when the sweet grapey liquid hit my tongue.

"Where did you live before?"

"Have you heard of Stockton RE?"

I nodded my head, "just on the outskirts of Callie Bay."

Daniel lit up at my recognition of his hometown. “Yeah, that’s the one. I’m impressed, normally people look at me blankly when I say that.”

Could fate really be on my side? Someone who knew what it was like to live in the clouded world of skyscrapers and penthouses.

“I’m a CB original,” I said proudly, lifting my head and straightening my shoulders. Daniel laughed at my movements, and I couldn’t help the one that bubbled from me. I struggled to remember the last time I’d felt this relaxed in someone else’s company.

You felt relaxed when Seb’s head was between your legs.

We sat and ate our food in silence, only coming up for air to announce how good the food was, and when we finished, Daniel chivalrously paid the bill despite my objections.

“I need to use the gents. I’ll be back in a moment.” As he left the table I began people-watching around the restaurant again.

There were a lot of guests here, the owner must have had a lot of good friends. Though I couldn’t blame people for enjoying the food. It was one of the best meals I’d eaten out, and the company had made it even better.

My eyes wandered to the glass windows, and at the fountains that sprung to life behind them. As the water fell in a shower before springing upwards again, I noticed a figure standing on the other side of the road staring in my direction.

Leant against a motorbike, the man that had appeared at the community garden was standing arms folded, visor closed, watching in my direction.

Seb.

My palms were clammy and sweating, and I rubbed them against my dress, the material clinging to my skin with every swipe. Rabid thumps attacked my ribcage, and I started counting in my head, trying to stop the panic from morphing.

It didn't seem impossible anymore that Seb might actually follow through on the threats he'd made about Daniel, and fear grappled with my muscles at the trap I was walking straight into.

One. two. three. four—

I couldn't escape him. But that wasn't why I panicked.

I panicked because I didn't *want* to escape him. The thrill of his chase, *his obsession*, snaked inside me.

"Everything okay?" My head whipped behind me. Daniel appeared; his eyes narrowed together as he stared down. I looked back out the window, but the street was empty, as if no one had been out there to begin with.

Was I hallucinating, was my imagination playing tricks on me?

"Yes, sorry." I tightly smiled as he pulled my chair out and we headed towards the restaurant's exit.

The drive back to my apartment was silent, my mind going at war over the decision to invite him back in or not. Delilah's gathering was sure to have gone elsewhere by now, and even if it hadn't we could mingle with her friends, maybe have a few drinks.

"Would you like to come inside?" I blurted before I had a chance to reconsider asking.

Daniel looked at me from the driver's side of the car and put his hand on my knee, squeezing gently. "I'd love to."

I waited.

I waited patiently for the butterflies to come, to start flying around. But they didn't. My body didn't react to Daniel's contact at all, and a disappointed ache fluttered in my chest.

That was the only feeling his touch teased from me, disappointment.

Climbing the stairs, the loud thump of music coming from the apartment lingered in the corridor, and gave a half-hearted smile at Daniel over my shoulder.

"Delilah's got some friends round. I hope you don't mind." Daniel returned the smile and nodded.

When I pushed the door open I was met by the strong stench of marijuana, and drunken bodies spilt over every surface of our living room. Most of the guests were passed out on the floor, but Delilah was sat on the counter straddling Cherry, whilst the source of the herby smell sat burning by the window.

I walked towards it, snubbed it out and then threw it through the open glass. "What the fuck Delilah?"

She pulled her face away from Cherry and looked at me. Her eyes were glazed, and she could barely keep her head straight.

"Princess! You're home!" Delilah swayed as she detached herself from Cherry, and jumped down onto the wooden floorboards.

"Don't call me that." I folded my arms across my chest and her smile evaporated, a pout appearing in its place.

"Why? It suits you, plus *he* gets to call you that." She pointed behind me and sure enough, leaning against the wall, arms folded was hell himself.

And he was smiling at me like I was dinner.

Daniel, obviously feeling uncomfortable in the situation, moved closer and whispered against my ear. "You want me to go?"

I collected all of my strength and gave him an apologetic look. "No. No, it's alright. Go through that door, it's my room. I'll be there in a second."

Seb didn't take his eyes off Daniel until he was safely tucked away behind the door, and I was surprised that Daniel did the same, his own glare challenging and deadly.

As soon as the door closed Seb was pushing from the wall, heading straight towards me. I backed away, my legs moving as quickly as they could, but I was soon slamming against the wall with Seb's hand wrapped around my throat.

"What game are you playing princess?" His voice was low, the scratch behind his words intended only for me.

"I'm not playing a game you psychopath!" I looked back towards the kitchen, expecting to see Delilah and Cherry there, but they had gone, obviously deciding to give me and the devil some privacy.

Traitors.

A dangerous smile appeared at the corners of Seb's mouth, and his hand trailed down my body, and under the hem of my dress. I clenched my thighs together, attempting to pacify the frantic need that was gathering between them.

Seb noticed, a sadistic grin dancing on his face. "I know you need me as much as I need you."

"You're delusional." I snapped, but it came out weak and unconvincing, my voice horsy against his fingers trapping the air in my throat.

He ran his tongue down the side of my neck and pushed his fingers against the inside of my leg attempting to tease them apart.

"Don't touch me." I just about managed to say, the voices in my head arguing with my mouth.

"Why? Scared you might like it? Or is it because you already know you will?" His eyes were like furnaces branding my heart.

Owning my heart.

"If you're going to play with fire princess, make sure you're ready to burn."

Seb suddenly let go of me, leaving me panting and breathless against the wall. He stepped over the bodies sleeping on the floor and threw himself on the sofa, his eyes refusing to detach from mine.

I eyed a couple of glasses in the kitchen, my fingers twitching at my sides. I wanted to be the one to finish this fight. "Don't tempt me to throw something at you. You obnoxious arsehole."

Seb smirked, and it made my stomach summersault. "You're killing me here Harriet, no one ever teach you it's rude to tease? Seems you have a lot to learn."

I needed to put as much distance between us as I could before I threw myself into his trap. I quickly flew across the room and into the security of my bedroom.

"If you want to make me out to be the villain that's fine, but let's not forget who was begging me not long ago."

I slammed the door as soon as I was in my bedroom, my ears bouncing with the last of his words hammering through them.

I was trying so desperately to hold it together, and as I counted silently I laid my forehead against the cool wooden surface.

"Wow, that's…full on."

Daniel whistled behind me, and I turned to find him sitting upright in amongst my duvet. Despite the confrontation outside he still radiated a cheery aura, and I was thankful he didn't ask me any questions as I undressed, careful to hide my scars, and pulled a knee length t shirt over my head.

Scooting in beside him, I let his arm crowd around me and pull me tightly against his body. I begged my heart to open for this man, begged it to release the butterflies. But it ignored me, and as I fell into blissful sleep, my dreams were haunted by hypnotising dark eyes and an addictive smoky scent.

Chapter Sixteen

Seb

Icy water attacked my windpipe, and I was suddenly awake, coughing and spluttering as I sat upright. Looking down at me, a scowl on her face, was the angel herself.

"Did I go to heaven?" I smirked as I wiped my wet hair from my face.

"Who are you kidding? You'll never get into heaven."

"Why would I want to when I know you'll be coming to hell with me?"

Harriet ignored my flirt, placed the now empty glass on the TV cabinet, and walked towards the kitchen where she poured two cups of black coffee.

The scent filled the air, and I innocently smiled as she turned to face me, leaning against the counter. "If you think one of these is for you, you really are a psychopath." I narrowed my eyes at the same time a giant oaf walked from her bedroom door.

I don't know why he looked so full of himself; I knew he hadn't fucked her. I stayed awake most of the night listening, waiting for the moment he dared to touch what was mine.

All I needed was an excuse to go in there.

The posh twat didn't even look at me as he crossed the room to my girl, clearly he was too good to spare me a single drop of attention.

Smithy was right. He *was* a stuck-up grad school kid, and he had no idea who he was playing with.

When he did finally look in my direction, I tilted my head to the side and leaned back on the sofa.

"Morning." He called, and I watched as Harriet rolled her eyes at my silence. I nodded my head at him, but that was all he was getting from me.

Delilah's bedroom door suddenly swung open, catching all of our attention and from it, Cherry and her came through, ribbons of laughter spilling from their mouths. They abruptly halted when they noticed the tension, and Delilah looked from me to Daniel, before finally settling on Harriet.

"Bit of a crowd in here this morning." *I couldn't agree more.*

"I should probably go." Daniel interrupted the silence, and I watched as he leaned down to give Harriet a kiss. When she moved, directing his lips to her head, a dangerous satisfaction rolled inside of me. As if she could feel it too, her eyes immediately fixed on mine.

Good girl little siren.

Daniel was oblivious to her rejection. "I'll meet you outside the box office at seven babe. The film starts at half past." Harriet smiled up at him and nodded her head as he began stepping away.

Babe. The guy was full of imagination.

Interesting that she was entertaining his narrow mind when it was clear she had no intention of pursuing him.

As soon as Daniel stepped outside the door, I was on my feet. "Cherry get your stuff. We have to go."

"Yes Sir," Cherry said sarcastically. She untangled her body from Delilah's before stepping back into the bedroom.

Pulling on the handle of the apartment door, I quickly raced down the steps, hoping to catch Daniel before he left. And luckily for me, as I opened the door he was just rounding the edge of his car.

"Daniel!" I shouted, and his head flung upwards.

"What do you want Seb?" He slammed the door with a huff, and walked back to the pavement, leaning against the passenger door.

"Something going on between you and Harriet?"

A smirk raised at the corner of his mouth, and he folded his arms, looking nonconcerted by my question. That was mistake number one.

"Why, you jealous?"

My fingers tensed at my sides, this guy was pushing my buttons, *and* being cocky about it.

Mistake number two.

"Just looking out for her."

"Don't worry arsehole, I'll look after your *princess*. I'll make sure she's well taken care of." He winked at me, and the sultry tone in his voice sent me over the edge.

Mistake number three.

I flung my body towards him before he could move. "If you touch her, if you even *think* about her again, I will cut your hands off and feed you each fucking finger one by one." Daniel laughed, and it provoked my psyche even further into insanity.

"You don't scare me mate—"

"I'm not your fucking mate. Stay the fuck away from her, or you'll be eating shit through your gummy mouth for the rest of your pathetic lonely life. No one ever tell you I enjoy collecting teeth for trophies?"

"Seb…" Cherry's soft voice called from behind me, and I stepped away from Daniel, my chest rising and falling as the deadly mist blurring my vision started to disperse.

He didn't say anything else as he got in his car and sped away, leaving me and Cherry standing on the sidewalk alone.

"There's a spare helmet under the seat." I began walking towards the bike, but Cherry's nails dug into my arm.

"Let's walk, it's nice out here and we both had a lot to drink last night. Bikes plus hangover don't mix well." I nodded, and when she looped her arm through mine and we began walking towards our home, we settled into a comfortable silence.

Out of the corner of my eye, I spotted Cherry chewing the corner of her mouth. "Whatever you want to say, spit it out."

"What's happening between you and Harriet?" Whenever I'd brought a girl around the Carnival before no one had batted an eyelid, so the question confused me.

"She's so…innocent Seb."

"Harry is far from innocent." I inhaled the cool air that was battling against our bodies. "She's going to help us."

Cherry looked at me, her eyes full of questions. "I find that hard to believe. She looks like she wants to strangle you every time she sees you." I stayed silent. "Besides, how does a girl from the big city help two lowlifes out of a criminal enterprise?" I laughed at her use of dramatic words.

"Just trust me."

"Do you at least care about her? Tell me you're not using her for our benefit, she's a sweet girl Seb, kind. I don't want to see her get hurt. I feel bad enough that I stole her purse. If something happens to her it'll be our fault."

I stopped in my tracks and turned Cherry to face me. "Even if I wanted to, I can't stop."

Cherry nodded, satisfied by my answer, and we continued on our walk, "what about you and Delilah?" A huge grin coast across her face, and I noticed the tinge that began painting her cheeks.

"God, Seb. She's everything. She's smart, funny. All of my lady bones shake when I see her."

"I don't need to know about your lady bones." I pulled a face and we both vibrated as laughs bounced between us. Settling into silence again we rounded the corner, and Cherry paused in front of the Carnival gates.

"I think I love her Seb. I think I've always loved her, and it scares the shit out of me. I feel like I'm drowning when I'm around her, and I don't know how to swim." I pulled Cherry into my arms, offering her a comforting embrace.

"Looks like we'll both need to learn how to swim."

Chapter Seventeen

Harriet

I pulled my phone from my bag and looked at the time again. *Seven fifteen.*

Daniel was late.

I skipped between my feet, wrapping my arms around my body. The air was cold, and each time the frosty breeze bit against my skin goosebumps erupted. Maybe Daniel had already arrived and was waiting in the movie theatre.

Hoping I was right, I pushed against the heavy glass door and towards the counter.

I'd thought ahead and bought my ticket for the film online, we were going to see a new horror movie that had just come out and had raving reviews. When I was met by the bright smile of the ticket attendant, I held my phone out and she scanned the screen, a loud chime coming from her device as she did.

"Good choice. I've heard this one's even gorier than the first." I wasn't sure whether I should be slightly alarmed by the gleam in her eye. "You want screen four." I thanked her and began walking towards the designated room.

Above the entrance, a big flashing four signalled the correct way, and I shoved my body against the door. Inside, the theatre was already blanketed in darkness, and small spotlights guided the direction of the stairs.

For a film that was supposedly so popular, there were only five other people in here. A couple sat on the first row, closest to the screen, another couple further up on the other side of the aisle, and in the back corner, someone sat by themselves.

But no Daniel.

I took a seat in the back of the theatre and pulled out my phone bringing Daniel's name up on the screen.

Clicking the green dial button I held the phone to my ear, but the call went straight to voicemail. A generic voice spoke back to me and as the beep rang, I whispered into the speaker.

"Hey, it's me. I'm not sure whether you forgot or…well I hope you just forgot. But I'm at the movie. It's pretty empty, no one will notice if you come in late, so…yeah. Maybe I'll see you soon." I hung up the phone and switched the button to silent before I shoved it into my bag.

Pulling my jacket off, I made myself comfortable. I'd opted for a tartan skirt, and loose button-up blouse that I'd tucked into the waistband. The scars on my leg were beginning to fade, and the newest ones were healing well, so I'd decided not to cover my legs, hoping that if he decided to touch them again, the skin-on-skin contact might ignite some feeling that was hidden away in my depths.

I'd never been much of a fan of horror, but halfway through the movie I found myself leaning forward, my eyes covered by my hands as I sneaked glances through my fingers. The attendant outside was right, this film *was* gory.

I flinched as the man on the screen ran straight into a room that was hiding the killer.

"Enjoying the film?"

Every hair on my body stood up at the husky tone snaking through my ears and at the familiar smoky scent wafting through my senses.

"Seb? What are you doing here?" I whisper shouted at the intruder sitting next to me.

"I'm partial to a horror film every now and again." I rolled my eyes and looked back towards the large cinema screen, trying to give it my undivided attention again.

I leaned back in my seat and crossed my arms, and from the corner of my eyes I could see the grin refusing to budge from his face.

"Are you the reason Daniel isn't here?"

Seb didn't look at me as he spoke quietly. "I'm much better company."

I huffed and stayed silent. I was trying to calm the butterflies that were piercing against my ribcage, and the hurricane that was throwing its weight around in my head.

A rough finger stroking my thigh pulled me away from the internal argument I was having, and my head flung in Seb's direction.

"Seb—"

"Watch the film Harriet."

His voice was demanding and stern, his words leaving no room for argument. As his fingers traced patterns further and further up my leg, my hands gripped the armrests of the seat and I gritted my teeth, attempting to stop the moan that his touch was enticing from me.

So much for staying away from him.

Seb's fingers dipped below the hem of my skirt, and as it travelled closer towards my aching bud, his fingers brushed over the silky material covering the sensitive nerves and I squeezed my thighs together. But his hand was too strong, and his fingers dug into my soft skin as he forced my legs apart.

"Don't close your fucking legs." That bite in his tone sent a cascade of goosebumps rioting over my skin, and my chest thumped hard with every swipe of his fingers.

"Take them off."

I spun my head in his direction, and I was met with a threatening glare. "What…?"

"Take them off."

"You're joking."

"Do I look like I'm joking?" I shifted at Seb's demands, but not because I was uncomfortable. Because it evoked a stampede of excitement straight to my already aching clit.

"It wasn't a request Harriet. Or maybe you'd like everyone to hear what happens when you fail to give me what I want."

I looked back at the screen, and then at the heads of the other people in the theatre, my nerves dancing around. Without another word, I took the bait and raised from the chair. Hooking my fingers in the elastic of my underwear, I pulled each of my legs out one by one.

I'm pretty sure if this man told me to strip I would do it. I was at complete mercy to his demands, whether I wanted to be or not.

Where was my willpower when I needed it?

Seb held his hand out next to me, and I didn't need to ask what he wanted. I dropped the crumpled fabric into his hand, and he tucked them neatly into his back pocket.

"Good girl."

My body flittered from his praise, and a smug sense of satisfaction wrapped itself around my chest. Seb's finger's assault on my leg continued. Each time his fingers rose they would tickle back down again, and soon I was panting in frustration, each stroke coaxing small moans from my lips.

"Careful princess, someone might hear you."

I hadn't realised I'd closed my eyes until I opened them and began blinking rapidly. Remembering where we were I shoved against Seb's hand and flattened my skirt down, my skin turning heated as I tried to refocus on the film.

"We're not doing this here."

"Why? Scared you might not be able to control those beautiful songs of yours."

"No." I lied.

A low growl vibrated from Seb next to me, and my seat shifted as he turned and leaned in closer. "Do you know what happens when you refuse to give an addict what they want?" I shook my head, my eyes refusing to leave his penetrating stare.

"They turn feral."

He was suddenly on the floor in front of my seat, his hands looping under my arse and dragging me forward. I let out a squeal at the movement, but it was quickly replaced by a quiet hum that danced from my lips as his tongue lapped against my pulsing clit.

The noises he made were carnal, "your cunts so fucking wet already." His mouth was immediately covering me again, each flick of his violent tongue drinking me up.

I slammed my hand over my mouth as a moan escaped and tightly closed my eyes, my other hand desperately gripping the strands of his thick hair. My legs began to shake, and his mouth retreated from me.

Not again.

"Not yet." He began placing delicate kisses down the inside of my thigh, as his finger teased my entrance. I bucked my hips, wanting more of him. I was desperate, needy, and this time I couldn't blame it on being intoxicated.

At least not by alcohol. Whatever aphrodisiac he was injecting into me was responsible for my lack of objections against his daring demands.

He gently eased a finger inside of me, and as he did a delicate moan left my mouth.

"Harriet…"

His voice was a warning. I innocently smiled at him, and as I did he began moving his finger, curling it up inside me. I brought my hand back to my mouth and bit down in an attempt to stop the hums floating away.

He picked up his speed, inserting another finger inside me. As he did he stilled, giving me a moment to adjust, but I didn't want to wait. I moved my hips, grinding myself against his touch and a deep growl evaporated from his body.

My hand travelled down my body, and my fingers began delicately circling my sensitive clit. "That's it princess, show me how you touch yourself."

His words were all the encouragement I needed, and soon my release was beginning to build inside of me again.

"Seb, please…please don't stop." I kept my voice as low as possible, and as I closed in around the pleasure coiling up inside of me Seb rose, not detaching our bodies, and leaned forward resting his weight on top of mine.

His lips crashed against mine, his tongue invading my mouth and battling with my own. Moments later I was falling apart.

With each wave that shocked through my body, my muscles tensed and trembled. I wrapped my arms tightly around his neck, as though it could offer some support to my shaking limbs.

Slowly we separated, and after gently withdrawing his fingers, Seb brought them up to his lips and sucked them dry. My eyes widened, and my mouth parted slightly at the gesture.

"Don't worry. Next time I'll share. Today I'm feeling greedy."

As Seb moved to sit back in his seat, he positioned himself against me, "so sweet." I blushed at his words, my thoughts recoiling with where we were and what we had just done.

I frantically looked between the two couples seated in the rows at the front, but neither seemed to have notice what had happened back here. As if sensing the panic building in me, Seb took hold of my hand and laced his fingers through mine. "Relax Harriet. No one saw us."

I tried to watch what was left of the film, but my mind was working overtime. The harder I tried to stay away from this man the more he dragged me under, struck my dreams with his hungry talons.

I watched his thumb gently stroking across the palm of my hand, and I knew I was headed to hell.

And I was letting him take me there.

Chapter Eighteen

Seb

The lights came to life in the theatre, and my eyes squinted as they adjusted. Looking over at Harriet, my lips curled into a grin. Her skin was still flush with a pink hue, and her lips were swollen from my assault. Her normally neat and tidy hair was wild and unruly.

I was drooling.

If she looked this good after I'd fucked her with my fingers, I could only imagine how good she'd look after I'd fucked her with my cock.

It couldn't come soon enough. But I needed to be patient.

Her taste still lingered on my tongue, and I licked at my lips hoping to savour the flavour. If I could bottle her taste up I would. That mixed with her delicious vanilla scent would be enough to get me through the rest of my existence.

I didn't release her hand when we began walking down the steps and towards the exit. The theatre was quiet when we left, and the air outside was raw against my skin. Next to me, Harriet shivered, and I removed my jacket, looping it over her shoulders.

"Thank you." She looked at me with such softness, so much kindness, that it hit me right in the chest, and the unfamiliar emotion caused a wave to riot through me.

After every challenge I'd pushed on her she still looked at me like I was the star that brightened her night.

I wanted to be the phantom that haunted her dreams.

She bit down on her lower lip, and I brushed my thumb over it, forcing her to release the soft pink skin.

"You got something to say princess, say it."

Harriet shifted on her feet nervously, an internal conflict evident in her opal eyes, but then let out a heavy sigh and her shoulders dropped.

"Do you want to come back to mine?" I raised my eyebrow and my lips curved into a smirk. Her cheeks camouflaged into a scarlet tinge, the streetlights illuminating her beautiful face. I pulled her chin upwards, my lips landing softly against hers as my tongue teased her mouth open.

Drawing back, I looked between her eyes. "Sure."

We travelled back to hers in her Mustang, and I had to admit, it was a comfy ride. The leather interior gave it an edgy vibe that suited her, and I couldn't keep my eyes off of the beautiful siren and the way she looked so carefree driving it.

It reminded me of how I felt when I rode my bike.

"It belonged to my mom. The car." Her fingers tapped the steering wheel. "She died from an overdose. Angie had been an addict most of her life." I reached over and stroked my hand across her thigh, encouraging her to continue.

"I was eighteen when she died. It had only really been the two of us. I didn't know how to cope without her." We stopped at a set of lights as they faded to red, and she turned to face me. "I shouldn't have said what I did the other day. I don't like that you're involved in drugs. At all. But it's unfair to put my mother's death on you."

I remained silent. There weren't many words I could offer her that could lend much comfort, when I was ready I would share some more of my past with her, and she would understand what had led me to the life I live now.

Pulling up outside the apartment building, she switched the engine off and we sat there for a moment, a peaceful silence resting between us.

"I know that there are healthier ways to deal with emotions, I've seen shrinks and had appointments with healthcare professionals. They always tell me the same thing. Write your feelings down, keep a diary, let the words absorb the feelings." I was surprised that she was sharing the depths of her secrets with me, but I kept my face emotionless, not wanting to scare her off with the anger that was coiling inside of me.

I was glad she felt comfortable enough to share her past, but the endless tragedies she had lived through made my fingers itch.

Her hands fumbled in her lap for a moment.

"When I met you something just snapped in me. It was overwhelming. It was as though you became the journal. You absorbed the pain." She smiled, and I swiped my thumb against her cheek as a small tear slithered down.

"I tried so hard to fight it. Especially after my birthday. I didn't want to be caught up in that…world, I still don't. But I want to be caught up with *you*, and I know that means I have to accept that as part of your life."

She paused. "I don't want to put anything on you Seb, I don't expect anything from you. But if you plan to disappear, plan to leave, I need you to tell me. I don't think I can go through that pain again." I closed the gap between us and pulled her towards me, our lips melting together.

"I'm not going anywhere." A soft smile graced her face and I wanted to capture the look. I never wanted her to look at someone else the way she was looking at me.

Like I was her saviour.

I couldn't tell her yet, but she was doing the same for me. I wanted to bathe in Harriet's light, let her rays burn off my sins. "Shall we go up?"

She laughed nervously, "yes, sorry." As she swung and began to move her arm to the door handle, I quickly caught her.

"Don't ever apologise." Harriet nodded and I released her arm as we both began manoeuvring from the car.

Her bedroom wasn't at all like I had expected, something about her made me think she would be a fan of monotone, but this space was everything but.

It looked like fairies had thrown up all over the walls. Splotches of yellows, pinks and purples covered the surface, and her bedding was a rainbow of medley colours.

I should have known that chaotic imagination of hers wouldn't settle for black and white.

On the walls, she had posters taped up, most of them of old rock bands, some of cringy feel good quotes, but all of them felt like they were a reflection of her, as though she was sharing a small part of her fractured soul through colours.

On top of an old set of drawers, a cardboard box sat with 'Do Not Touch' sprawled across it in black marker pen.

"Very passive aggressive." I pointed to the box, and Harriet peered around me.

"Oh, yeah. You can have a look, they're old records. They belonged to my mom."

The box was packed tightly with vinyl records, some in immaculate casings, others in between pieces of tissue paper.

"I didn't think you had any belongings?"

"I had them delivered from an old storage container. Most of her stuff is still there, I don't want to get rid of it."

"Your mom was a fan of vintage?" I turned around to see Harriet bundled under her duvet, only her face visible amongst the colourful patterns as she popped two tiny pills in her mouth and swallowed.

"My mom was the pinnacle of vintage. She loved the rock and roll lifestyle, I guess she embraced all of it." A sad smile crept across her face. I didn't want to take advantage of her vulnerable state, but I needed to find out what had brought her here.

"Why did you come to Bromlin?" I crossed the room to the bed and kicked off my shoes, before lifting my T-shirt over my head. Harriet's eyes widened, and I couldn't stop the cocky grin that spread across my face at seeing the hungry gleam in her eyes.

"I—" She looked down, her hands fumbling on the bed sheets. "I walked in on my fiancé with another woman. But you already knew that." I'd figured Felix was responsible.

Low life.

I lowered down onto the bed and raised my arm. Harriet quickly moved forward, leaning against my chest, and my hand went straight to her head pulling her dark brown hair through my fingers. "It wasn't the first time it had happened, but for whatever reason, I decided it would be the last."

I nodded at her admission, "good. If that idiot hadn't been stupid enough to sleep with someone else, you wouldn't be here."

"I don't know, fate has a funny way of working itself out. I'd kept a hold of the leaflet for this place, normally I would just throw them straight away. I think I was always meant to find Bromlin." She smiled against my chest.

"And you know I would have always found you." I echoed.

I loved her optimism, the way that she so easily found the positives in every scenario. Her lightness was a barricade against my darkness, and after every second I spent with her, I could feel it chiselling away.

Years of loneliness, self-hate, the constant abuse as a result of The Carnival. Harriet was helping to fight it all off.

I gently kissed the top of her head as she yawned, "sleep Harriet."

Minutes later I heard the gentle inhale and exhale of breath as it left her delicate lips, my own body surrendering against the blissful sleep entering my mind.

Chapter Nineteen

Harriet

I couldn't remember the last time my sleep had been undisturbed. Normally I either struggled to fall asleep, or I would wake up in the middle of the night, panting and struggling to breathe.

I rolled over and came face to face with the man responsible for quietening my mind.

Seb was still fast asleep, his muscled chest rising and falling with the air that danced around inside of him. My eyes roamed over his face, he looked calm when he slept.

His hair was a tussled mess, and his eyelashes delicately fanned over his eyes. No one could deny that the man was stunning. Dangerously handsome, and sure to break the hearts of anyone who dared to get close.

That was me. I was daring to get close.

Now wide awake, I gently rose from the duvet and untangled my body. Gathering Seb's shirt from the floor, I pulled it over my head and began tiptoeing out of the room, careful not to wake him as I closed the door behind me.

"How was your date?" Delilah's mischievous voice called from across the room, her interruption to the silence startling me. I headed towards her and perched on the countertop as she passed a cup of black coffee into my hands.

"Daniel didn't show." I tried to fathom disappointment in my tone, but even I couldn't hide the relief that stole its place. Seb hadn't confirmed whether he was responsible for Daniel standing me up, but I had a suspicion that he had something to do with it.

"So who's in your bed?" Delilah's brow rose as she looked at me over the rim of her mug, her eyes sparkling in playful delight. I took a long gulp from my own and hummed when the liquid warmed my throat.

"Seb." I wasn't going to try and hide what was going on between us anymore. Even if I didn't understand it.

He was an anchor, dragging me into the pits of hell, and I wanted to dance among the flames.

Delilah laughed and pulled herself up onto the counter next to me. "How are you doing it?" She looked at me with confusion, and I peered down, my legs swinging nervously. "With Cherry and The Carnival."

Delilah took a long drink from her cup and placed it down next to her. "Cherry and I have known each other for a long time, I think it was inevitable that we would eventually end up together. I have to accept that The Carnival is part of her life, whether that's for another month or another year." I shuffled backwards and crossed my legs, Delilah did the same.

"The Carnival saved her when she needed it, and I respect that if I want to be a part of her life I have to share her. But I also know it's all temporary. We're learning how to navigate it."

I nodded at her. "If Seb tells you he wants out, you have to trust that's the truth, otherwise it'll never work. You'll destroy yourself if you don't."

Delilah was silent for a moment, chewing on the inside of her mouth. "I've known Seb for a while Harriet, I've never seen him this consumed by someone before. When you two are in a room together it's like the whole place is on fire. We all feel it."

I pondered her words.

"You two are like peanut butter and jelly. Tasty apart, but when you're together you're bloody delicious. Everyone knows it." I couldn't stop my bleating laugh at her choice of words.

She was right though. If I hoped for this thing between me and Seb to go somewhere, I needed to trust him. Delilah jumped down from the counter just as my phone began to play melodically from my bag.

"I'm headed over to see Cherry now, need anything whilst I'm out?" I shook my head as I rummaged for the source of the music.

"No, thanks. I'm headed out to the community garden this afternoon in case I'm out when you get back."

Delilah waved as she left the room, and my brows tightly creased when I saw who was responsible for interrupting my morning. I took a deep breath and pressed the answer call button. Holding the phone to my ear, I tried to relax my voice and calm the riots marching through my head.

To think I'd been floating on a cloud twenty minutes ago.

"Hey Dad."

"Harry. How are you?" My eyebrow rose, my dad was never one for small talk. He was direct and got straight to the point. His friendly question threw my walls up.

"Fine, did you need something?" There was a cough on the other end of the phone, and I could feel the hesitation pouring from him as though he was standing beside me.

"I want to see you. Can I take you for lunch?"

"Why?"

"Does a father need a reason to take his daughter to lunch?"

I scoffed, deliberately not trying to hide it from him. If my father wanted to see me, there was a reason for it. Richard Wolston always had an ulterior motive.

Suddenly two large arms wrapped around my waist like a vice, and small pecks were being planted across my neck and shoulder. My body shivered against the touch, and immediately my tense muscles began to loosen.

"Fine, I'll text you the address for a café I know. I'll meet you there." I was reluctant to share the life I had created in this little town with my dad, but I knew I couldn't keep ignoring him. If he wanted to make amends, I needed to be the bigger person.

Ending the call I spun to face Seb, a devilishly striking grin peaking at the corners of his mouth. His voice was raspy as he spoke, and need began to pool in my core.

"Who was that?"

"My Dad. He wants to meet for lunch." Seb's hands travelled down the backs of my thighs, and he pulled me upwards, my legs wrapping tightly around him as he walked me to the counter and planted me back on the cool surface.

Who needed a sofa when you had an island?

"Do you want me to come?" He spoke against my neck, and I smiled. His need to protect me sent a gentle wave of peace through my body.

"No, I'll be fine." He planted a shy kiss on my mouth before pulling away and leaning his head against mine.

"What's your favourite food?" His question caught me off guard, and a small chuckle left my throat.

"My favourite food?" He nodded against my head. "Delilah's waffles." From the top of my eyes, I spotted his mouth lift into a grin.

"Delilah's waffles." He echoed as he laughed, and the sound warmed my heart.

"I don't want to share you. With Delilah's waffles *or* your dad." His hands disappeared underneath the shirt that was drowning me, his fingers tickling my bare skin.

"You aren't sharing me. I think you've made yourself clear on the consequences. I'd rather not have hands *or* eyeballs turn up on my doorstep."

Seb let out a groan. "I should be going now anyway; I have some things to take care of." Reluctantly I unlocked him from the cage I was creating with my legs, and he collected his belongings from the dining table.

Spotting the pout on my lips, he smirked and walked back across to me. His finger looped underneath my chin, and he dragged me against his mouth, his smoky taste invading my senses.

"I'll be back later. Make sure you're wearing that T-shirt. I like seeing you in my clothes, and I'm positive I'll like tearing them from you too." I blushed and let him leave.

The room felt empty without his dangerous aura crowding it.

Taking a deep breath, I hopped down from the counter and allowed the fog weaving through my body to carry me to the bedroom.

I pulled up outside the café I had texted my dad the address for. Hesitation overwhelmed my body, and as it did, sadness started to invade me.

I hadn't known much about my dad growing up, my mother had kept him private, only referring to him as *'the scumbag that knocked her up'*. But every time she mentioned him, I saw the grief in her eyes, saw the longing that his memories brought her.

After she died and I went to live with him, I struggled with the image she had painted. But every day we spent together, the less and less I saw him for the monster she had created. Richard Wolston may not have been the father figure I had wanted growing up, but he was trying to make up for it.

That was until I did the one thing that threatened his reputation.

I walked away.

I spotted the grey suit in my wing mirror before my eyes landed on his face. The last time I'd seen my dad he was the fresh face of youth, but from here he looked worn and old. Tired, as though he'd aged ten years.

Pulling my courage together, I opened the car door and the wind immediately swarmed my face and sent my hair flying. My dad spotted me as soon as I turned in his direction, and I couldn't decipher the look on his face. He looked almost disappointed to see me and my stomach sank. I tried to smile at him but it felt tight and forced, and I knew it wasn't convincing.

"Hey Dad." He walked ahead of me and held open the café door, letting me guide us in first.

"Harry." His tone was flat.

He followed inside, and we soon settled into a secluded table in the corner, one that had a full view of the outside world but kept us hidden from the bustling one inside.

A bubbly waitress came towards us as soon as we sat down and we both ordered coffees, mine with extra sugar. Her smile was bright, and I wished I lived in her head, wished I wasn't feeling uncomfortable in the presence of my own dad.

"When is this phase going to end?" I looked down at my hands, and my fingers began fiddling with the fray of my top. I hated how he looked at me, how he spoke as though I was a petulant child throwing a strop.

"I like it here Dad." He scoffed and shook his head, his eyes staring out of the window.

"What is there to like. It's a dyer little town, with no prospects." My defences spiked up, I'd learnt to adjust to this *'dyer little town'* and I hated the association he created by pairing me with his impression of it.

"I've made friends, I have a job."

"You already have a job."

"I fit in here, and Felix he isn't what you—" His hands slammed against the table just as the waitress returned with our drinks. The explosive noise caused her to jolt back before she shakingly placed the two mugs on the table and hurried away.

My dad's voice was low as he leant across the table, "Felix has given up everything for you. *I* gave up everything for you. Do you have any idea what your little stunt has done to my reputation? You're behaving like a spoilt, ungrateful child." His words sent a pang of hurt through my body, but it was quickly extinguished as anger crept into my muscles.

"Felix was sleeping with other women dad. What do you expect me to do, just sit around and accept that as my life?" Silence skirted between us for a moment, and I didn't miss the lack of shock that crossed my father's face.

I waited for the penny to drop, waited for him to hear what I was saying, for him to hear the truth about Felix. But he just stayed silent.

That was when I knew.

"You know." The anger evaporated, and in its place, the familiar caress of numbness laced my insides. My dad seized the mug in his hands and took a small sip, his face turning up at the bitter taste.

"Yes." Now it was my turn to not look shocked. I should have known. Hell, my dad probably watched him leave the clubs and bars with the women who ended up in our bed.

Gave him his blessing.

I was grateful for the numbness. If it wasn't for that I was certain that I would be sick.

"He works hard Harriet. He works hard to give you the best life, the best things. If his way of winding down is a night or two off from you, I don't see the harm. You know you're hard work, you yourself have admitted to that. Felix took a lot on when he met you, and you never complained about the lifestyle you had."

The words bounced around in my head. *I was hard work.*

"I—" I couldn't speak, the words stuck in my throat.

"You really are like Angie. When you don't get your own way you stomp your feet. I didn't sign up for your tantrums."

I rose abruptly, knocking the table as I did. Speaking to no one in particular I stared at my half-drunken coffee, "I don't want to see you again." My dad stood, challenging me.

"Sit down Harriet, you're causing a scene." I let my eyes wander to his, staring knives, hoping they would physically fly from my pupils.

"Did you ever stop to think that maybe I wouldn't have been such *hard work* if you hadn't abandoned my mother? Abandoned *me.* She would probably be alive still if it wasn't for you."

"Your mother was a junkie Harriet. It might be hard for you to face, but she brought her fate on herself. If you stay here, you'll end up like her."

He tightened the tie around his neck. "It would be sad to see you end up dead."

Sad… to see me end up… *dead?*

My lungs were punctured, and I couldn't breathe.

Tears began pricking at my eyes, but I refused to allow him to witness my collapse.

I grabbed my bag and ran straight into the bathroom as my eyes dampened. Soon tears were flooding my face, and I was struggling against the tightness in my chest and the haziness blurring my head.

I locked myself in one of the stalls, my body shuddering as I tried to regulate my erratic breaths.

Each one stabbed my chest, and the pain became unbearable.

It was no use, the numbness was consuming me, and my body was being held prisoner against the intrusive thoughts that commanded me.

Grabbing my bag up off the floor, I desperately fumbled around in it until the cool metal cylinder of my lighter brushed my fingertips.

Retrieving it from my bag, I flicked the spark wheel and a flame roared to life. My eyes glowed in its ember, and the numbness stroked, anticipation at knowing what was coming sending sickening thrills dancing in my veins.

I released my finger from the spark wheel and the flame dimmed along with my spiking adrenaline.

One. Two. Three. Four. Five

The counting wasn't working. My lungs heaved against the struggling air trying to leave and enter them.

Is this what dying felt like?

I looked up at the ceiling, trying to blink the tears away, and hooked my fingers in the belt loops of my jeans. As I shimmied them over my hips and let them sit just above my knees, I clenched my eyes in one final attempt to still the explosion that was detonating behind my ribcage, but it was pointless.

I couldn't put my broken parts back together this time.

Flicking the spark wheel again, I moved the glow to the edge of my thigh. As the flame tickled against my skin I took deep breaths and the sensation began to intensify, the burn scolding my skin.

I clasped my hand over my mouth as the pain began to overtake the numbness, and a fresh set of tears stung my cheeks.

I counted again, but this time it wasn't to calm me.

One. Two. Three. Four. Five.

Five was my cut-off point, but unlike usual I didn't move the flame, I let it keep slicing my skin. It was only when I could smell my skin burning that I dropped the lighter, the metal casing clanging against the tiled floor as it fell.

The numbness screamed at me, begged to dance with the pain again, and fragmented sobs vibrated my broken body.

The pain caught up, and my leg was suddenly ablaze with an overwhelming agony that paralysed my entire body. My legs were powerless against the heaviness, and as I dragged my phone from the ground and pushed the call button, I settled into a calm stare, allowing the friendly butterflies to dance in the numbness.

Chapter Twenty

Seb

"We have six new clients on the books for tonight. I need you all in your finest, especially you Cherry. We know the men have a thing for your red hair." Saffron smirked. "Seb, I'll need you controlling the income flow."

She stood with her hands on her hips, her uptight frame staring down at all of us. "If I hear so much as a peak that our new friends are unhappy, none of you will see sunlight for a week."

I knew first hand that the threats were real. Being locked away from the rest of the world was one thing, but what she didn't divulge was the battery that came with it. The hours of torture that would be rained on us if we disobeyed Saffron's orders.

Cherry fidgeted on the sofa next to me, and I looked in her direction. Purple bruises were beginning to form on her legs, and red marks wrapped like ribbons around her throat, turning her pale skin a scorching red.

I ground my teeth and locked my arms tightly across my chest. "I think Cherry needs a night off." Quiet murmurs began whispering from the other performers and Saffron's eyes blazed in my direction, a venomous smile curling on her mouth.

"It's a good thing I don't pay you to think then isn't it." She looked at Cherry wincing in her seat, "I'm sure Cherry understands what is required of her to keep our clients happy." My fists tightened, and my entire body tensed at her lack of concern, greed seeping from her.

Cherry had been put through the rings these last couple of nights, from men who wanted her tied and bound, to one who cut off her air supply until she passed out.

I hadn't met the ones that had hired her last night, but when I did I would make sure they never came fucking back.

"I'll see you all later tonight." Saffron walked away, her stilettoes tapping against the floor, but before she left she turned back towards us, her chin motioning to Cherry. "Cover the bruises, no one wants to see those."

The gentle hand on my leg was the only thing stopping me from going after her, and as I turned to face Cherry her soft smile pulled me from the demons marching inside my head. "It's okay." I wished I had the same optimism as her, but it was impossible.

Things were getting worse at the Carnival; the clients were getting more and more flippant with the girls. More reckless. Their need for control and power causing their inhibitions and sadistic fantasies to shield their judgment.

More performers left the rooms bruised, and with each one that appeared on their skin, my patience wore thin.

The men treated the marks like trophies. I needed to find a way to get us out of here, and soon.

The room fell into mindless chatter, and I followed Tony as he walked towards the kitchenette. "Know anything about these new clients?"

He shook his head as he pulled two bottles of water from the fridge and threw one across to me. "They're out of town, that's all I could find out. Everything else about them is locked up pretty tightly. I'll keep digging though."

My phone vibrated in my pocket, and as I pulled it out I patted Tony's shoulder. "Thanks, anything you find out I want to know."

Harriet's name appeared on the screen in bold letters, along with the photo I'd taken of her whilst she slept. She looked so peaceful when she wasn't trying to hold herself together for the world around her.

A smile curled at my lips, and I welcomed the comfort that spread through my chest as I hit the answer button.

"Princess." I couldn't hold back the grin that covered my face, but when the end of the line stayed silent my smile began to falter. "Harriet?"

Quiet sniffs sounded through the speaker, and my stomach dropped as I pushed the phone closer to my ear and Harriet's tiny voice spoke.

"I…I need you, can you come get me?" Her voice was broken, and I struggled to hear each word.

"Where are you?"

"At the old house café off Turner Street." I mentally calculated how long it would take me to get there, and without an ounce of hesitation, I scooped my keys up and looked towards the tent's exit, making sure my path was clear.

"I'll be there in five, don't fucking move." I pressed my finger against the end call button, not waiting for her response. I moved quickly, my eyes narrowing on the escape route.

"What's going on?" Cherry's voice called from behind, a nervous rattle lacing her words. I could only imagine the feral look on my face if *she* was concerned.

"Something's wrong with Harriet. I need to find her." Cherry nodded and grabbed my helmet from the sofa, passing it to me as I rapidly moved.

"Okay, I'll keep things running here until you get back." I smiled at her before darting through the separation in the fabric and sprinting to my bike.

I rode into the parking space behind Harriet's blue Mustang and jumped from the bike, beelining straight for the café's entrance.

"Sebastian." A familiar slimy voice called my name, and I turned around to see John walking straight towards me. I tried to hide the tick in my jaw at the man's poor timing.

"John, good to see you." I masked the nonchalance in my voice and shook his hand as he stretched it out in front of him.

"I trust everything is in place for tonight?" My brows creased together in puzzlement, "I'm bringing some associates to meet your girls tonight." So John was the high paying client that Saffron was talking about.

"Yeah, Saffron told us all this morning to expect you." John nodded and stashed his hands in his pockets.

"And Cherry?"

"She'll be there." A grin I couldn't decipher appeared on his face, and he silently turned heading in the direction of a black beamer parked on the opposite side of the road.

Focusing my attention back to the café, I shoved my body into the glass door and searched around.

Harriet was nowhere to be seen.

A bubbly waitress past in front of me and I stepped in her way, causing her to freeze and look up at my towering frame.

"I'm looking for a girl, about five foot seven, brown hair." I continued looking around the café as I spoke, and when the waitress remained silent I stared down at her, letting the anger seep from my eyes.

She made the right decision when she told me Harriet was in the bathroom, and I stalked in the direction she pointed. Slamming open the women's bathroom door, I walked past each of the stalls until I stood in front of one that was closed.

"Harriet?" A quiet sniffle came from behind the door, and as soon as I heard the latch turn, and the lock changed from red to green, I was pushing it open.

Harriet was sat down on the seat, her eyes circled in red rings and bloodshot as she looked up at me and sadness trickled away from her.

My vision travelled from her face to her legs when I spotted her jeans sitting halfway down her thighs. Across her left leg, an angry blistering mark sprung from her skin.

I sank to my knees in front of her forcing her to look at me, and as I did the walls holding her tears at bay fell apart and she began sobbing uncontrollably into me. She fell forward against my body, and I let her weight wrestle mine to the ground, my arms tightly wrapped around her as quiet wails screamed from her body.

One of my hands rested on the back of her head, and I pulled her closer, tucking her between my neck and shoulder. Confusion stormed through me, my eyes frantically searching for an explanation as to why my siren was lying severed in my arms.

We sat there for what felt like hours, her body gently shuddering against mine as her tears began to calm and her breaths regained a steady rhythm.

Stroking my hand down the side of her face, I guided her eyes towards mine. Staring back at me was an agonising pain I'd never seen, the glazed expression of a completely fractured woman.

"What happened?" I kept my voice levelled. I didn't want to spook her with the anger that was threatening to spill under my skin.

"My dad," she spoke through breathy inhales. "He said it was my fault that Felix cheated on me. He said—" She took a deep breath, attempting to keep the tears at bay between hiccups. "He said I'd end up like her if I stayed here. He said I'd end up dead."

Burning rage filtered through me, the man was venom. I needed to keep him as far away from Harriet as I could. My gaze was distracted by the angry welt that was glaring from her thigh.

"I'm going to take you home, can you stand?" She gently nodded against my neck, and as she pulled away I captured her face between my hands and brushed the pad of my thumb over her cheek.

"You don't need him. Don't let his words dim your light." A small smile peeked on her lips, and it sedated the roar inside me slightly. "You're too fucking bright to let him destroy you."

I pulled her upright against my body, her legs stumbling slightly from the denim fabric restricting her movements.

Without speaking, I pulled at the waistband of her jeans and tugged upwards, careful not to press the fabric against her burn too roughly. She winced as the denim covered her thigh and I made a mental note to keep spare clothes for her under my motorbike seat.

Not that I would ever let something like this happen again. I refused to entertain the thought that I couldn't fix this.

I would drown in her pain if I could, if it meant she never had to feel an ounce of hurt again.

Threading my fingers through hers, we left the bathroom and when we passed the people in the crowded café she kept her head low.

Harriet began pulling me in the direction of her car, but I gently tugged her back. "We're taking my bike. I'll have Tony bring your car around later." Her eyes widened when she spotted the black motorbike parked behind her Mustang, her eyes darting between me and the vehicle.

"I knew it. This whole time, you *were* the man on the bike." I smugly grinned and began lifting the spare helmet from under the seat. Passing it to her, I shrugged.

"You thought I was lying when I said you would never escape me? I couldn't stay away from you princess. From the moment you gave me that feisty middle finger, I was hooked." She didn't say anything as I moved her hair behind her and began pulling the helmet over her head. I was pretty sure she would go into shock soon and wanted to get her safely home before that happened.

I helped her onto the bike, careful to make sure her leg was comfortable before I lowered in front of her. Pulling her arms from behind me so they wrapped around my waist, I called to her. "Hold on tight."

As the engine roared to life, her arms squeezed tightly, and I relished in the feel of her body pressed tightly against mine. I'd never ridden with someone else, but having her here, having her share the euphoric feeling the rides gave me felt like I was finally beginning to mend the hole in my chest.

It didn't take long to get back to her apartment, and as I silenced the engine and hopped off, I helped her to lift the helmet from her head.

Before she could stand, I quickly dipped and captured her lips between mine. I couldn't offer her much reassurance, but I knew that she felt comfortable with me, and right now that was all I had to offer.

"Harriet!" A high-pitched voice shouted, and we both turned in the direction it was coming from. An older woman with sparkling grey hair began skipping across the road towards us. When she was closer a wariness crossed her eyes, and she raised her brow at me.

"Hi Josie." Harriet pulled her into a tight hug, and the woman's body instantly relaxed.

"Are you coming to the garden later?"

Harriet shook her head, "I'm sorry, I actually have plans tonight," she sheepishly smiled at me, and Josie's brow rose higher.

"That's okay. It's nice to meet your *plans*." She winked as though the two shared a secret only they knew about.

I had to admire Harriet. I knew she was in pain, the corner of her eye kept wincing when she shifted her weight, but she didn't let the woman in front of her see. That was when the realisation hit me.

She'd had to pretend before.

"We're having a charity event this weekend, you should come. Bring your friends. There will be some high benefactors there, we're hoping to raise enough money to finish off the garden."

Harriet curtly nodded, "I'd love to, I'm sure my friends will come too." Josie's eyes roamed over me and I lifted the corner of my mouth in a dazzling smile.

She was obviously important to Harriet which meant I needed to make a good impression.

"Great! I'll let you two go. Enjoy your evening." She spoke in a hushed tone that I knew wasn't intended for me, but It was hard not to hear every word when she was standing only inches away. There was something mysterious about Josie, and her playfulness mixed with the kindness she was exerting felt familiar.

After the two shared another hug, Harriet began leading us up the stairs and towards the door of her apartment. As soon as we stepped over the threshold into the living room, I lifted her from the ground and planted her on the sofa.

I ignored her squealing protests and hooked my fingers through the waistband of her jeans and gently pulled them down, being careful to manoeuvre them safely over the fresh burn on her thigh.

"Where's your first aid kit?"

"In the cupboard above the sink in the bathroom." I nodded and left to grab it, returning moments later, and opening the clasps. I pulled out a tube of antiseptic cream and a couple of wipes.

Tearing one of the packages with my teeth, I dabbed it on the welt, and she hissed as I swiped it over the sore.

"I'm sorry for dragging you out." I glared up at her, my hand pausing.

"What have I told you? Don't ever apologise Harriet." We settled into silence as I continued wiping at her wound. "You're my priority. You'll *always* be my priority."

My interruption seemed to take her by surprise as she tried to lean forward, but the angle I held her leg at stopped her from moving very far.

After I'd finished wiping down her leg and smothered antiseptic cream across her skin, I stood up, fetched two mugs of coffee, lowered myself into the space next to her, and folded my arm over the back of her shoulders.

"Will you come to the charity event with me?" I wanted to talk about what had happened at the café, find out what had made her spill over the edge, but it seemed she wanted our conversation to go in a different direction.

"If you tried to take anyone else, I'd tie you to the bed so you couldn't leave."

I noticed the hitch in her throat at my words and the way her thighs tightened together. It would be too easy to throw her down on the sofa and have a taste of my favourite delicacy, but I didn't want to push her.

As much as I wanted to be the distraction she craved, I couldn't. Not this time.

"What happened with your dad?" I didn't want to push her, but I needed to know how to fix this.

Harriet hadn't said much about her dad, but whenever she did speak about him, it wasn't highly. Her body froze momentarily, before she shuffled in closer to my body, her tantalising vanilla scent wafting up through my senses.

"He knew what Felix was doing, said that he deserved a night off from me because I was *hard work*."

Every muscle in my body tightened, and I had to battle against the demon in my head demanding I hunt the man responsible for making her feel like she deserved any of this.

But I knew she would never forgive me. No matter how Harriet felt right now, he was still her dad. A vial cretin that didn't deserve her, but still family. The *only* family she had.

She didn't notice the change in my body, and it was probably a good thing. I didn't want her to see the poison dripping in my eyes.

"He said if I stayed in Bromlin, I would end up like her." She fidgeted nervously, "my dad knows I would never touch drugs. It felt more like a threat."

She looked up at me beneath her feathery lashes. "I'm scared Seb." The way her voice broke and she curled herself smaller sent another wave of anger flying through my body.

"You're safe Princess. I will never let anybody hurt you, family or not." She sweetly smiled, the edges of her mouth meeting her beautiful doe eyes.

"The day my mom died, I'd entered this storytelling competition. My work had been shortlisted for an award. I was so proud of myself, and despite my mother's dedication to her addictions, I knew she would be proud of me too." I watched her from above, her fingers weaving the edge of my shirt through them.

"She'd been struggling more, I have no idea what was causing it, but she was more irritable and more…unpredictable. She was talking to herself a lot. My mother had always struggled with her mental health, a bit like me."

A quiet laugh sounded from her as she continued. "It runs in the family. Maybe my dad's right, maybe I am destined to end up like her."

A growl racked through my chest and caught Harriet's attention; her eyes glassy when they set on mine. "Don't say shit like that. You're not your mom." Harriet began to move her head down, but I caught it with my thumb, stopping her from being able to look away.

A stray tear slipped from her eyes. "I don't know how to stop Seb. I don't know how to live without the pain."

"Give it to me. Every tear, every hit, every hateful word you want to scream. Let me have it. Be the knife, the fire. Whatever you need to be to make the pain go away. But please, *please*, don't fucking hurt yourself." Harriet remained silent. "You're too fierce to let this world darken your light."

Her tears had stopped and in their place, a coy emotion turned the corners of her mouth upwards.

"You're a siren Harriet. You're smart, you're brave. You're fucking perfect. Everything you've managed to achieve whilst you've been here is a credit to you. Don't let him take that away. Don't let him make you forget how strong you are."

She remained still for a moment, and then she was shuffling upwards until she was straddling me, her legs either side of mine. Hands locked around my neck, and her fingers tugged at the ends of my hair as she began pulling me towards her mouth.

She tasted like caramel, sweet and velvety, and I couldn't resist her tongue as she teased my mouth open.

When her body began grinding on top of mine, all the air dissolved from my lungs and my chest vibrated as I hardened beneath her.

"Princess," I warned, but she kept going, her own body shuddering as she began to move quicker. I pulled back slightly, noticing the tantalising grin that was dancing on her face. It mirrored the one I'd flashed at her many times exactly.

"If you start, I won't be able to stop you."

She began to still, surprise that she had listened to my warning masking my face. But then she leant close to my ear, and her voice sang straight through me.

"Then don't."

My cock hitched at her seductive words, and before I could respond she was shuffling off the sofa, her body kneeling between my legs.

"I want to taste you."

She looked so fucking breathtaking on her knees, her crystal eyes glassy as she stared up at me, her chest rising and falling in nervous staggers. The complete picture of innocence.

She looked like fucking euphoria, and I nearly came from that alone.

I leant towards her, my finger hooking under her chin and my thumb stroking over her lips. "You look beautiful on your knees." A red flush painted her skin and I leant backwards, folding my arms.

She raised her eyebrow at me, and then her hands were on my black jeans, messy movements fumbling with the buttons that kept me hidden away. The redness didn't leave her skin as she continued to pull at the buttons, and a huff of frustration left her body.

"If you want help all you have to do is ask," I smirked at her, and she cocked her head at me.

"Can you help, please?"

"Help you do what?"

Her eyes poured with fire, and I couldn't help but chuckle in amusement at the look that she was blinding me with.

"Get your jeans off."

"Why?"

"Because I can't get them off."

I leant towards her, the smirk on my face growing with each blade that flew from her eyes.

"No. Why do you want them off? I need your words."

Harriet blinked, her eyelashes fanning as she tried to find the words I wanted to hear. "I want to taste you."

"You've already said that." She leaned back on her knees and pouted. Teasingly, I pulled at the buttons, and one by one they sprang apart.

"I'll help, but next time I want to hear you tell me how much you want my cock, how you want to roll your tongue across every inch as I fuck your face."

Harriet's eyes widened, and she froze.

I loved the reaction she gave me when I caught her off guard. She wasn't as innocent as she wanted people to believe, and I wanted her to embrace the deviant that lay dormant inside her.

I quickly made work of pulling my jeans and boxers over my waist and down in one go, and when my cock sprung out, Harriet's mouth parted, and she whipped her eyes to my face.

"What's wrong little siren? Not feeling so brave now?"

Harriet pulled her shoulders back as her tiny hand wrapped around my length and began pumping me. Her strokes were slow, delicate. Each one a meticulously planned movement to drag this out as long as she possibly could.

I went to speak, but quickly shut my mouth when she moved forward and flicked my head with her tongue, her eyes refusing to break the trance they had on mine.

A hiss left my throat as she covered me with her mouth, her tongue gently brushing down the side of my cock as she moved lower and took me further into her mouth.

I had to admit it, I was impressed.

Most of the women I had been with had struggled with my size, but as her mouth hid more and more of my cock, it became apparent that she was ready to rise to the challenge.

She slowed, and her throat constricted as I hit the back of it with my tip.

Pulling her hair from her face and holding it tightly, I wrapped the strands around my fist.

"You're doing so well princess. You look so pretty with your mouth filled."

I held her there for a minute, just as tears began appearing in the corner of her eyes. As soon as I released my hold, she was lifting from me, desperately inhaling air through sputters.

I expected her to stop, but as soon as she had taken a deep breath of air, her mouth was swallowing me again, and this time she didn't hold back.

She took my cock deep into her mouth, her tongue attacking every thrust. I strung my hands through her hair again, encouraging her head lower with every swipe.

"Relax your throat."

Harriet followed my direction, and I jerked my hips upwards whilst I held her head still.

"So fucking good." I gasped through gritted teeth, my head rolling back.

I didn't want to tear my eyes away from her, but it was so goddamn hard with the way her mouth was taking me, each inch of my cock hidden away by her sweet pink lips.

My release edged closer, and I tried to keep it at bay. I wanted to drag this out as long as I could. Stay in the bubble of ecstasy she was holding me hostage to. But as I looked back down at her, her stunning chestnut eyes stared at me and I fell apart.

My whole body shuddered as I poured my release into her mouth, but still, she didn't move.

She swallowed everything I gave her, and when my body finally began to sedate she gently removed my cock from her mouth with a pop, and swiped her thumb at the corners, a massive grin spread across her face from ear to ear.

I leant forward, swiping a tear that was falling stray at the corner of her eye.

"You're a fucking sight Harriet." My hand caressed her cheek. "No one else touches you. Is that clear? You're Mine."

Harriet raised from the ground and planted herself back on the sofa next to me, her body cuddling in against mine.

Everything about her stroked the demon lurking in my depths, sedating him with every smile, every word, and as we both began drifting into oblivion thoughts of sweet vanilla and velvety caramel held my dreams captive, and my siren's face flashed through my mind.

Chapter Twenty-One

Harriet

My eyes fluttered open, and I wrapped my legs around the feathery duvet. I wasn't sure how I'd gotten into bed, but I was glad it was where I was waking up. Sun rays beamed through the window and warmed my skin as I rubbed the sleep from my eyes.

I immediately thought back to last night, my mind refusing to stop drooling over Seb and the possessive words that branded me.

Mine.

I'd never felt like this before. Safe.

The feeling conflicted in my head. I knew Seb was in some dangerous business, and I knew that he was only showing me half of him, worried that I'd be scared off if he allowed me to see all of the demons he carried. But somehow I knew, no matter what he showed me, I was stuck.

This tiny, turbulent town had stolen my heart, along with the devil that haunted it.

A crash in the living room made me jump and I shot upright, suddenly aware that I was lying in my bed alone.

Where was Seb?

The room outside was silent and I hurried out of bed, pulling his shirt from the floor and tugging it over my head. I gently pad to the door and peeked around the corner.

Seb was standing in the kitchen, one hand pulling harshly at his hair whilst the other held his phone to his ear. I stood there for a moment watching him as he paced around.

"What the fuck do you mean she's hurt?" I'd never heard Seb sound worried before yesterday. But listening to him now, it wasn't worry that was spilling from him.

It was fear.

"Fine. *Fuck!* Fine. I'll be there soon, just… just make sure she's okay." I walked out of my bedroom as he ended the call and stood frozen in the middle of the kitchen.

"Everything okay?"

Seb spun around and quickly strode towards me. As soon as he met me on the other side of the room his body crowded mine, and I laid my head against his chest, the thumping behind his ribcage pounding against my ear.

"I'm sorry. I have to go." I looked up at him, my eyebrows creasing. Seb smiled but it was forced, his eyes covered in a blanket of fear. When he released the grip he was shrouding me in and began shoving his feet into his boots, I wriggled anxiously, not quite knowing what to say.

"I was thinking we could get together with Cherry and Delilah tonight. Watch a movie? I'll cook." I smiled, but he refused to look in my direction as he knelt on the floor tying his laces.

"Yeah. Maybe."

I knew that whatever was causing his uptight demeanour had nothing to do with me, but I couldn't help but feel a little hurt at the way he brushed me off.

When Seb finally stood up and spared me some of his attention, I didn't try and hide the hurt that was on my face, but instead of comforting me like he would usually he just sighed and ran a hand through his hair.

"I'm sorry Harriet. I'll make it up to you." Before he'd even finished he was out of the door, and I was left standing in the middle of the living room, with just his T-shirt reminding me he had been there.

After I'd finished cleaning the burn on my leg and covering it with a dressing, I changed into a pair of ripped washed light jeans, and a white tank. The sun was beaming outside, and I wanted to feel comfortable in the heat in the garden.

The weather was strange these days. I was used to snow in winter, not sunshine.

Opting for a pair of wellies, and scooping together my phone and purse, I left the apartment and headed to the garden across the road.

Josie smiled when she saw me, her contagious grin forcing me to mirror one back.

Josie was an infectious person, and in light of everything that had happened recently, I was grateful I'd met her. "Harriet? I wasn't expecting to see you today." I shrugged and looked around the garden.

"My plans changed. Anything I can help with here?"

"Oh yes, your *plans*." The smile on her face was mischievous. "Do they have a name?" A blush crept over my cheeks, the butterflies in my stomach igniting.

"His name's Seb." I didn't know what else to say, I couldn't share with Josie the details of Seb's life. I had been quick to judge him, someone who didn't know him was sure to make unfair assumptions even more quickly.

"He's cute." Josie glinted at me.

"Yeah, he is." Sensing I wasn't going to share much about my mysterious companion, Josie nodded in the direction of a small planter we'd installed last week.

"The vegetables have finally arrived. You can help plant them."

"Sure." I headed in the direction of the empty wooden box. Kneeling in the dirt, my face twinged when the skin pulled on my leg, but I ignored it and started parting the soil, creating my hole for the first plant.

A little while later a shadow cast over the area I was working on and I looked up, shielding my squinting eyes from the sun.

"Hey Harriet." A timid voice spoke as my vision cleared, and my eyes widened at Daniel standing behind me.

"Daniel. Hey." I was a little surprised to see him here. Though I was glad he did, I was still annoyed that he had stood me up, and my pride ached a little at his rejection.

Even if Seb *had* been responsible, he could have at least sent me a text.

"Listen I'm sorry about the other night. Something came up."

I stood, brushing my soil covered gloves against my legs. "It's okay, the movie was rubbish anyway." Daniel laughed nervously and then looked around us. Satisfied that no one was intruding on our conversation, he edged closer.

"Harriet you need to leave, this place isn't good for you. Seb, *he* isn't good for you, do you even know what he—"

"I know a lot about Seb. I appreciate your concern, but I'm fine. Besides, I like this town. I don't want to leave."

Daniel shifted nervously and edged closer. My body demanded me to move, alarm bells sounding in my ears, but I held myself steady, refusing to allow him to intimidate me.

"Harriet this is all going to come crashing down, this little fantasy you're living in. I tried to stop you from being dragged into that underworld. You're going to end up collateral damage if you don't get out now."

His voice lowered to barely a whisper. "The guy threatened me for god's sake. You need to wake the hell up."

I was losing my patience with everyone thinking they had some say in how I chose to live my life, thinking I wasn't capable of looking after myself.

"Like I said, I appreciate the concern." I started to move, but Daniel's grip on my arm stopped me.

"How long will it be before Seb's asking you to join him." He hissed.

Daniel didn't know Seb like I did. He would never ask me to join The Carnival. If I thought for even a second he was capable of expecting such a formidable request of me, I would have run for the hills.

I brushed him off and returned to the little plot of soil I had been moulding. Daniel stood there for a few minutes, but after I refused to spare him another glance he hurried off, and I watched as he shoved past Josie and through the metal gates.

Josie looked at me as he left and I shrugged my shoulders, not wanting to get into it with her. My apprehension spiked at Daniel's words, but I shook it off, not giving it the authority to bother me. I was finally settled somewhere I belonged, and I refused to allow anyone to break down the little realm I had crafted.

After a few hours, the planter I had been tasked with filling was overrun by colourful vegetable plants, and I stood back admiring my work.

A soft hand on my shoulder startled me, but when I looked over at Josie beaming it settled, and warmth danced around inside my body at the approval.

"This looks great Harriet. Thanks for your help today." I didn't say anything, sensing she wasn't finished. "It's none of my business, but is everything okay with Daniel?"

I kept to the truth, or at least the parts I could divulge. "He stood me up, and I moved on." It was a sprinkle of what had happened, but it was all I could give her.

A musical tune sang from my pocket, and I was guiltily relieved at the interruption. Apologizing to Josie and moving away, I smiled at Delilah's name as it danced on the screen.

"Hey! I was going to call you, do you—"

"Harriet, are you near the apartment?"

My stomach sank at the panic in her words. Something was wrong.

"Yeah. What's going on?"

"We need your help, can you come home?" I was nodding as though she could see.

"Yeah, I'll be there in five." I ended the call and walked back over to Josie, attempting to still the tremble in my voice. "Sorry, I need to go." Her brows furrowed together, obviously picking up on the worry in my voice, but she didn't ask questions as I ran off towards the other side of the road.

I flew over each step, furious adrenaline throwing me upwards. I was scared of what I was walking into, whatever was going on was bad enough to spook Delilah.

I fumbled with my key in the lock, and before I could push the handle the door was swinging open and Delilah was staring at me, her eyes red and swollen with the tears staining her face.

"Delilah? What's wrong?" I stepped over the threshold, and she gently closed the door behind me.

"Cherry needs your help."

Cherry?

What help could I possibly offer Cherry?

My brows creased in question, and I followed Delilah into her bedroom.

The minute I stepped through her bedroom door I froze. Seb was sitting upright on the bed with Cherry's head lying in his lap, her body covered only by an open robe and her underwear.

But it wasn't her lack of clothing that had me freezing. It was the marks that covered her arms and legs. Purple bruises were forming over her normally porcelain skin, and around her wrists, her skin was raw and angry. Her stomach was covered in raised slash marks, and her legs had what looked like teeth marks embedded into them.

Someone had carved patterns onto her body, patterns they wanted to scar.

Her eyes were open, but she didn't notice me as I entered the room. Neither did Seb, who was sat brushing his hands through her hair, whispering gentle words of comfort to her.

A knot formed in my throat at the look that was being passed between the two of them, and I suddenly felt out of place, as though I had interrupted a private moment.

My frail heart cracked.

Finally, Seb looked up, but his face was emotionless. Glassy eyes looked straight through me as if I wasn't there. Creeping over, the mattress dipped under my weight as I sat on the edge.

"What happened?" I had a feeling I knew, and I wasn't sure that I wanted to hear someone say it out loud. So when no one answered me, I was both relieved and annoyed.

Getting a closer look at Cherry's body, and the cuts that covered her, I suddenly realised why they needed my help.

They couldn't take her to the emergency room.

I eyeballed Seb, begging him to look at me, but he remained consumed by the woman lying in his arms.

"You want me to clean up her cuts." I whispered. Seb nodded, and then rose from the bed, not sparing me a single glance as he left the room.

Delilah shuffled closer, her voice raw from her cries. "Here's the first aid kit, there's a needle and lighter in the front pocket." She dropped the small box next to me on the bed, along with a tiny sewing kit, and quickly followed Seb out of the door.

When I looked back at Cherry she was staring at me, "I didn't know you were a doctor."

"I'm not," I replied, "but I have some experience patching cuts up." Cherry nodded and turned her head back to look at the ceiling. I pulled the lighter from the front of the first aid bag, followed by the packet of sewing needles and thread. Swiping my thumb over the spark wheel, the lighter roared to life, and my eyes danced with the flame.

I was caught in a trance, the fire stroking my mind.

We love the flame.

After holding the needle in the heat for a few minutes and threading the string through the loop, I looked at Cherry. "I'm sorry, this is going to hurt a little."

A sad smile teased the corner of her mouth as a tear scurried down the edge of her face. "Can't hurt any more than it already does."

I expected her to jolt, move even a little bit when I began to pierce her skin with the needle, but her body remained still as I sewed up the gashes.

"I see why he likes you." I hadn't noticed Cherry staring at me, my attention taken up by the concentration of the needle and thread, but when she spoke I lifted my eyes to meet hers.

"You're gentle."

I laughed under my breath and went back to decorating her skin. "I'm glad you think so, I would expect this to make you flinch at least."

"You've done this before?"

"Only on myself." Sadness crept into Cherry's eyes, but I tried to ignore it and resumed my focus on the intricate task in my hand.

"I wasn't talking about the needle."

I knew she wasn't, but I desperately wanted to avoid talking about Seb, especially after I'd just seen the way he looked at her. I stayed silent, hoping she would too, but she seemed adamant to want a conversation.

"I'm sorry that I stole your purse." I'd forgotten about that. So much had happened since I'd arrived here, the stolen purse seeming inconspicuous against everything else. My mind wandered to the Polaroid I kept hidden in the back of it, my mom's face lighting up in my head.

I paused my hands and forced myself to smile at her.

"It's forgotten about." Sensing I had nothing more to say, Cherry nodded and resumed her stare at the ceiling.

It took about an hour to close up all of the cuts that patterned her skin, and I was still none the wiser at what had happened.

All I knew was that she hadn't caused them herself. Someone else had tried to brand her.

I looked down at my top, blood had dried into the white fabric, and my hands were covered from where they'd weaved against her skin. I was sure my face probably had some blood on It too from the amount of times I'd moved my hair from obstructing my vision.

"You need to keep an eye on them. If any of the stitches open they could get infected. They don't look too deep though. They should heal well within a couple of weeks."

Cherry smiled at me in thanks, and I forced a tight one back at her. I rose from the bed, and as soon as I opened the door Seb was in the room and flying across the bed, pulling her close and uttering sweet words into her ear.

My legs were starting to crumble, as though someone had hit me straight in the stomach. Tears threatened to blur my vision, and I refused to stand here as a third wheel to their affection.

When I looked down at my hands again, they were saturated in blood. Scarlet covered every part of my skin up to my elbows and heat rose up my neck.

Delilah spotted me from the kitchen as I ran from the bedroom.

"Harriet?" I couldn't speak, fearing if I did I would open up the dam holding the tears at bay.

I walked straight from the living room into the bathroom and wasted no time stripping from my clothes and into the shower. I needed to wash the stains from my skin.

I needed to wash the stains from my body. Needed to get the blood off.

Turning the water up to its hottest setting I allowed the showers to cascade over my body, and when it began to burn, my skin chaunted.

Not long after I'd adjusted to the temperature, I heard the bathroom door creak open and a gust of cool air from the apartment barged its way in. I didn't look in the direction of the door, I didn't need to. I knew who was invading my privacy. I heard the heavy clank of boots as they hit the tiled floor, and the thud of a metal buckle on a belt as it smacked the ground.

Even when Seb's body stood behind me in the shower, I refused to look at him.

"I shouldn't have asked you to do that." I closed my eyes, pleading with my voice not to betray me.

"You didn't, Delilah did."

"Thank you." There was a desperation in his voice I couldn't quite decipher.

Every muscle in my body wanted me to turn around, to look at his stunning features and black devilish eyes. But I couldn't. A small tear escaped, and a whimper fell from my mouth.

"Harriet?" My name on his lips was all I needed for the barrage to break and allow the tears to consume me.

I was suddenly frantically scratching at my skin, the blood I'd cleaned off reappearing in blotches, refusing to be washed away.

The voices grew louder in my head. Their deathly screams demanding me to surrender to the black hole carved in my head.

My body shook as I covered my eyes with my palms, begging for quiet, and the air rocketing through me lodged itself in my throat. Rough hands grabbed my shoulders and spun me, but still, I refused to look at him.

"Princess, what's wrong?" Seb tried to pull my hands away from my face, but I held them there tightly, the scorching water from the shower now burning against my back and trickling over my naked body.

I silently screamed.

My chest became tight, and my breaths shallow, as I struggled with the grappling air.

My oxygen was getting thinner and more hoarse, my frantic panic growing with every second that passed.

I pulled my hands from my eyes, and they began clutching at my throat.

"I can't—"

My throat burned. *Why does it hurt so much?*

"Seb, I can't breathe." Immediately he reached behind me, stopping the lava that was waterfalling across my skin. My chest heaved and my head became hazy, the lack of oxygen making me dizzy.

Seb stepped over the edge of the bathtub and guided me out after him. My legs moved in a numb stumble and suddenly I was crashing against his bare body. My mind wailed at me to count but the numbers were jumbled and chaotic, and I couldn't concentrate over the fireworks going off in my head.

The last thing I saw before my vision turned black was Seb's eyes and the grim reaper dancing behind them.

He'd come to take me home.

Chapter Twenty-Two

Seb

We stayed planted on the bathroom floor for hours, my arms cradling Harriet's broken body against mine. She had drifted in and out of consciousness, but when I finally got her to hear my voice her breaths settled, and she was soon blinking away her fog. I kept her tightly tucked against my chest as I stroked a hand through her hair.

"What happened?"

"You passed out." I continued running my fingers through her hair, hoping it would soothe away the rest of her haze. "What started the attack?"

"There was so much blood." Her voice quivered. I wasn't going to tell her there wasn't. I didn't want her to feel any more out of control than it was likely she already did.

"Harriet, when was the last time you took your meds?" I could see the cogs turning in her head as she counted.

"I don't know. I've been distracted. A few days? Maybe a week."

I sighed. At least she didn't try to convince me she was still taking them. I wasn't about to start dictating what she should and shouldn't do, but I also wasn't going to let her lead herself on a path of self-destruction.

"We need to make sure you're not distracted. They're important." I didn't want to patronise her, I wanted to *look out* for her.

We sat in silence as the steam slowly evaporated in the room, the remnants of the scorching water no longer lingering.

"Do you love her?" The quiet squeak that bounced off my chest was mumbled, but I managed to decipher her question.

It broke my fucking heart.

"Yes," I knew what she was asking, and I owed her the truth. But as soon as I said it, I knew she would misunderstand.

"Cherry's like family to me. She's my sister in every way apart from blood." Harriet's gentle breaths flickered on my chest. "When I think of the men who did this to her, I want to hunt them down, unleash hell on them." The gentle body in my arms stiffened and pulled away to look at me.

"What happened to her?" I couldn't look at her, I didn't want to see the judgment that I knew would be circling the depths of her eyes.

"She had some clients. I tried to tell Saffron she shouldn't accept their money, but she didn't listen." My jaw clenched as I spoke through gritted teeth.

"The same guys hired her a few days ago and left her covered in bruises, I didn't know they'd come back again."

My voice was low. "There's always someone who takes it too fucking far."

I didn't know who the men were yet, I'd asked Tony to try harder to uncover who they were after the first encounter with them, but everything was locked up in a tight vice, their lives a secret they intended to keep safe.

Harriet was quiet in my arms, and then she began to pull away, but I wasn't ready to let her go.

"I don't want you to compare what we have with what me and Cherry have. She'll never be you." Harriet continued to pull away, and I had to loosen my grip before we both fell forward.

"And I'll never be her."

My heart shattered at the sadness in her voice, the way she refused to look at me.

How the fuck had I let this happen?

I'd been so caught up with my anger at what had happened to Cherry, I'd missed my siren falling apart. I hadn't thought about how she would feel being put in this position, how what she was being asked to do would haunt her.

I needed to find a way to make this right.

As Harriet stood and wrapped a towel around her body, I copied her movements. Her shaking hand clasped the door handle, but I slammed my palm against the wooden surface as it began to open.

She stayed facing the exit. “Princess, I am nothing without you. *Nothing.* Please, let me make this right.” She turned to face me, her shoulders dropping as she searched my eyes.

“I’m scared Seb, I’m scared that I’ll be the one who gets hurt at the end of this. You keep saying you want out of the Carnival, but every day you seem to get sucked further into it.”

I didn’t try and stop my eyes when they pleaded with her, and when she scanned the ground trying to avoid me, I placed my hands on either side of her face and pulled her eyes level with mine.

“What happens next time someone takes it too far? Does she end up dead? Do *you* end up dead? You hide everything from me, hide *me* from everything. You’re not giving me a chance to handle it.”

“You have nothing to fear Princess, and you’re right. I need to do better.” I pulled her against my lips, and gently kissed her. I tasted a salty tear as it dropped down her face and slithered between our lips. Pulling backwards, I swiped it away with my thumb.

“And you don’t have to worry about me. I’m not going anywhere. Not unless it’s with you.” For the first time, she smiled at me, and it seemed genuine.

Satisfied that she was starting to listen I stepped backwards, letting her open the door and leave the bathroom. I stood there for a few minutes after she left, my mind still whirling in chaos.

I needed to find the men responsible for hurting Cherry, part of me dying to itch the scratch. But I was also very aware of Harriet's growing presence in this town. It wouldn't take long for people to find the connection between the two of us, and I wasn't going to put her in a position that could get her hurt.

I needed to be careful how I handled this, there were too many people that could get caught in the crossfires.

I left the bathroom, and followed into Harriet's bedroom, absorbing the vanilla scent as I closed the door behind me.

When we emerged from the bedroom and I saw Delilah sitting with Cherry on the windowsill, a slither of relief filtered through my body. I was glad that Cherry wasn't still lying helpless in bed, and grateful to Harriet that she had managed to aid with the injuries.

I knew it wasn't possible, but Cherry's body was already looking better thanks to the gruesome cuts now being stitched up.

"There's a vintage fair tomorrow just outside of town. The'll be cars and stuff. Music, food. You wanna go?" When Harriet walked ahead of me into the kitchen, I grabbed hold of her wrist, tugging her back against my body, and wrapped my arms around her waist.

"What do you think? Fancy a day out?"

I could feel her body warming at my public display, and I nipped at her ear, keeping my voice low so only she could hear,

"Keep blushing, and I'll turn your whole body pink."

She tried to look at me over her shoulder, but I kept my chin tucked into the crevice of her neck, stopping her from being able to move.

"Sounds fun." Her cheek lifted as a smile covered her face, and my body instantly relaxed. I'd hidden her away from my friends, from the other performers, but that had only made her feel more of an outcast.

I was going to rectify that. Besides, it was about time people knew who she belonged to.

Knew who had captured the heart of the Grim Reaper.

There was always a risk that the enemies I was creating would find her, but the more people on my side who knew what she meant, the more protection she would have.

The more chance I had to keep her safe.

"Great!" Cherry cheerfully beamed at us, "Tony's coming, and a load of the other performers. We'll take the minibus." Cherry began tapping away on her phone, and with both her and Delilah distracted, I started planting small pecks across Harriet's bare neck and shoulder, goosebumps erupting with every stroke of my lips.

"Would you two like to come to the community garden's charity gala this weekend?"

My lips froze. Harriet's question shocked me. Josie had mentioned bringing friends, but I didn't think she would extend that invitation to Cherry, who was now squealing like a child.

"I've never been to a gala! Does this mean we can go shopping for dresses?" She leapt from the window, her eyes clenching slightly as she landed, the movement obviously causing her skin to pull against her new stitches.

Suddenly she was stealing Harriet from my arms and wrapping hers around her tiny frame. I raised my eyebrow at Delilah, who just shrugged her shoulders when her eyes made contact with mine.

She was obviously as taken aback by the unexpected display of affection as I was.

"Thank you Harriet, I'm glad you're here." It took a lot for Cherry to say thank you, the same way it took a lot for her to say sorry, so I was well aware of how big a step this was for her.

Once my friend had finished suffocating Harriet she returned to her perch next to Delilah, and the two settled into a quiet conversation.

I followed Harriet into the kitchen, and as she passed me a bottle of water from the fridge, I watched her. She looked nervous, her hand fiddling with the bottle cap.

"Everything okay?" She began chewing her cheek, looking everywhere but at me. "Harriet…"

"Daniel was at the community garden today."

What the fuck was that piece of shit arsehole doing near her?

My jaw clenched, but I stayed quiet, waiting for her to continue. "He told me you threatened him."

Bastard.

"I did." I needed to stop shadowing the truth from Harriet. If I expected her to be honest with me, I needed to do the same. Her eyebrows shot up.

As if she really believed I hadn't.

"Something wasn't right about him. I didn't want him near you, still don't." She took a long sip from her bottle, and from the corner of my eye, Delilah and Cherry leaned their bodies forward, their attention stolen by our conversation.

Nosey fuckers.

Harriet nodded as her throat bobbed and she swallowed. "He knows about the Carnival. He told me everything would come crashing down, that I'd end up collateral damage." Her words provoked a dormant anger inside of me, and I grappled against it as I tried to remain calm.

"If he comes near you again, if he speaks to you again, you tell me straight away. I don't want him—"

"Seb, I don't need a babysitter." She sighed, "If you keep trying to protect me, you're giving them something to poke at. Daniel, my dad, they're looking for something. It can't be you."

I understood what she was saying, but it didn't mean I had to like it. I nodded and pulled her arms until she stood against me, her hold wrapped around my waist and her body moulding perfectly to mine.

"Do you guys wanna watch a movie? I think we've had enough doom and gloom for today." Delilah was already heading towards the television set and pressing buttons on the remote before any of us spoke. She was right though, having a distraction would help, even if it was the cheesy rom com she had picked.

Harriet laced her fingers through mine, and we were soon cuddled up on the sofa next to Delilah and Cherry, the four of us content in the company of each other as we watched the film.

Chapter Twenty-Three

Harriet

I was the first one to wake up, and I was surprised to see we were all still squished together on the sofa. Delilah laid with her legs over the arm and Cherry was sprawled out against her. Seb was slumped across our half, his arms leisurely stretched behind us.

My body was stiff as I sat up and lifted my arms above my head hoping to loosen my tight muscles.

I delicately stepped towards the kitchen and began brewing the coffee. When tip toes on the floorboards caught my attention, I turned to see Cherry crossing the floor towards me, a sleepy smile on her face.

My eyes immediately narrowed on her legs, "how do you feel?"

She shrugged. "As good as I can I guess."

I shifted uncomfortably between my feet. "Why did this happen to you?"

"Seb didn't tell you?"

"He told me some bits." Cherry took the mug of coffee I handed her, and I poured my own.

"I thought I knew what to expect, I've been with men who like to…exert their control before."

I walked to the window and perched myself on the sill, lighting a cigarette. As Cherry joined me, I held the packet out to her and she thankfully pulled one out.

"I'd already had an appointment with two of them and they'd left me pretty sore. Nothing I couldn't handle though." She laughed quietly to herself.

"This time it was different though. There were four of them. As soon as they came in I knew something was wrong. Normally Seb is there to greet them and explain the 'rules', but with him not being there I think they felt those didn't apply to them. Honestly, I'm not sure they would have listened if he had been."

I silently counted. Seb hadn't been at the Carnival because he'd been here with me. A pang of guilt hit my chest.

If he hadn't been with me, none of this would have happened.

This is your fault.

Cherry didn't notice my body turn rigid as she continued recalling the memories. "Normally, we spend a few minutes talking, they tell me what they want, what they like. These guys wasted no time." Her voice turned sad, and I reached across tightly squeezing her hand.

A mumble from the sofa caught both of our attention, and we looked just in time to see Seb and Delilah fall together in a sleepy heap. I looked at Cherry, attempting to stifle the laugh that was threatening to spill behind my lips. She had the same expression, and soon we were giggling between ourselves.

"You're good for him. I've never seen him so…" Cherry paused and looked back at her sleepy friend on the sofa.

"So what?" I asked, my curiosity piqued by her opinion.

"In love."

Her words jolted me, the last thing I had expected her to say was that she thought Seb loved me. I looked back at him, my mouth instantly setting into a grin when I did.

He looked peaceful when he slept, like he was made of clouds instead of storms, and I let out a slight laugh.

I loved his storms.

This man was anything but peaceful, he was chaos and danger, a hectic tornado that didn't care who he swept up. But he was my chaos, *my danger*, and my heart jumped at the villain I was surrendering to.

Cherry and I devoured another cup of coffee before Delilah and Seb began to stir on the sofa, and I watched Seb as he sat up disorientated his eyes darting around the room.

As soon as he landed on me, sat against the window, his shoulders relaxed, and a smile crept over his face. Suddenly he was up and stalking towards me, a lethal glint bounding around in his eyes.

He didn't say anything as he grabbed my hands, pulled me upwards, and began dragging me towards my open bedroom door. I looked behind at Cherry who just gave me a little wave and a wink as we disappeared into my sanctuary.

As soon as we were inside his body was against mine, and he was walking me backwards until my calves hit the mattress and I tumbled to the ground. I sat staring at him wide-eyed, my chest rising heavily as he began dragging his T-shirt over his head and unbuckling the belt around his waist.

I was paralysed, his stunning body lighting up from the sun reflecting through the window, the grin on his face poised firmly as though the hellion himself was holding it in place.

My tongue darted out and swiped across my bottom lip as I bit down, and Seb stilled, his eyes turning into furnaces of dark burning coals. He slowly crouched, his glare never leaving mine as he spoke calmly but with a dangerous edge that sent goosebumps over my body.

"You look beautiful." I wanted to protest.

I was well aware of how I looked In the morning, and it was far from beautiful. But I kept my lips closed as his fingers brushed strands of fallen hair away from my face.

His thumb swept over my lips, and I darted my tongue out, brushing it against the tip. A low growl crept from the depths of his chest as he watched me intensely, his eyes refusing to break their connection.

"Tell me what you want princess." I closed my eyes. It was impossible to say everything I wanted, all of the words were jumbled in my head. My focus was entirely consumed by the sensation of his thumb and the trail of sparks it was leaving on my mouth.

"I want you."

I knew my mistake as soon as I spoke. When I opened my eyes, Seb's sneer confirmed he'd noticed, and his eyebrow rose.

Before he could correct me, I quickly spat my words out.

"I want you to fuck me." Seb's body vibrated as a chuckle left his lips, and I burnt with embarrassment.

"You're learning, but you can do better than that." My brows furrowed, and the violent heat continued to spread throughout my body.

He was going to make me beg.

I wasn't a prude by any means, but the way this man continuously made me beseech for what I wanted had swarms of heat mixed with desire sketching under my skin.

I spoke quietly, as if I didn't intend for anyone to hear my words.

"I want to feel your cock inside of me. I want you to fuck me until my legs are shaking, until I can't stand."

Seb was on top of me in one swift movement, His fingers digging into the sides of my legs as he pushed me further back on the mattress. My chest hitched, but my brain didn't have time to catch up with my body as frantic hands pulled my shirt up and over my head, leaving my body exposed apart from the thin layer of underwear.

His mouth covered mine, his tongue battling for dominance as his snake inked hand wrapped around my throat. The sensation sent heat pouring in between my legs, and when one of his hands found my nipple and began teasing it in between his fingers, a breathy moan slipped between our mouths.

His tongue consumed me like a man desperate for water, his urgent movements throwing a wild rage of ecstasy plummeting around in my head.

Suddenly he pulled away, and I couldn't stop the huff when he did, my want for him growing with every slither of his fingers.

"Needy little thing aren't you."

Seb's touch moved from my chest and trailed down my body until he sat, gently brushing against the fabric separating him from my throbbing mass of nerves.

"I can feel how wet you are already." He pushed harder against the fabric, and a whimper danced from my tongue. "That's it, sing for me."

My eyes rolled back as he pulled the fabric to the side, and immediately pushed two fingers inside of me. My hips rolled, and another breathy moan swept over my mouth.

"So fucking tight. Imagine my cock inside your pretty pussy." His words caused my stomach to tighten, and my body to shudder. His fingers continued to move as he slowly edged a third inside and his sadistic smile curled his lips as I cried out in bliss.

"So fucking pretty." Seb used his arm to push my legs back, and my knees were suddenly inches away from my chest, my arse being motioned upwards.

His fingers plummeted deeper from the new angle, and the moans that swept over my mouth became louder.

"You're my favourite music. Let go of the edge Harriet. Let me catch you."

My orgasm crept up on me, and suddenly my entire body was convulsing as waves of raw sublime coated me and held my body hostage.

Seb didn't stop his fingers from moving as I rode out the waves, and each time he pushed inside of me, my body coaxed another raging tsunami.

My trembles began to calm and my breath steadied, but as I rose onto my elbows, Seb's hand gripped my throat again and slammed me back down onto the mattress.

"We're not finished." A snarl left his lips, and the butterflies ignited inside of me again, the throb between my legs needy and desperate. *How was that even possible?*

"You wanted me to fuck you. So I'm going to fuck you."

Seb had never been particularly gentle, but he'd never been rough with me either. The sudden power that he was holding over my body both struck fear and excitement inside of me. I trusted this man wholeheartedly, which just provoked the little voice in my head, demanding I give him my all, demanding I spilled my darkest desires.

Seb grabbed my hips and was suddenly flipping me onto my front. With one swift movement I was dragged backwards, my arse in the air and my body on all fours.

"Spread yourself for me." I was glad he couldn't see my face, because I was certain I was turning a fluorescent shade of red. A sharp sting across my arse shoved my body forward as Seb's hand connected with my soft skin. My clit throbbed at the contact and my eyes blinked hysterically.

"Don't make me ask you again princess." The top of my body fell down onto my duvet, and I shyly pulled my arms behind me, following his demands and opening myself up for him.

A honeyed vibration floated in the air, and goosebumps rocketed over my skin with each second that passed.

Seb's rough hands gliding over my arse provoked a cascade of sparks across my skin, and when he brushed the head of his cock against my entrance my heart picked up and began thumping chronically in my chest. It was as though someone had put a defibrillator on my heart and was trying to bring me back to life.

"Tell me what you want." Seb's voice was low and desperate, his own resilience to remain patient crumbling away.

The torturous tease was the last straw. I couldn't hold onto the pride that kept me stubborn.

"I want you to put your cock inside of me, I want you to stretch me open and fuck what's yours." My voice trembled a little.

"I want you to own me."

"Good girl," Was all Seb said before he was slamming into me, his size stretching my walls and shoving my body forward.

A star-crossed cry screamed from my lips, and I rammed my face into the pillow, attempting to mute the sound.

His hands roughly gripped my waist as he moved, his cock driving in and out of me with force and speed.

"So, fucking, tight." His words were raspy, and he spat them out through gritted teeth. My arms fell away from my arse, desperate to grab onto something.

The feel of his hand against my prickling skin vibrated the walls again and he brought it down in a hard smack. The sensation flittered over my skin. The sting from the contact, mixed with the ecstasy he was creating was a whirl of conflicting feelings.

I fumbled with the duvet, my fingers clawing at it with every turbulent hurdle of pleasure that stormed through my body.

Seb's hands moved from my waist and up my back, settling over my shoulder. "Your cunt's so fucking greedy. Look how well you're taking me."

He held on firmly, keeping my body from rocking with his movements, and he slammed into me, over and over again.

Incoherent words dripped from my lips, and I struggled to remain present with each thrust of his cock.

"Breathe Princess." I hadn't even realised I'd stopped.

Fuck heaven, I wanted to stay in hell with this god of a man forever.

The heat swirled around as my orgasm began to creep up again, "I'm going to come." My voice broke. Seb removed one of his hands from my shoulder, and quickly brought it underneath my body, his fingers finding my sensitive clit. He circled his fingers around it with such violence that every touch barrelled torment through my quivering state.

That threw me over the edge.

My head flung back as waves flooded my body, cries of delight and pleasure singing from my lips.

I didn't even try and stay quiet. It would have been impossible.

My body shook in a chaotic frenzy, and soon Seb's movements became static until he slammed into me one final time and stilled, his own cries vaporising from his lungs.

We stayed connected to each other for a few minutes before Seb began to slowly edge out of me, his warm seed spilling down the backs of my thighs as he removed himself.

I felt exposed, still kneeling on the mattress, but I couldn't move, and as I tried to decide the best way to manoeuvre myself, a warm fabric was being pressed against my swollen clit and Seb's voice returned to a familiar gentler tone.

"You did so well princess."

He helped me to turn and began pulling me upwards by my arms. My legs were a numb shaking mess, and I struggled to stay balanced.

I did ask him to fuck me until my legs shook.

Seb wrapped me tightly in his arms, and my thumping chest settled against his soothing hold. A few moments later a pound on the door startled us both, and Cherry's muffled voice bounced through the wood.

"If you two are done in there, the minibus will be here in twenty."

Crimson heat travelled up my neck, and my eyes widened at Seb who had a mischievous grin spread from ear to ear across his features. I groaned and covered my face with my hands now knowing that Cherry and Delilah had heard everything from my room.

Seb's body shook with laughter, and he kissed the top of my head. "Don't be embarrassed, the way you fuck is nothing to be ashamed about. You're a goddess Harriet. And that fucking voice." He fell down on the bed with a moan, taking me with him, and his hands ran up and down his face as strings of laughter travelled from his mouth. I fidgeted from his arms, releasing myself from the hold he had on me and grabbed a T-shirt to fling at him.

The noises he made were contagious, and as I sauntered towards the drawers in the corner I couldn't stop my own laughs from falling from me.

"I never know how to be with you. Every push you rise to meet. You're a secret little songbird. What else are you hiding?"

I looked at Seb in confusion. "I want to know your deepest fantasies Harriet. I want to know what will truly draw out that little demon sleeping inside of you."

I didn't know how to answer him, and thought back to the encounters we'd shared. "The movie theatre. I liked the movie theatre."

"Which part?"

Chewing on the corner of my mouth, I avoided his intense stare. "Knowing someone could see us." I kept my words to a whisper, not really believing what I was admitting.

"You want other people to watch you scream for my cock?" I nodded.

"Maybe."

"Maybe?"

My walls were crumbling. "Yes."

When I finally looked at Seb, I expected to see the familiar smirk, but it wasn't there. Only intrigue gleamed from his eyes.

"You're full of surprises."

My mind began to wander, and I became distracted by the strange feeling aching my chest. More pounds on the door absorbed me from my daydream, and when Delilah shouted that the bus was early, I looked over at Seb standing arms folded, leaning against the wall.

An obsessive spark twinkling in the depths of the coals.

That was the moment I knew I was doomed. That was the moment I knew that the shackles had tightened, and I would never be able to escape.

I was sinking, and I welcomed the burn.

Chapter Twenty-Four

Seb

The vintage fair wasn't too far out of town, and by the time we had finished making the final stops to collect the rest of our group we were well on our way towards the grounds it was held at.

The bus was a chaotic frenzy of jeers and laughter, everyone making the most of the day off and the freedom we were granted on this occasion.

I'd stolen a seat at the back hoping it would give me and Harriet some privacy, but Cherry and Delilah decided to commandeer the two seats in front of us, and didn't stop talking for the entire journey.

I couldn't keep my hands off Harriet. Keeping my fingers locked between hers, I pulled her onto my lap and leaned her back, so she was supported by the window. She giggled as I trailed my lips from her ear to her shoulder, and the sound wrapped tightly around my heart.

I didn't care who saw us, I didn't care what opinions they had of me. I'd always had to be the tough one, the one ready to protect. A façade I had carried heavily on my shoulders for the last eight years. I was still those things, but now I didn't have to hide my other side, the side that wanted people to see that the beautiful girl on my lap belonged to me, that I had the capability to love and be loved.

I wasn't just the fucking monster they all knew me to be.

Delilah threw something and it hit me straight between the eyes, jogging me from my thoughts.

"Is this what it will always be like now? You two incapable of keeping your hands to yourselves?" I stared at her, not quite sure what answer she was hoping for, when Cherry's head popped up over the seat in front of us, her red hair flying around from the fans blowing above.

"They're in love." She sang in a childish voice, "it's cute."

I didn't react to her choice of words, but next to me Harriet was shuffling uncomfortably and pulling at the edge of the sundress I'd made her wear.

The one I'd made her wear with no underwear.

Her eyes darted around, looking everywhere but at me, and I narrowed my eyes on her. "Problem?"

She shook her head nervously and bit down on her lip, the movement causing a rush of heat to go straight to my cock and stir it awake.

"Love is a strong word." She spoke quietly, keeping her sight firmly plastered downwards.

"It is."

"It shouldn't be used flippantly."

"It shouldn't."

Harriet sighed. "Do you? Do you love me?"

I rubbed my thumb over the back of her hand, but still, she didn't want to look at me.

"I'm not stupid enough to ignore that you still have a lot of things to figure out Harriet, but I'm also not stupid enough to let you go."

Finally, she looked up, her eyes glassy and dim.

"I love you. But I'm okay with you not loving me yet."

"I'm not a good person Seb. I'm not stable or normal. I've done a lot of questionable things."

"If you told me every terrible thing you've ever done, I'd still come back. Stop trying to scare me off Harriet, It won't work."

She smiled and looked back down again, her face glistening against the sunlight striking her through the window.

For the rest of the journey we sat in mostly silence, content in enjoying each other's company. A couple of the performers had come over and introduced themselves, and Harriet gracefully mirrored their forewords. They all seemed enamoured by her, but who could blame them.

She was a siren who demanded attention, and everyone here could see that. Even if she couldn't.

Tony came over as we began to pull into a field, offering us both a bottle of water. He loosened the cap on his own and chugged back half before wiping the back of his hand over his mouth.

"Nearly there, boss. Hey Harriet." He smiled at my girl, who was now back on the seat next to me, "you look nice."

"Thank you, Tony."

"So you two are a thing now?"

I narrowed my eyes at him, but he ignored the warning and leaned against the back of Delilah's chair.

Neither of us said anything, but that was all the confirmation he needed. "Does Saffron know?"

What the fuck.

My body vibrated and Harriet noticed, her hand moving to lay on my forearm.

"Thanks again for the water, Tony." An angelic smile appeared on her face, and her hand tightened, but I kept my eyes fixed on the hungry gaze he was roaming all over her.

The bus came to an abrupt halt, and Tony turned away from us, walking back to the front of the bus. Something about that minor interaction seemed off. Tony was good at recognising when he was pushing my buttons, so he knew exactly what he was doing.

My fists clenched at my sides, anger spilling around inside of my head, but as soon as the sweet scent of vanilla morphed into my senses, it began to ease, and I was soon relaxing, my arms around Harriet.

"Saffron, is she a problem?"

I didn't want to scare her off with horror stories, but I also didn't want to patronise her with half-truths and loose lies.

"Saffron takes no prisoners. There's a chance if she finds out about you, she'll try to use it against me." Harriet stared at me. "I will never let her get near you. You have nothing to worry about. She can't hurt you whilst I'm here."

As soon as we stepped into the muddy field, the cool winter air was spinning around us, throwing our clothes into a maze of psychedelic patterns. I looked at Harriet, who was holding her dress down with her hands. A tiny slither of guilt gnawed inside me at putting her in this predicament, but I also enjoyed seeing her squirm, her face reddening as the wind picked up and threw the material into the air.

She was so fucking beautiful. Her red face brought back memories of her red arse when my hand had connected with it.

Fucking delicious.

Before the driver could leave, I quickly ran back onto the bus and pulled a rucksack from the overhead compartment. This bus was only used by the performers, so it was safe to keep our belongings in there.

I pulled out what I needed and left the vehicle, giving the door a tap to let the driver know he could leave. With a salute, he drove away.

I ran back over to Harriet who was still desperately trying not to flash everyone. "Here, put these on." I dangled a piece of black fabric in front of her, and as she snatched it from my hand her eyebrow rose.

"Do I even want to know why you keep a pair of boxers on your minibus?" I folded my arms and laughed at her.

"Probably not." I moved to shield her body as she stepped her legs in and shimmied them upwards. I smirked at her as she stared down at herself.

"This is your fault." She huffed, but I knew she wasn't too upset, her words lacked the bite she exuded when something really pissed her off.

"You look good in my clothes."

Slinging an arm around her shoulder, we began walking in the direction of the crowds of people and the bellowing music that chimed through the air.

The further we trudged into the field, the more Harriet's body relaxed, and she was soon settling into my side, her fingers lacing through mine on her shoulder. It was unusual to feel so relaxed, so open. I was beginning to get sick of keeping her away from the Carnival. Being able to be with her in public was a treat, and one I intended to make the most of.

"Seb look!" I followed the direction her hand was pointing, and she began jumping with excitement on the spot. "It's a record stall!"

I didn't even have a chance to respond to her before she let go of my hand and was speedwalking to a tiny tent that had the words 'Vint Recs' hanging from a banner over the doorway.

From outside the place looked small, the tent couldn't have been much bigger than about twenty feet wide, but when I stepped through the separation in the fabric and followed Harriet, It was as though I'd stepped through to another world.

This place was a vinyl collector's dream.

Around the edge of the tent freestanding shelves covered every side, and each shelf was stacked with vinyl in cardboard boxes. In the centre, tables were the same, their surfaces covered with rows and rows of old music. Tiny lightbulbs in mason jars hung from strips around the perimeter giving it a secluded yet cosy feel, and low jazz music played from the speakers.

In the corner, Harriet hurriedly pulled tubes of rolled up paper from a box and bundled them into her arms. When she turned and saw me, her face lit up.

I'd seen Harriet happy. But this wasn't happy, this was ecstatic. She was radiating a fierce joy, her eyes beaming with light as she skirted around the tables and began hoisting more memorabilia into her arms.

I watched her for a moment, her enthusiasm bubbling to the surface, when a man knocked behind her and the collection of purchases she was cradling scattered to the ground.

I was at her side in seconds.

Harriet was fumbling around on the ground, trying to pull together the fragments of joy she had held in her arms just moments ago, the man blurting his words of apologies at her.

When he grabbed her arm to help her stand, the switch inside of me flicked.

"I've got her." I pushed passed him and hooked my arms underneath her elbows, her skin turning a bright shade of tomato.

"It was my fault." I hadn't looked at the man yet, but there was something about his voice that struck a nerve.

When I finally gave him my attention, a menacing smirk was staring at me, and I racked my brain to decipher where I had seen him before.

"Harriet, go pay. I'll be there in a second." She nodded sheepishly and smiled up at the man tightly before scuttling off to the cash register.

"Pretty girl you've got there. Harriet. Nice name, easy on the tongue." I didn't take my eyes off him as he looked past me, a sadistic smile creeping up at the corners of his mouth.

"Who the fuck are you?" My teeth ground together, and my patience hung thin. At my sides my fingers tickled, itching to show this man who Harriet belonged to.

"Brunettes always were my favourite. Though I think I prefer her in the cheerleading costume. You should have her wear that next time."

Realisation hit me, as though a stack of rocks had been thrown over my body. My eyes widened, and a sudden panic began to swarm as I watched Harriet at the counter completely unsuspecting of the lion's den she had wound up in.

She was now talking with another man, smiling at the words that were being spoken between the two of them.

"I told you. She isn't for hire."

The man in front of me crossed his arms and nodded, but his expression remained flat, unbothered.

"So you said. Does Saffron know you're hiding her away, keeping her to yourself?"

My blood boiled as he provoked the carnage that was unfolding inside of my body.

"Go near her again, and I'll fucking kill you."

I didn't give him a chance to respond before I was stalking to the other side of the tent and slinging my arm possessively around Harriet's waist.

How had they known we would be here, that *she* would be here?

A knot formed inside my throat. I had done everything I could to keep her away from the dangerous exploits of the Carnival. I had been stupid to think it wouldn't find her.

Fucking naïve to think we could be normal. *Have* normal.

As soon as we stepped outside, cool winds swept through my lungs, and I welcomed them as the breeze calmed my thumping chest.

I looked down at Harriet and she was still beaming like a small child, her face a picture of angelic innocence and completely oblivious to the leaches trying to get close to her.

"My mom loved this band." She held one of the posters out and it unravelled showing four men with various instruments and the name 'Cobra Shift' in bold letters at the top.

From the corner of my eye, I spotted Delilah and Cherry barrelling towards us, their feet tripping up in the wet mud under their feet.

"This place is great, how have I never been here before?" Delilah squealed as she looked at Harriet guarding her new possessions in her arms.

"Because you've never been with me." Cherry dipped her head and planted a soft kiss on Delilah's lips. "They've got some bands playing on the stage at the front, we should go and watch. Harriet, they have some holding lockers in the tent over there."

Cherry pointed at a small tent on the other side of the field. "I think they charge, but you can put your stuff in there, so you don't have to carry it around." Harriet nodded, and I placed my hand on her lower back guiding her forward.

"We'll meet you guys at the stage, save us a space." The pair turned, walking hand in hand back in the direction of the booming music.

After safely depositing Harriet's purchases into the arms of a young attendant, we joined our friends and the rest of the performers at the front of the barricaded section of the stage.

Bodies were writhing and dancing to the low base and melodic tunes, and when Harriet leant her body back into mine and began moving, my legs matched her movements.

I whispered against her ear. "I'm staying with you again tonight."

Her head shifted slightly to look at me over her shoulder. "I'm glad I didn't have to ask. For once you're not forcing words from me." I chuckled at our private joke.

"I'm just helping you discover who you truly are."

It wasn't long before we were pulled into the crowd of the other performers, and we were all dancing along with the music pouring from the stage.

"I'm going to grab a drink, do you want anything?" I shouted into Harriet's ear. She shook her head and moved closer to Delilah and Cherry, their bodies dancing together as matching smiles covered their faces.

I didn't take my eyes off of her as I stalked to the canopy-covered bar and ordered two bottles of water. Harriet might not want anything now, but I knew she would soon.

I watched the three of them from afar, my beautiful girl sandwiched in the middle of the two other women. Her body twisted gracefully, her hands dragging through her hair forcing the strands to move as they lifted into the air and then tumbled back down.

She was the image of beauty. Like a siren, she captured the hearts of everyone she met. Even the performers who had never seen her before were smiling at her, just as enamoured by her forceful radiance as I was.

My throat constricted as my mind wandered back to the man in the tent, at how his eyes had greedily roamed over her body. I knew at that moment what I needed to do.

Hide her away so no one could get close.

I'd made a mistake showing her off, and now she would be forced to pay the price.

As soon as we'd attended the charity gala this weekend, I'd steal her away. If it were my choice we'd go sooner, but I knew how much she loved that garden and wanted to see it flourish.

I was going to cause her so much disruption and heartache, I wasn't going to take that away from her as well.

All of a sudden, the sky opened, and rain began pelting down. Most of the gatherers ran to take shelter in one of the nearby tents. But of course, Harriet, Delilah and Cherry remained firmly fixed in place, their bodies erupting into fits of laughter as they continued dancing.

When Harriet spotted me staring, she tilted her head, her eyebrow rising. One of her hands firmly planted itself on her hip, whilst her other waved at me, commanding me to join the trio.

I grabbed the water bottles off of the counter and began trailing towards her. After all, who was I to deny the princess of her wishes.

Chapter Twenty-Five

Harriet

My feet ached and my dress was soaked through, but I didn't want to stop dancing, I didn't want to leave the little euphoric bubble that was clouding my body. So when Seb told me we needed to go, I folded my arms, pouted, and stared at him like a child who had been told off for misbehaving.

The smile on his face dissolved me. Its normally devilish curls were nowhere in sight, instead, a soft twinkle lifted from his eyes, and my insides tightened.

With our fingers laced together, we quickly collected my new posters and vinyl from the holding tent and headed towards the minibus that had arrived, ready to take us back to reality.

Seb rummaged around the rucksack that was sitting in the locker above our seats and pulled out a dark hoodie. Without saying anything, he swept my dripping, tangled hair behind my shoulders and pulled the jumper over my shivering body.

It flooded my frame, but I loved it. Burying my face against the sleeves and inhaling, I closed my eyes when his familiar smoky smell warped into my senses.

I wanted to suffocate in the smell.

When I finally opened my eyes Seb was staring at me with a look I couldn't quite decipher.

"Sorry." I said sheepishly, "it smells of you." He smiled and took one of my hands in his.

"I want to show you something tonight, once the bus drops us off."

"What is it?"

"It's a surprise."

I raised my eyebrow at him, and a low chuckle shook his body. "Nothing to be worried about."

It was impossible to worry about anything when I was with him.

I leaned my head against his shoulders and allowed my heavy eyes to close as my muscles began to warm against the cold dampness. I was definitely going to get sick from standing in the rain, but it was worth every second.

Everything that had happened, every decision that had brought me to this moment, flashed behind the back of my eyelids like static memories. I'd had no idea what I was doing when I arrived in Bromlin, I still didn't. But nothing could make me regret my decision to pack up my life and move.

I thought back to Felix, about the years we'd spent together, and a twinge of sadness hit my chest. Sadness mixed with guilt. I had a different perspective now about our life together.

Maybe my dad had been right, maybe I was a lot to handle.

But I also knew now that wasn't my fault, and it wasn't Felix's either. He just wasn't the person who was going to fight away my shadows, help me recover from the shackles that had caged themselves around me since my mom died.

"Harriet? What's wrong?" Seb spoke softly as his thumb brushed my cheek and swiped away a tear I didn't know I'd let fall.

"Nothing." I looked up at him, his eyes pulled together in worry. "I was thinking about everything. About my mom." He stayed silent, and I continued speaking. "They're happy tears. I'm happy Seb."

His face relaxed, and he pulled me in closer against his chest.

"Me too princess."

"Where are we going?!" I tried to shout, but my words were muffled by the helmet covering my face. As Seb's motorbike roared and weaved around the other cars, I held on tighter scared to let go.

He hadn't heard me, his concentration stolen entirely by the quick manoeuvres he was making with his bike.

Up ahead, I spotted the familiar steel gates of the Carnival come into view, the normally illuminated sign hidden in darkness. I narrowed my eyes, confusion skating around in my mind.

This was Seb's surprise?

As we began to slow, my arms loosened from the vice they were creating, and my muscles began to slacken until we came to a firm stop.

Seb jumped off the bike first, and pulled off his helmet, revealing a smirk and his dishevelled hair. When he held his hand out, I took it and swung my body from the seat, his rough fingers causing aggressive sparks to light in pinpricks across my entire body.

I'd never tire of that sensation, never tire of his touch.

Now standing, Seb pulled the helmet from my head, and I was silently grateful for the braids I had created in my hair before we left, their tight weave stopping my hair from becoming a wild mess of matted tangles.

Seb didn't say anything as he led me towards the gate and fished a key from his pocket, loosening the padlock and chains from around the enormous bars.

I expected him to take me in the direction of the performer's tent, but instead, we began walking in the opposite direction, straight into the middle of the Carnival's grounds.

When we passed the haunted walk ride, my chest tightened. Memories of Seb on his knees, my leg laying over his shoulders whilst his tongue had ignited my skin sent shockwaves aggressively hurdling through my body, and I had to tear my eyes away to stop myself from dragging him inside.

So much has happened since my birthday.

After a few minutes, we came to a stop just outside a barricade that led up to a Ferris wheel and Seb turned to face me, a grin stretching from ear to ear lighting up his face.

I looked from him to the Ferris wheel and back again, my face contorting into confusion.

"What are we doing here?" I asked, looking back up at the enormous metal wheel looming above us.

"I wanted to show you something." Seb sounded like an excited child, and as he disappeared around the other side of the frame I shifted on my feet nervously, anticipation grazing underneath my skin.

Suddenly the wheel came alive with bright colours that dazzled the sky. A medley of reds, blues and greens flashed into the air and illuminated the darkness.

My eyes widened with awe as Seb returned, and I flicked my eyes between him and the waterfall of colours.

"This isn't it." Seb began unhooking the safety chain that stopped anyone from passing onto the ride. When he started climbing the steps my legs eagerly followed, and soon I was clambering against the metal floor of the Ferris wheel.

He lifted one of the bars from across the seats and held his hand out for me. I crept forward slowly, and when he manoeuvred me into position, I let him.

"I'll be right back." I remained silent as he ran towards a small shack on the far side of the ride. As soon as he was inside, the wheel began to shake and I gripped the edge of the safety bar. The ride shuddered and I started moving, my feet dangling as the metal floor below me disappeared.

Before I was lifted far off of the ground, Seb ran back and launched himself into the seat, yanking the metal safety bar back down across our laps.

We began floating into the air until we stilled at the top. I looked around, my throat getting lodged at the scenery engulfing us.

From up here you could see for miles.

Bromlin was a mess of lights and glares, and tiny people moved like ants around the streets. When I looked to the other side, I spotted a lighthouse in the middle of the expansive body of water, its light circling around like a vulture looking for its prey.

I was speechless.

Everything looked so small, so inconspicuous. I looked to Seb who was watching me intensely. "It's beautiful," I admitted, turning my attention back to the dazzling lights of the world beneath us.

We sat in silence for a few minutes, both of us captured by the stillness of our company, when Seb reached out and tucked a strand of hair behind my ear.

"You see the lighthouse?"

I looked back over at the water behind him and nodded.

"Just past that, there's a small town, Rosewood." He paused, "I want you to come there with me."

"Like a holiday?"

"No."

I was confused.

"Like *live*. I want you to move there with me."

All of the air evaporated from my lungs. Seb was asking me to *live* with him.

"You don't want to live here?" I asked, "what about the Carnival?"

He sighed, his chest heaving heavily as he leaned back against the bench.

"There's so much going on here Harriet. The Carnival, it's changing, growing. Something big is coming and I..." He stared into my eyes, a wave of hesitation flashing through his. "I want you as far away from it as I can get you. Rosewood is a good start until I figure something else out."

I sat there in silence. I didn't like the way Seb sounded as though he was almost scared, and his unease filtered through to me. I fiddled at the hem of my shirt, hoping it would offer some comfort.

"But I like it here Seb." He laid his hand on top of mine and squeezed.

"It won't be forever, just until things calm down."

I swallowed, nerves racking around inside of me.

"When do we go?"

"Monday. That gives us a few days to sort everything out after the community garden's event tomorrow."

Three days.

I had three days before I was going to have to pack up and move again. Start over. *Again.*

I was finally settled, *finally* somewhere where I belonged, and it was being ripped away from me.

I slowly nodded my head but kept my eyes firmly fixed on our hands in my lap. His fingers traced delicate patterns over the back of my hand, and I sighed.

"What's going on Seb?"

"I can't tell you."

"You're asking me to leave my life behind, temporarily or not, I deserve to know why. I deserve to know why *I* need to leave."

Seb dragged his fingers back through his hair, his jaw ticking as he thought. "Is it not enough that I just want to keep you safe?"

"Safe from what?"

"From everyone." Seb's hands separated from mine and tightened on the bar. "Fuck, Harriet. If anything was to happen to you because of me. Because of this cesspool of a life. I can't risk losing you, please, just trust me."

I looked back out towards Rosewood, sensing I was fighting a losing battle.

"It's only temporary?"

Seb nodded. "As soon as things calm down here, we'll come straight back. I promise." He lifted one of my hands and planted a gentle kiss on my fingers.

"Okay." I smiled but it didn't reach my ears. I did trust him, but it didn't mean I had to like the secrets that came with that trust.

We sat there for hours, our bodies huddled together as we gently rocked in the breeze. My mind was hurtling with questions for Seb, all of which I knew he wouldn't answer.

"It's you and me Harriet. You and me in this tiny fucked up world."

I enjoyed the irony and let out a small laugh, "two fucked up people in a fucked-up world."

His voice was a whisper. "There's no one else I'd rather be fucked up with."

When Seb took me home, I didn't invite him in.

I'd told him earlier he could stay, but I needed some time to myself, time to understand and convince the voices that the secrets were worth it.

Of course they were. *He* was worth it.

I was still sad about the predicament we found ourselves in. After I changed and clambered into bed, I pulled the photo of my mom from my purse and skirted my fingers around the edge attempting to scorch the image into my fingertips.

Eventually, I fell asleep, and when the shadows came knocking in the dead of night, I let them in, and danced with them in my dreams.

Chapter Twenty-Six

Harriet

"Cherry, I'm not sure about this."

I stared at myself in the mirror as she tugged the zip on the back of my dress, gluing me into the tight-fitting fabric.

"What's not to be sure about? You look fucking amazing!"

She was right, I *did* look amazing.

Dark emerald silk fitted like second skin to my body, with a corset-styled bodice that was covered in intricately designed petals and leaves weaving in swirls around my chest. The lack of straps left my shoulders bare to the breeze, and my skin glittered with a delicate brushing of bronzer Cherry had forced on me.

My hair had been styled into barrels woven on top of my head, with two small strands curled and framing my face.

Delilah had helped too. She'd painted my face in a hypnotising dark kohl, and a fierce red lipstick settled on top of my normally rosy lips.

I hadn't had time to pick out a dress for tonight, my mind was still preoccupied with my impending departure. So when Cherry offered to pick something up for me, I quickly accepted her generosity.

What I hadn't expected was for her to pick something that was as equally dangerous as it was beautiful.

Her gentle hands laid on my shoulders as she captured my stare in the mirror. "You look stunning Harriet. Seb's a lucky man."

I quickly spun and wrapped my arms tightly around her neck, not wanting to let go of the woman who'd become a vital part of my survival in this town. Her hands ran up and down my back in comforting strokes.

"Hey. What's wrong?" I let out a small sniffle as I stepped back and released her from my hold, a sheepish smile tugging at the corners of my mouth.

"Sorry. I'm just… I'm so glad I met you." She smiled at me, her eyes bright, as she wrapped me back up and returned the sentiment.

A knock on my door distracted us both, and as Delilah entered she whistled, her eyes flicking between the two of us.

"Wow. Harriet, are you sure Cherry and I can't tempt you to experiment a little with your sexuality?" I laughed at her as Cherry moved to her side.

"Are you crazy? Seb would fucking hunt us if we won that argument." She chuckled.

Delilah was wearing a dark maroon dress suit and a black bowtie. Her raven black locks had been braided at the sides and fell down her back in waves. She and Cherry matched each other exactly.

"Speaking of the devil, Seb's going to have a heart attack when he sees you."

Cherry laughed, "it's not Seb she should be worried about, it's every other man that looks at her."

I smiled at the pair as they stood arm in arm, Cherry's body towering over Delilah's from the platform stilettos she was wearing.

When I had tried to slip on my high-tops earlier, they had been very quickly thrown out of reach and a pair of black heels dropped into my lap. I hated wearing heels, but sensing I would lose if I argued, I slipped the shoes onto my feet and stumbled around.

Three harsh knocks on the front door of the apartment caught our attention, and Delilah unwrapped her body from Cherry's as she headed in the direction the noise came from.

I heard Seb's voice before I saw him, mutters passing between him and my roommate just outside my door.

When he appeared in the doorway he froze, his eyes widening as they roamed over my body.

"I'll leave you two to it. The limo will be here in five." Cherry smirked as she looked between the two of us and crept from the room.

We stood in silence for a moment, our chests rising and falling as we stared into the space separating us.

The black suit cloaking Seb caused my throat to hitch. It masked his body perfectly, but despite his normally intimidating ink being hidden it didn't stop him from radiating a contagious danger that had my insides combusting.

His hair had been neatly combed, and I desperately wanted to run my fingers through it and mess it up. It would seem I wouldn't need to.

Seb's hand rose and swiped through his black strands, his attention never parting from me.

"Do you like the dress? Cherry picked it." I smiled at him but it was small, and my fingers fidgeted in my lap, his intense glare making me nervous.

Seb slowly stalked forward not stopping when he reached me, and forced my body to back up against the wall. His hands lifted and planted themselves firmly on the wall either side of my face.

His head hung in the space between us, and when he lifted it his eyes were heated pits of gasoline, shooting daggers straight into mine.

"You're trying to fucking kill me princess." Desperation dripped from his voice, and I shifted in the small space around my body. "The limo needs to hurry up and get here before I throw you on the bed and rip that dress from your body."

Heat slithered up my neck, and I pressed my thighs together, hoping Seb wouldn't notice the effect his words had on me.

Of course he noticed.

A devilish smile curled on his face, and he tilted his head as his fingers danced across my shoulders and down my arms, igniting a runway of flames as they moved.

"You look like a fucking goddess Harriet."

"Limo's here!" Delilah shouted from the living room, distracting us from our trance.

I smiled at Seb expecting him to move to let me pass, but he didn't, he stayed fixed in place.

My voice was low and shaky, "we have to go."

Seb continued to stare, and as he leant closer his breath fanned against my ear. "I will kill any person who so much as looks in your direction tonight, let alone dares to lay a finger on you. No one touches what's mine."

The threatening promise behind his words sent a throbbing need straight to the bundle of chaotic nerves between my legs, and my throat sputtered as my voice tried to catch up.

Finally, he stepped backwards, taking his relentless heat with him.

Though I was glad to be able to breathe steadily again, my body missed his comfort and immediately I felt naked, every inch of my body craving the fiendish touch of his fingers.

After scooping up my velvet clutch bag, phone, and purse, I followed into the front room where Cherry and Delilah were waiting patiently.

"Ready to do this?" Cherry smiled between us, and we nodded.

"Then let's take a dash of Carnival to the party."

The limo, courtesy of Josie, pulled up outside an impressively huge historical building, its dark grey stones illuminated by lights that shone upwards into the sky. Crowds of people mingled on the pebbled driveway, their bodies covered in accentuate and lavish colours and fabric.

The night's cool air immediately hit me when I stepped out of the car, and I suddenly felt out of place. I knew all of the people in attendance tonight were guests who had made large donations to the community garden in the past.

I was just a city girl who worked in a tech store.

The gentle touch of Seb's hand on my back forced me from my thoughts, and I smiled up at him as I spotted Josie hurtling towards us from the corner of my eye.

"Harriet!" She called as she closed in on us, "I'm so glad you came, and you brought friends. This is already looking like a successful night." She wobbled on her legs, and I laughed at the empty champagne flute she was holding in her hand.

Spotting the direction of my vision she turned, pointing towards the entrance door that was littered with bodies passing through it.

"Go through there, make a left. Bars in the back corner." She winked at me and then turned her body towards Cherry and

Delilah. "Thank you so much for coming. Really, it means the absolute world." The two of them smiled at the intoxicated woman as she staggered off in the direction of another car.

"She seems like fun," Cherry laughed, and we began walking towards the entrance of the gala.

As soon as we entered through the colossal, elegant doors we were wrapped up in the world that had been created inside.

White drapes covered in flickering fairy lights hung across the ceiling and flowed down the walls, whilst tables were scattered around the space, stacked high with white porcelain vases spilling with an assortment of beautiful flowers and greenery.

In the centre of the room, a stage stood tall and proud in front of a dance floor already packed with gyrating bodies. Lights twinkled around the space and my eyes remained fixed on the enchanting fairytale that had morphed around us.

Seb's hand wove around mine and we headed across the room towards the bar. It was crowded and bodies shoved to get towards the front. Sneaking off to the edge, we spotted a parting and lodged our bodies in.

"This is cosy," Delilah chuckled, and we all joined her laugh, the sweet sound cascading in ribbons as it fell from our mouths.

I overheard one of the groups to our side talking about the donations table and made a mental note to make sure to head there after we'd collected our drinks.

When we finally made it to the front, Seb ordered four glasses of champagne, and I couldn't stifle a giggle at seeing the tiny flute in his large, tattooed hands. Seb raised his eyebrow at me.

"Something funny?"

I took a sip from the glass, my lipstick staining the edge as I stood with my arms crossed, biting down on my bottom lip. A low growl vibrated through his chest, and he brought his thumb up and swiped it across my lips.

"Keep doing that, and we won't last another hour here."

"Give the girl a break Seb. You're so brooding and stern. I'm surprised she's still standing." Cherry laughed as she hooked her arm through mine and dragged me away from the bar, leaving Delilah and Seb staring at us.

I looked at her in confusion. "You know as well as I do, you keep looking at him like that and he's going to bend you over that bar."

My skin burned at the words, but I nodded knowing she was right. I needed to stay on my best behaviour, at least until the speeches were out of the way.

After that, if the devil wanted to dance I would gladly be his partner.

Cherry pulled the now empty champagne flute from my hand and dropped it onto a nearby table before leading me towards the dance floor. Immediately we began moving in rhythm to the music, our bodies in perfect sync as we held hands and spun around together.

I was going to miss her so much.

My mind wandered to thoughts of leaving this town again. But I refused to be sad, I refused to believe that this would be the end of the little friendship we had quickly formed.

Nothing was permanent.

I trusted Seb, and if whatever was going on with the Carnival could somehow implicate me, I needed to know I was doing the right thing, making the right decision.

A smoky scent began to morph itself around me, and when Seb's hands wrapped around my waist and pulled me backwards against his body, I sank into his broad muscles.

"I have something to show you."

"Last time you said that we ended up a hundred feet in the air."

"No Ferris wheels this time. I promise." His fingers laced through mine and we gracefully navigated the crowds of people, and in the direction of a staircase that towered up to the second floor. Fleeting excitement wound its way through my muscles as we climbed each step.

Seb guided me towards a balcony edge that was covered in clear glass panels, giving us a panoramic view of the ballroom beneath our feet.

I scanned the crowds, my eyes lighting up when I spotted Delilah and Cherry caught in a hypnotising dance in the centre of the floor. Fondness skirted over my skin at the sight of the two women, so desperately holding each other.

I knew firsthand what that desperation felt like.

Cool air fanned my shoulders as Seb's muscles pressed against my back. "There's a lot of people here. Clearly Josie has many admirers to achieve such an immense turnout." I nodded; my words caught in my throat at the sensation of his fingers brushing over my arm. When they began to trail slowly over my chest, teasing my nipples under the fabric, I stilled.

"You wanted an audience princess, now you have one." Memories of our conversation in my bedroom flooded my ears. Seb had asked me what fantasies I had, and here he was delivering them on a silver plate. "I wonder if they'll notice the way your skin twinkles under my fingertips or how your chest freezes under my words."

His hands began a torturous roam of my body, travelling from my chest and towards the apex of my thighs. I was beginning to feel clammy, but it wasn't from fear. It was from excitement.

Flittering hums danced on my lips, and I closed my eyes, savouring every flame he enticed from my skin.

"Tell me what you want." His voice was carnal, need dripping between each word.

"I want you to fuck me. I want you to fuck me for everyone to see." I was done being the shy girl who didn't go after what she wanted. I was ready to take everything this man would offer.

Seb's fingers intertwined with the bottom of the material of my dress, and soon the fabric was bundled around my waist, every inch of my bare skin on show for the world to see.

I was a performer, ready to dazzle my audience.

I hadn't heard Seb moving behind me, so when he began manoeuvring my hips backwards and his cock lined up with my already dripping entrance I jolted slightly.

"Let them hear you sing, let them hear your sweet music."

In one movement, Seb's cock was pushing inside of me, each tantalising inch teasing me wider. Animalistic moans escaped my mouth, and with each thrust, he coaxed more and more from my body.

"Fuck." He hissed through gritted teeth.

Below me, I watched as more people crowded the room, and with every person that joined the hundreds, my adrenaline spiked, and more breathy moans evaporated from my mouth.

"More. I need more." Seb slammed into me over and over again, his cock hitting the spot that could force me into submission.

I struggled to keep myself steady, struggled against the force of Seb's movements, each one knocking me closer to the guarded glass.

"Do you enjoy being on show, enjoy knowing that at any moment someone could look up and see your pretty pussy being fucked, see you being owned?"

Shivers ran over my skin, his dirty words battling the truth lying dormant inside of me. I did enjoy it. Every second was pushing me closer and closer to the edge, begging for someone to see. Watch me as I relished in becoming the tarnished Persephone being dragged into the underworld by Hades.

The grunts coming from behind me stole me back to reality, and as the throb threatened to unleash my pleasure, I quickly dropped the fabric of my dress and slammed my hands against the glass.

Euphoria spilt from my lips in tight ribbons that filled the space around us. My legs buckled, and I was nearly falling to the ground, but Seb's tight grip around my waist held me still. He thrust inside me one final time before filling me with his come, almost forcing me to combust at the seams.

We stayed there panting for a few moments, Seb whispering incoherent words into my ears, but I couldn't hear any of them, my hazy senses too preoccupied with the cloud I was floating on.

I suddenly felt empty as Seb stepped away and hid himself back in the confines of his trousers. In between my legs dampness dripped down my thighs, and I blushed.

"I need to go to the bathroom." I flattened down my dress and began walking around Seb, but his forceful hand stopped me, and he soon had me flush against the glass, his lips curled into a dangerous smirk.

"No. I want you to remember what we just did. I want the evidence dripping down your thighs when you walk."

It felt dirty, *sordid*. But his demand sent another coil of heat straight to my clit, and the butterflies erupted all over again. At my silence, he growled. "Is that clear Harriet?"

"Yes." I squeaked.

"Good." He wrapped his arm around my waist and began guiding me back in the direction of the staircase, each step forcing my legs to dampen with the remnants of his pleasure.

When we finally weaved between the crowds, we resumed our position like we hadn't just fucked on the balcony of the ballroom. I looked up to where we had been stood. The glass was a reflective panel, you couldn't see behind it.

Seb had tricked me, and I revelled in every part of the deception. My haunting devil was teasing me, and I would be ready to return the taunt.

The music slowed around us, my mind wandering to our soon departure from our dream.

"I can see you're sad. You know if there was any other way to keep you safe I would do it." My head rolled back against his shoulder, and we swayed together as the music began to slow. Around us couples moved together to the gentle harmonies.

"It doesn't matter where we go, as long as I go there with you. You're my home." It was the most truth I'd ever spoken.

I turned to face him, to make sure he knew I trusted him. But as I did, a recognisable face over his shoulder made the voices in my head scream.

What are you waiting for? Go!

Noticing my hesitation, Seb narrowed his eyes on mine before turning his attention to where I was staring. His entire body went rigid as five men approached us.

"Great." I sighed, Seb's eyes a frenzy as he looked back at me, a panicked expression sitting on his face. I smiled, confused by the look on his features.

"You're about to meet my dad."

Chapter Twenty-Seven

Seb

My grip on Harriet tightened as John descended on us, followed by the three men at the Carnival and another who was lurking in their shadows.

Alarm bells roared in my head as overwhelming panic grappled with my muscles.

"You're about to meet my dad."

Dad? What the fuck. John couldn't be Harriet's dad.

I thought her dad's name was Richard.

What the fuck is going on?

As he got closer, Harriet squeezed my hand firmly and began leading us towards them, my legs screaming at me to throw her over my shoulder and run in the other direction.

"Dad." She was sharp, her voice missing its normal fluttery tone. John looked between the two of us, a snarl curling at one corner of his mouth.

"Harry. I didn't expect to see you here."

Harry. That explains why she reacted so badly when I'd used the nickname.

Her grip tightening in my hand didn't go unnoticed, but I was too preoccupied by the hungry eyes devouring her from behind John to acknowledge her hold.

"Josie's a good friend of mine, and I help out at the garden."

He nodded and then turned his attention to me.

"Who's your friend?"

The fucking son of a bitch knew *exactly* who I was.

"This is Seb." John held his hand out towards me, and I shook it, mentally stopping myself from squeezing too tightly.

Break his fucking hand.

"Richard Wolston, pleasure."

Richard Wolston? I already knew who Harriet's dad was thanks to the information that Tony had managed to dig up about him online. I had no idea that he was involved in the Carnival though.

My head became heavy, my mind meticulously calculating how quickly I could get Harriet away from the den of vipers circling around us.

I was too stunned to speak, and from the corner of my eye, I noticed Harriet giving me a quizzical look. But I couldn't tear my eyes away from the man standing in front of me, or the four acting as starved bodyguards behind him.

"These are associates of mine," Richard spotted my glare and gestured to the men behind him, "Carl, Andrew and Tony." The three men smiled at Harriet, and she innocently shook their hands. "At the back is James, he's not much of a people person."

I hated the way each of them slid their fingers over her skin when they shook hands, the way each man purred their introduction.

The figure at the back was glaring, and when she looked past Richard's shoulder I spotted the uncertainty clouding over her eyes.

"Have we met?" Harriet's eyes narrowed on James, and a sheepish grin rose on his face.

"In the record tent at the vintage festival. Sorry again about bumping into you."

"It's okay."

"Seb, could you grab my daughter and me some drinks?" Richard's voice was acid in my ear.

He had to be fucking joking if he thought I was leaving her—

"Seb, I'll be right here." Harriet smiled softly up at me, her hand resting gently against my thumping chest. I wanted to scream at her, tell her everything I knew about this man, but I couldn't.

God knows what would happen to her if I opened my mouth.

My lips remained tightly pressed together as I backed away. I walked in the direction of Cherry who was jumping around chaotically in the middle of the dance floor.

My fingers dug into the soft skin on her arm as I tore her attention to me.

"Cherry. Go to Harriet." I pointed in her direction. She looked like a sheep being circled by wolves. Cherry's muscles tightened in my arm and she darted her eyes back to mine.

"Seb." Her voice stuttered. "That's them, the men that…the ones who…" My eyes widened, realisation hitting me like a tonne of bricks. These were the men responsible for hurting Cherry, and I had just left the most valuable diamond with them.

Richard was a fucking snidey vulture. Pretending to be an elite when really he was just as corrupt as the rest of them.

A raging furnace of fire and venom seeped from my body. "Fuck!" I shouted, my voice barely a whisper over the roaring music. I turned back to see Cherry shaking, I needed to do something, find a way to give me back control.

"Find Delilah," I shouted and she frantically nodded, but when I turned back towards Harriet, she was being motioned away by Carl, his slimy hand dancing across her lower back.

She searched for me over her shoulder as he pulled her away, her doe eyes desperately seeking me out, but too many people were blocking our path.

I needed to get us the fuck out of there.

I madly searched the room trying to find anything that would get us out of this, but everywhere I looked I was faced with dead ends.

I spotted Josie in the corner, mingling with some other guests and quickly crossed the room until I was standing in front of her.

"Josie, do you have any cars ready to leave outside?" Her eyes were glassy, and she stumbled on her unbalanced feet as she grinned up at me.

"I'm so glad she found you Sam, you make her happy." I rolled my eyes, now wasn't the time for sentiments.

"It's Seb—Josie, this is important." I planted my hands firmly on her shoulders trying to stop her from wavering around.

"Are there cars out front?" She looked thoughtful for a moment and then began enthusiastically nodding her head.

That was all I needed.

Running in the direction I'd seen Richard take Harriet, I turned a corner and quickly came face to face with the last member of their group, the one who remained at the back like a leach.

James.

I calmed my steps, his mouth curling into a sadistic grin as I got closer.

"Your girls a feisty one." I narrowed my eyes, pulling my shoulders back.

"I wonder if she fucks as good as she kicks." I was puzzled for a moment until blurred memories of Harriet running from the alleyway hit my vision.

Tony had given me the details of the man that had attacked her, and it *wasn't* this guy. My thoughts were jumbled.

I was dragging him against the wall before I knew it, my hands tightly holding him up by the collar of his shirt.

"I should fucking kill you for laying a finger on her." James snarled at me.

"Go ahead. Add murderer to the list of things you've got going for you. I'm sure that will make you that much more appealing. Tell me is her arse as tight as it looks? Actually don't spoil the surprise. I'll find out for myself."

All I saw was red.

I swung my fist into his jaw, the crack of bones splintering under the force. James whipped his head back to look at me and spat crimson red blood onto the ground.

From the corner of my eye I noticed a waiter appear, their legs freezing when they spotted me holding James against the wall, and the blood that was bubbling from his mouth.

"Fuck off!" I shouted, not daring to look away from the leach I had in my hold. The waiter scurried away, and I bared my teeth.

"Where is she?"

"Oh, she's being taken real good care of." A gruesome laugh vibrated from him, and I pulled his body forward before slamming him back, the sound of his head hitting the surface echoing through the walls.

I pulled him forward again, ready to inflict another round of battery on his head, but Delilah's voice distracted me from the smoke.

"Seb! We found Harriet. Go, we'll follow you out."

I didn't hesitate.

My hands released James and he fell to the floor in a clamber, his chest coughing against the air that was harshly travelling back into his lungs.

I should have fucking suffocated him.

"She's waiting out the front, Cherry's with her."

I didn't thank Delilah, my desperation to get to my siren forcing me through the concord of gatherers.

As soon as I was in the cold night air, my eyes frantically searched for the emerald dress, and as soon as I spotted it I was running at Harriet. My body rammed into hers, knocking her balance.

"Seb. What's going on?" Fear laced her voice as I took her head between my hands, and crashed my lips against hers.

"I'm going to find Delilah, we'll meet you back at the apartment."

I nodded to Cherry as she disappeared back into the old building. Flinging my arm tightly around Harriet's shoulders, I led her down the cobbled steps and towards a chauffeur-driven car waiting at the bottom.

"I'll explain everything, I just need to get you out of here." Harriet's eyes blinked quickly, a collection of tears pooling in them, and she nodded as I opened the car door and motioned for her to get in.

Rounding to the other side, I threw myself into the seat next to her and gave the driver the address. He quickly sped away from the building, and I tried to calm the thump assaulting my chest, my imagination whirling through every possible scenario at why Richard and his clan of goonies had been at the event tonight.

Surely he wouldn't put his own daughter in the hands of a cruel and brutal world.

As soon as we arrived at the apartment I was flying from the door and dragging Harriet from the other side of the car. My body moving in a chaotic frenzy.

Harriet ripped her arm from my clutches as we climbed the steps, "Seb!" She shouted, her voice shaking, "you're scaring me."

My fingers dragged through my hair, the tension in my body crying for a release, and when I faced the door to the building, my body's movements became involuntary.

I was suddenly throwing my fist through the panel, glass shattering at the forceful impact.

A yelp came from Harriet, and I stood there for a moment, begging the riots to sedate.

"Your dad has something to do with the Carnival." I didn't look at her, I couldn't.

"What do you mean?" Her voice was barely a whisper, and the quiet words tore at my chest.

"He's been giving Saffron money, helping her to find new girls, buy better wares to sell." Bile began prickling in my throat.

"I've met with him before. He goes by the name of John in the underworld, he wants to be a part of the Carnival's expansion proposals."

Harriet was silent behind me, and I turned towards her, ignoring the searing pain that was coming from my arm and the blood that was coating my fingertips.

"I need you to go upstairs, pack a bag and wait for me. Do not leave that apartment unless you leave it with me. Do you understand?" I whisper shouted at her, and she anxiously nodded her head.

"Delilah and Cherry will stay with you until I get back. We have to leave tonight."

A tear began to fall down her cheek, dragging her dark makeup in tracks with it.

I cupped her face and leaned my forehead against hers, "it's going to be alright, but we need to leave."

I opened the building door and watched as she hurried up the steps. Before we could go I needed to get some things from the Carnival. It was Saturday, which meant I should be able to get in and out without being detected. The performers always used the weekends we were closed to blow off some steam.

I ran to my motorbike parked on the sidewalk and quickly commanded it to life. Not bothering with a helmet, I flew off down the road and in the direction of the gated hell hole I called home.

The second I was at the steel gates, I was unlocking the padlock and throwing the heavy bars apart. Running across the muddy field, I went straight for the high-top tent, creating a mental checklist of everything I needed.

I would pack light and make sure I only carried the necessities to get us to Rosewood. Anything else we needed we could pick up when we got there.

When I entered through the parted fabric of the entrance, something immediately felt off. The air was stale, and a strange smell filtered into me as it was carried by a breeze.

I tried to locate the source of the smell, but the space was empty.

A clicking noise, followed by the drag of shoes against the floor pricked my ears, and as I stepped further into the tent Saffron suddenly emerged, followed by Carl, Tony and Andrew.

Hanging between Carl and Tony was Cherry, her body lifeless, and I immediately froze.

I knew what drugged looked like, I'd seen it so many times before.

"Seb, nice of you to join us." Saffron rolled her eyes as if I'd kept them waiting for hours, but I was too preoccupied by Cherry, and the blood dripping from her skin, to take any notice.

All of the stitches Harriet had crafted had been torn open.

A growl vibrated through my chest and Saffron tutted at me as though I was a naughty child. "Now there's no need for that. Just tell us where the girl is." Cherry's body began to stir in between the men's hold, and the silent voice in my head screamed at her to open her eyes.

"Seb I'll make this very simple for you. You either tell us," The clicking noise sounded again, and suddenly Saffron was holding a revolver to Cherry's head. "Or I'll kill her. What will it be?"

My eyes widened, and I desperately pleaded with her. "Saffron, leave Cherry alone. This has nothing to do with her."

I hated begging. *Hated* giving this vulture what she wanted. But it was my only choice.

Saffron stepped forward, her eyes burning into mine. "Maybe not. But you *stole* my paycheck from me."

My mouth opened and closed as I looked between the men, Cherry and then back at the viper puppeteering the show.

"Do you really think I'm that stupid that I wouldn't notice your late-night rendezvous?. That I wouldn't notice the girl you spent them with?" She spat, her words filled with poison. "After all these years keeping my bed warm, I'm surprised your attention was so easily taken by a shiny new plaything."

"Where's Delilah?" I needed to stall, give myself time to figure out how to get Cherry out of this cesspool.

Saffron laughed, and it made my skin crawl, her cackle lighting pinpricks over my body.

"In a back alley somewhere. James is taking care of her."

Cherry's body stirred again as if recognising her girlfriend's name. When she finally looked up, the sadness that covered her eyes broke my heart, and my knees crumbled.

Saffron walked closer and used the barrel of the gun to lift my eyes to hers. "This can end easily Seb. This is the last time I ask you. Where's my girl?"

My girl.

Snatching my head away, I stared at Cherry. "Surely you wouldn't sacrifice the life of your closest friend for that of a pathetic toy."

When Cherry's gaze met mine, a soft smile graced her face and one of her eyes was swollen closed. Her smile was gentle, *calm*, and I allowed that calmness to wash over me as I took a deep breath.

But I remained silent.

"You're wasting my time Seb. Where is she!" Saffron screamed, her spit sending a light shower over me. I snarled, the corner of my mouth lifting as I bared my teeth at her.

A gentle tone fell from my redheaded friend. "I finally learnt to swim Seb. I'm not drowning anymore."

If I could just distract them, I could get to her. I could—

"I don't have fucking time for this."

Everything moved in slow motion, a loud ringing noise capturing my ears and holding my senses hostage, as Saffron pulled the trigger on the gun.

A roar bellowed from my throat, burning as it mixed with bile spilling to the ground. Carl and Tony released Cherry and she slumped to the floor, and a pool of crimson soaked the ground around her.

Saffron had shot her in between the eyes.

I tried to move, tried to crawl towards her, but I was paralysed, every muscle in my body aflame.

My vision became blurred as dampness coated my eyes.

She fucking shot her.

Muffled voices argued, but I couldn't hear them over the wails that were rioting in my head.

Clinking shoes walked further towards me, and Saffron forced the tip of her heel under my chin, jolting my head upwards.

"I'm moving you to the East Coast Carnival." Her words fell on deaf ears, I couldn't focus on anything apart from Cherry's lifeless body curled on the ground.

This had to be some sick twisted nightmare. Any moment I would wake up and none of this would be real.

It couldn't be real.

"You had so much potential. You could have owned this empire if you hadn't of been stupid enough to let a girl distract you."

As she stomped away I heard her speaking to the men, instructing them to move the body, and I wanted to lunge, wanted to force her to turn the gun around on herself.

"Oh and Seb." I looked up at her, not moving my head. "If you resist, if you try and pull any more *stunts*, I'll kill Harriet."

They were the last words I heard as I watched Carl drag Cherry's body into one of the rooms, leaving a trail of bright scarlet liquid on the floor behind her.

As soon as the room was empty I collapsed further into the ground, begging it to swallow me and steal my last breaths.

The agony was shattering, but I welcomed the pain as I lay there, and my world turned black.

Chapter Twenty-Eight

Harriet

Bright light stirred my eyes open, and I winced at the sun reflecting through the window. My body groaned with aches as I attempted to shake off the disorientation.

I'd fallen asleep.

I frantically looked around the apartment living room as memories from last night hurtled back into my mind.

I shouldn't still be here.

Attempting to get to the bathroom, I stumbled across the floor as my emerald dress clung to my skin. "Hello?" I called out, expecting Delilah or Cherry's voice to answer me. I narrowed my eyes. Seb had said they would be here.

The apartment felt eery, its silence unwelcoming and threatening.

Padding into the bathroom, I paused when I caught my reflection in the mirror. The remnants of my beautiful makeup was smeared across my face, and I frowned at my hair sticking up in a wild nest of curls.

Leaning over the sink and turning the tap on, I splashed cold water onto my skin and scraped away the caked makeup with a cloth.

My eyes flicked in the mirror, bloodshot and raw, either caused by tiredness or by the tears I'd cried myself to sleep with.

I ran the water through my hair and retied it into a loose bun on top of my head, a few of the strands slipping through my fingers in the fumble.

Leaving the bathroom and heading straight for the drawers in my bedroom, I pulled out a pair of leggings and a plain white T-shirt. After struggling with the zip on the back of the dress, I finally managed to rip my body from it and my skin sang as cool air hit.

When I thought I'd heard the front door open, I poked my head around the corner of the door, but I was met with emptiness, and more unease began to scratch up my body.

Seb had been adamant about Cherry and Delilah meeting me here, why would he think that if they weren't. Knowing them two, they'd probably ended up back in Cherry's room. I shook my head as I laughed, my heart warming at the thought of my two closest friends.

After a few minutes of pacing the living room, I made the decision to go to the Carnival and find Seb. Maybe he had changed his mind about leaving, maybe he had been mistaken about my dad.

A sharp pang erupted in my stomach.

Why would Seb think my dad had something to do with that place? He was many things, but I knew him.

He would never sit by idly whilst young women were taken advantage of and drugs were fed to unsuspecting victims, if anything my dad would try and stop that.

He had his reputation to think of after all. He wouldn't be caught dead involved in the corrupt underbelly of the Carnival's illegal activities.

I wrapped my arms around my body, remembering the feel of Carl's fingers as he stroked across my bare skin at the gala, the way his slimy voice whispered unwanted compliments into my ear.

"You're fucking gorgeous Harriet. You've already stolen the show, we just need to move you to the spotlight."

Shaking off the apprehension, I grabbed my phone from the kitchen counter and quickly flicked across the screen, expecting to see a missed call, a message, anything that would offer up some explanation about where everyone was.

But as I pressed my fingers against the glass and tapped in my password I was met with blankness. Strange.

I pulled the hoodie Seb had given me from behind the sofa and let it swamp my body. His smoky scent was still floating on the fabric, and I let it consume my senses, its familiarity soothing my raging chest.

Before leaving I took one last look around the space, hoping that whatever it was that had stopped Seb from returning last night meant I wouldn't have to leave my little safe haven.

I was surprised to find the Carnival gates unlocked when I arrived outside. The only time the gates were open was when the Carnival was hosting a show or a fair, and I knew there wasn't anything planned for a week. Cherry had promised to show me how to beat the ring toss game, and I'd been excited before Seb had told me we were leaving.

The sky was thick with fog, the frosty air finally settling over Bromlin now we were drawing into the height of winter. I hugged Seb's hoodie closer and began to walk towards the performer's tent.

Across from me, I spotted a mop of curly red hair approaching and I waved at Tony as he got closer.

"Hey Tony," he was panting, as though he had been running for hours. When he finally stopped and looked at me, his eyes were dancing with concern, and I narrowed my own at him.

"What is it, what's wrong—"

"Tony!" A screeching female voice yelled, and from the parting of the tent a woman stood tapping her foot.

She was cladded in a grey dress and blazer, her blonde hair pulled back tightly into a neat bun behind her head.

She reeked of power.

This must have been Saffron. I'd heard her voice before, but seeing the woman in person was an introduction I never intended to experience.

Nerves began to wrack my body. Seb had never spoken kindly about the Carnival's puppeteer, and I immediately took a disliking to her. The way she had manipulated him as a child, forced this lifestyle on him, it was something that could never be forgiven.

She was also responsible for allowing whatever had happened to Cherry. As the circus master, she dictated everything that went on here. Everything from what games to run, to which women would service the men was under her control.

When she glared at me, aggressive goosebumps pricked my skin.

Saffron tilted her head and began stalking towards us. I wanted to run, and the voices in my head blared at me to get out of there, but I remained firmly in place.

I needed to find Seb, and I wasn't leaving until I did.

She stopped inches away from us and Tony shifted uncomfortably between his feet.

"Tony. Put the kettle on." Her voice was stern, demanding, but it didn't feel threatening.

When she held her hand out in front of me, I took it. Her hold was firm, and she smiled at me.

"Harriet I presume? I'm Saffron."

I nodded. "I'm here to see Seb."

She pursed her lips, "come with me, I'll get you a coffee whilst you wait." She seemed almost… gentle.

As Saffron walked in the direction of the tent I followed quickly behind her, and the moment we were inside, she was motioning to the sofas. "Have a seat, I'll get you a drink."

I'd never seen the tent this empty, normally it was filled with noisy energy, and apart from what sounded like furniture being moved around in one of the other rooms, it was silent.

Minutes later Saffron returned, a steaming cup in her hands. I gratefully took it and slowly sipped on the burning liquid. It was sweeter than the one Tony had made me, but it was still delicious and heated my skin against the frosty coldness of the outside world.

"I'm afraid Seb isn't here." I frowned as she sat on the sofa across from me.

"Do you know where he is?" Saffron looked over her shoulder at Tony and directed her head at one of the bedroom doors. The man hurried away, not looking at me as he did.

"What do you know about the Carnival Harriet?"

That felt like a trick question.

I wasn't sure whether Cherry and Seb should have disclosed as many secrets as they did to me about what really went on here.

Taking another large gulp of the coffee, my body began to loosen, and a cloudy haze swept through my head.

"You entertain people." I shrugged, but the movement was heavy, as though a weight was sitting on my shoulders.

Saffron smiled and took the mug away from my hands. I tried to grip onto it, but my fingers stopped working as more haze began floating through me.

"Sweetie, we do much more than entertain people. Let me show you."

Saffron held onto my hands and pulled me upwards from the sofa, my body not attempting to resist it and I followed into one of the bedrooms behind her.

Ice water splashed my skin, and fiery burns covered my entire body. My head whipped up and I tried to pull my arms from behind my back, but plastic dug into my wrists, holding them firmly in place.

"Good, you're awake." Saffron stood in front of me, all remnants of the woman I had met earlier completely evaporated from her body.

"We'll need to build up your tolerance if you have any hope of surviving here."

What was she talking about, tolerance to what?

My head became heavy, and it dropped forward. But when it did my eyes widened at my body, completely naked apart from my underwear.

I desperately tried to move my limbs, but my legs were strapped to the chair legs with more cable ties.

What the hell was going on?

Confusion barrelled around in my head, mixed with the remainder of whatever had forced me to black out. My eyes were blurry, but I could make out her walking around behind the fuzziness, and the silhouette of another figure hidden by the shadows in the corner of the room.

"What did you do?" I managed to say before the words felt too heavy in my dry mouth.

"I think the better question here is what are *you* going to do Harriet?" I narrowed my eyes at her, her voice jumbled as it entered my ears.

"Do you love him?" Saffron crouched in front of me, and I couldn't hide from her glare.

"If you do, then I suggest you listen very carefully." Her eyes skated over my body and landed on my legs. "Pity about these, they'll drop your value."

My… *Value?*

"Seb isn't here. I sent him to the East Carnival. His relationship with you was causing…complications."

Saffron leant against the doorway and folded her arms, the tip of her shoe resuming its tap. Her words were bouncing, chaotic and messy. I could barely hold on to any of them.

"He stays alive, *if* you join the Carnival."

My head shot up. "You want me to…to *join* the Carnival."

"Yes, you'll take Cherry's place."

What did Cherry have to do with this? My brows furrowed and I looked around confused. Moments later, my eyes finally adjusted to the room we were in. It was a bedroom.

Along the walls, various instruments hung like artwork. Chains, rope and some leather contraptions. At the end a trophy display of knives twinkled in the dim lights. Fear erupted over every inch of my skin.

"Cherry's dead. You'll replace her."

I froze my already paralysed body. That had to be a lie, Cherry couldn't be dead. I'd seen her yesterday; I'd been with her.

"You can blame Seb for that, his little stunt at the gala cost me a lot of money."

Voices in my head were a frenzy of deafening screams, but my face remained emotionless.

She wasn't making any sense, and disorientation held me captive. I tried to open my mouth, tried to speak, but no words would come out.

"Harriet. I'll put this as simply as I can. If you do not work for me, I will kill Seb. In fact, let's throw your little black-haired roommate in for good measure as well." Saffron began walking away from me, "you have until morning to decide."

This vile woman was using my friends as bait to lure me into her corrupt world.

"No." the word came out breathy and tight, my throat finally finding its voice.

"I suggest you reconsider. Unless you want more blood—"

"No. I don't need until morning." Saffron raised her eyebrow and smirked at me.

I challenged her glare with my own and spoke quietly, as if only to myself. "I'll do it, just don't hurt them. Please." I didn't want to beg, but god knew that I wasn't going to sit back and let her kill anyone I cared about.

Not again.

It all made sense. *This* is what Seb was trying to save me from. But like a naive child, I wandered straight into the trap.

Saffron nodded her head, and waved at the figure who began to emerge from the shadows, "good, because your first client is here."

Carl appeared in front of me holding a bundle of rope, and what looked like a paddle. I tightly shut my eyes, my body begging for release from the hard plastic slicing into my skin.

A sadistic smile crept over his face, and Saffron opened the door. Before she left, she turned towards me one final time.

"Oh, a word of warning. Carl bites."

Bite marks covered Cherry's skin.

She smirked as she closed the door, and I was left in the room with the masochist who was smiling down at me like I was dinner.

He leaned towards me, and ran his nose across the bare skin of my neck, inhaling deeply.

"I thought you worked for my dad?" I whispered, "why are you doing this?"

Carl ignored me.

"Sweet. You smell like vanilla." I quivered, my entire body trembling as the man's hands began scouring over my body, his fingers pinching my bare flesh.

"I could fucking *smell* him on you at the gala." His tongue licked at my neck before lethal words crawled from his lips.

"This will only hurt a little bit."

Pain erupted over me as Carl sunk his teeth into my shoulder, and I screamed out at the agony crashing over my skin. He was branding me, making sure anyone else that came near knew he'd been with me, knew his filthy hands had touched my body.

One. Two. Three. Four. Five

I tried to ignore the pain, tried to ignore the sickening feeling collecting inside me, and when Carl wrapped the rope around my neck and began guiding my face towards his now unzipped trousers, I thought of Cherry, about how strong I knew she would have been before she was murdered.

I thought about Delilah and her mischievous flirty one-liners.

I thought about Seb and his endless promises to protect me, and I prayed.

I prayed to fucking god that he found me before the numbness did.

Five Months Later

Dear Seb.

You were wrong. I'm not brave, or strong. I'm just like my mom.

Now I know how she felt before she decided to get out of this world.

I want out of this world.

I can't do this anymore. I'm sorry.

See you on the other side.

Forever yours,

Hx

Made in United States
North Haven, CT
09 February 2024